The Tenth Pan Book of Horror Stories

Herbert van Thal has compiled a number of anthologies which include some of the writings of James Agate, Ernest Newman and Hilaire Belloc and a volume on Victorian Travellers. He has also resuscitated the works of many neglected Victorian writers. In 1971 his autobiography, *The Tops of the Mulberry Trees*, was published, as well as *The Music Lovers' Companion* (with Gervase Hughes). He has recently edited Thomas Adolphus Trollope's autobiography and a two-volume work on Britain's Prime Ministers.

Also available in this series
The Pan Book of Horror Stories
Volumes 1–23

The tenth Pan book of
HORROR STORIES

edited by Herbert van Thal

Pan Original
Pan Books London and Sydney

This collection first published 1969 by Pan Books Ltd,
Cavaye Place, London SW10 9PG
14th printing 1983
© Pan Books Ltd 1969
ISBN 0 330 02369 1
Printed and bound in Great Britain by
Richard Clay (The Chaucer Press) Ltd, Bungay, Suffolk

CONTENTS

ACKNOWLEDGEMENTS

The Editor wishes to acknowledge the following permissions to quote from copyright material:

Mr Chris Murray and his agent, London Management & Representation Limited of 235–241 Regent Street, London WA1 2JT, for THE ACID TEST.

Mr A. G. J. Rough and his agent, London Management, for SOMETHING IN THE CELLAR.

Mr John Christopher and his agent, David Higham Associates Limited of 76 Dean Street, Soho, London W.1, for RINGING TONE.

Miss Dulcie Gray and her agent, London Management, for THE NECKLACE.

Mr Walter Winward and his agent, London Management, for SELF-EMPLOYED.

Miss Rosemary Timperley and her agent, Harvey Unna Limited of 14 Beaumont Mews, Marylebone High Street, London W1N 4HE, for SUPPER WITH MARTHA.

Mr James Connelly and his agent, London Management, for PUNISHMENT BY PROXY.

Miss Frances Stephens for THE END OF THE LINE and PUSSY CAT, PUSSY CAT.

Mr Martin Waddell and his agent, London Management, for THE FAT THING.

Miss B. Lynn Barber and her agent, London Management, for THE FLATMATE.

Miss Diana Buttenshaw for THE SKI-LIFT.

Mr C. A. Cooper for MAGICAL MYSTERY TRIP.

Mr David Lewis and International Magazine Features for LONG SILENCE, OLD MAN.

Mr William Sinclair and his agent, London Management, for TERROR OF TWO HUNDRED BELOW.

Miss Dorothy K. Haynes and her agent, London Management, for THE CURE.

Mr Alex Hamilton and his agent, Jonathan Clowes Limited of 20F New Cavendish Street, London W.1, for THE IMAGE OF THE DAMNED.

Mr Norman P. Kaufman and his agent, London Management, for A SHARP LOSS OF WEIGHT.

Mr Desmond Stewart and his agent, Anthony Sheil Associates Limited of 47 Dean Street, Soho, London W.1, for AN EXPERIMENT IN CHOICE.

Mr Robert Duncan and his agent, London Management, for THE EVIL ONE.

Miss Joan Aiken and Victor Gollancz Limited for MARMALADE WINE from *The Windscreen Weepers*.

Mr John Arthur and his agent, London Management, for MONKEY BUSINESS.

THE TENTH PAN BOOK
OF HORROR STORIES

THE ACID TEST

By Chris Murray

THEY PUSHED Marie into a large, well-lit room. At one end capacious armchairs clustered in a cosy arc round a high ornamental fireplace in which a cheerful fire blazed vigorously.

Marie gasped with surprise when she recognized the figure buried deep in one of the armchairs.

'Paula!' she exclaimed. 'What are you doing here, and where's Mark? Will someone tell me what this is all about?'

'All in good time, my dear. You'll know soon enough.'

There was an edge to Paula's voice and Marie shivered when she remembered the circumstances under which they had last met.

It had been in a night club in the West End. Marie was engaged there as a singer and after her performance one evening she had been invited to join a party at their table. With some reluctance, she had accepted on the understanding that she could only stay a few minutes.

Mark and Paula were in the party and they made a very clinging couple, with Paula doing all the clinging. When Mark saw Marie, however, he had quickly disentangled himself and transferred his attentions. By one of those strange quirks of fate, although he had been drinking to excess and his advances were rather too amorous for such a short acquaintance, Marie was attracted to him. This drew baleful glares from across the table and the other members of the party quickly became aware of the atmosphere that was building up and watched developments with interest. Marie, too, sensed the tension and animosity, but Mark seemed quite oblivious to everything around him, except her.

Paula, having failed to head him off, became more and more furious, until she could contain herself no longer. When it became obvious that she had lost her escort for the evening, she leapt to her feet, her eyes blazing. She was a beautiful girl, but at that moment her beauty was marred by the hate which emanated from her contorted face.

'All right, Mark Stevens,' she hissed. 'This is the last time you'll make a fool of me. You needn't bother to come crawling back when you're sober. And as for this little tramp . . .'

Her face was charged with malice as she looked at Marie.

'You haven't seen the last of me. You'll live to regret this night.'

Then she was gone, leaving an uncomfortable silence behind her. Marie made to get up and follow her, but Mark held her arm.

'Let her go, she'll get over it,' he advised. 'I didn't ask her here tonight anyway, she just tacked on. Now perhaps she'll take the hint that I'm not interested. Come crawling back indeed, cheeky bitch!'

Marie felt less complacent. It was difficult to forget the remark which she overheard from one of the other men at the table.

'Did you see her face?' he had whispered. 'She looked almost mad with anger. I reckon that girl would make a very nasty enemy. I've heard, incidentally, that she has a Sicilian background.'

Mark's initial infatuation for Marie blossomed into a genuine affection which became mutual. This was no chance flirtation and romance was very much in the air. Paula tried several times to retrieve the ground she had lost with Mark, but without success. Mark did not tell Marie about this, preferring to let her forget the unfortunate incident at their first meeting. Eventually, Paula appeared to take the hint and for a month nothing was seen or heard of her. But now, here she was, looking remarkably pleased with herself, though in a distinctly vindictive sort of way.

Marie had felt uneasy ever since her doorbell rang at 7 o'clock that evening. Mark was not due until 7.30, so she was far from ready.

The two men standing at her door looked like fugitives from an old gangster film. One was tall and gaunt with a long, narrow face in which the eyes were too hard and close together, the nose too bony and the lips too thin. His companion came only to his shoulder, but probably outweighed him by thirty pounds. Even the long drape jacket, which he wore, failed to conceal his considerable girth. Two small piggy eyes stared out from the mountain of flesh that was his face and when he spoke, his heavy jowls quivered grotesquely.

He told Marie that they were friends of Mark, who had asked them to call for her. She was to come quickly, just as she was, as he had a surprise for her, and to convince her they handed her a short note which she recognized to be in his handwriting. Mystified and still faintly suspicious, she had gone with the two men. Now, forty minutes of fast driving later, here she was. No Mark, only his ex-girlfriend, and the evening was beginning to assume distinctly unfavourable proportions.

'Mark won't be coming,' explained Paula.

'But the note?'

'Ah, yes, that. I always fancied myself as a forger and, as you can probably imagine, I am well acquainted with Mark's writing.'

Marie jumped when another voice spoke behind her. It came from the other armchair, whose occupant had been hidden in its cosy depths.

'So this is the girl you told me about, Paula. Most fascinating. I am not at all surprised that Mark should fall for her. It does seem an awful pity that . . .'

'. . . all right, Marcel, let me deal with this,' Paula interrupted sharply.

'As you wish, my dear Paula. I did promise to provide only the manpower. The floor is all yours.'

The speaker was a dark, sinister-looking character, with a small black goatee beard and evil piercing eyes. He might have been any age between thirty and forty-five and, although his English was faultless, his foreign accent was quite unmistakable. As far as Marie was concerned, he represented no improvement on her earlier company. Obviously more intelligent, he looked the more deadly in consequence. Her attention was diverted from him as Paula spoke again.

'I've been waiting a long time for this moment, you little tramp. Do you remember what I said when I left the Golden Bucket that night?'

Marie remembered only too well.

'So you and dear Mark are lovers now, I understand. Well not any longer. When I'm finished with you, Mark will never look at you again, nor will any other man.'

She spat the words out like drops of venom and Marie recoiled instinctively.

'You and Mark chose to humiliate me in front of my friends, now it's my turn. First of all, you will undress so that we can all see exactly what made you so attractive to Mark.'

'Now wait a minute, Paula, hasn't this gone far enough. All right, you've scared me, now . . .'

'. . . not far enough, by a long way,' Paula cut in. 'I said get your clothes off, unless you would like Gorky to help you.'

The fat man shuffled his feet and smiled. His companion stood with his back to the door, as a token demonstration that any chance of escape was impossible. Then it dawned on Marie that this was reality. She really was going to have to undress or be stripped involuntarily by the fat ape breathing down her neck. A quick look at his blubbery face, and then at Paula's, finally convinced her of that.

Slowly, she unbuttoned her coat and let it fall to the ground. With fumbling fingers, she undid the buttons of her blouse and, pulling the ends out, she removed it too. The skirt was unhooked and allowed to fall about her feet, followed by her slip, shoes, stockings, and suspender belt. She was now down to a revealing half-cup bra and tiny transparent panties, whose black tightness accentuated the creamy whiteness of her otherwise bare body.

'What are you waiting for?' Paula was looking triumphant as Marie paused just within the bounds of modesty. 'Those too.'

With hopeless resignation, Marie unclipped her bra and shrugged out of it. Then her last frail garment was peeled down over her thighs and, stepping out of them, she stood erect and stark naked.

'My word, Paula, this is much better than I expected.' Marcel could no longer remain quiet as he surveyed the girl's bare body. 'Raise your arms my dear and turn round so that we can have a good look at you.'

After a moment's hesitation, Marie obeyed. Anything was better than having that fat slob lay his hands on her.

Paula was not quite so appreciative, however.

'All right, Marcel, you can stop ogling her. That isn't the object of the exercise. First of all, we'll dispose of these.'

Bending down, she scooped up all Marie's discarded clothes, except her coat, and threw them on to the blazing fire, where they smouldered for a few moments, before bursting into flames. Very swiftly, they were reduced to a heap of black, crumbling ashes.

'You won't be using those again,' said Paula maliciously.

'Why did you have to do that?' After the unwarranted destruction of her clothes, Marie's fear could keep her silent no longer and her indignation spilled forth in protest.

'Shut up, you little slut,' Paula snarled. Her face wore that same murderous look as on the night she had stormed out of the night club. Then standing directly in front of the defenceless girl, she slapped her hard across the face.

'I warned you that I'd get even and now I intend to. No cheap little bitch is going to make a fool of me and get away with it, not that I really cared for your fine Mark. He is dull and conceited and I was only making a convenience of him. Nevertheless, that didn't give you the right to do what you did.'

She walked slowly round Marie, eyeing her carefully up and down.

'Mm, Mark never could resist well-built women,' she murmured.

Marie was certainly that. She had been engaged as a singer, but she would have been a much bigger sensation as an entertainer if she had been a stripper. She had a superb body by any standards and now it was naked, helpless, and completely in the power of this woman who seemed to have a fanatical obsession to harm her in the pursuit of some misconceived revenge.

'Your body is as attractive as I had hoped it would be,' Paula continued happily. And then more ominously: 'The more beautiful something is, the more effective is the act of destroying that beauty.

'I've thought a lot about how I would deal with you when this moment arrived. Of course I could have simply had you disfigured. Its amazing how a few well-directed strokes of a sharp knife can alter a pretty face out of all recognition, or so Marcel tells me. We could almost as easily have cut off your hands or your breasts, but none of these ideas was very original or seemed quite good enough for you. I wanted it to be something really special and, with the help of a chance remark from Marcel, I think we've got just the right corrective treatment.'

Her voice was cold and deadly as she added:

'When I'm through with you, you'll never steal another man as long as you live.'

Marie felt an icy finger of fear creeping down her spine. It was now obvious that Paula's hate had driven her beyond all reason and, with the help of these thugs, she had planned some terrible fate for her.

'We've talked long enough,' Paula went on. 'It's time my plans were put into effect. Come on.'

She led the way from the room into the large hallway, followed by Marcel. Marie came next and behind her came the two thugs, who drank in her voluptuous nakedness as she padded ahead of them.

In the far corner of the hallway a small door led to some steps which descended sharply. In single file, the strange little procession made its way down these dimly-lit stairs and along a narrow passage at the bottom, which must have run under the main structure of the house. The rough, uneven stone floor felt cold under Marie's bare feet and, after the warmth of the previous room, her body was chilled by the damp still air.

Paula unlatched a heavy oak door which blocked their path and, as it swung slowly open on protesting hinges, she touched a wall switch. The room beyond was flooded with light, and when everyone had entered the door was closed and secured behind them.

Looking anxiously about her, Marie saw that she was in a large cellar, the farthest corners of which defied the efforts of the artificial lighting, bright as it was, to expose their shadowy secrets to her gaze. In bygone days, this had probably been the wine cellar of the house, although now it contained no evidence of its earlier function.

The floor was in fact completely bare, apart from two large round metal plates embedded in it. They looked like manhole covers and lay about ten feet apart. High above them, near the ceiling, a pulley was suspended from a rail. The rail ran directly above the two metal plates and terminated against a huge stone pillar in the centre of the chamber. Against the pillar was a large mirror, which faced back along the line of the pulley rail.

Paula touched some more switches on the wall and the centre of the cellar was flooded with light. She then signalled to the tall man, who pushed Marie into their intense glare. He made her stop just short of the first metal cover and roughly grabbing her wrists, forced them together. From his pocket he produced some thick cord and proceeded to bind the girl's hands together. He then joined a free end of the cord to a rope, which dangled loosely from the pulley wheel overhead. Hauling on the other side, he slowly pulled Marie's arms up over her head. As they were drawn higher, the cords started to dig sharply into her wrists and only when she was at full stretch, with her toes barely touching the ground, did he knot the rope and secure it at that length.

Marie now hung there quite helpless, her nude body taut as a bow string. As long as she stood right on the tips of her toes, she could just take the weight off her arms. Any less of an effort, and the weight of her body was taken by her tightly bound wrists with agonizing results. Looking straight ahead, she could see herself clearly in the full-length mirror.

'Now I'll explain,' said Paula, stepping forward and eyeing the thin man's work with obvious satisfaction.

'The idea is quite simple. Under these two manhole covers are holes about the size and shape of a telephone box. They are deep enough to lower someone into until they drop below the surface of the ground. One of them is full of acid and you are going to be immersed in it until it completely covers you. I'll leave it to your imagination what you will look like after you've been left in there for about a minute. The acid will eat into every inch of your face and body and will turn it into a hideous mass of bubbling, erupting flesh. All the plastic surgery in the world won't be able to turn back the clock.

'Coming on to stage two. Although you'll be totally disfigured and will suffer terrible agony, the treatment must not be fatal and so we have the second hole into which you will be dipped after the acid has done its work. This contains a powerful alkaline solution which will neutralize the acid instantly before its effects become more than just mutilation.

'There is just one other thing. We did consider the possibility that in your agony you might swallow some of the acid to put an end to your misery. Well, as I've said, we don't want that and we don't want you to be blinded either. Otherwise you will be unable to appreciate fully what a thing of horror you've become, hence the mirror. Therefore, we've obtained some special pads and plugs. With these we propose to cover your eyes and mouth and plug your nose and ears. Apart from these, though, you will have no protection, so you can see how important it was now for you to be stripped.'

The growing pain in Marie's wrists was forgotten as she listened with increasing horror. She looked hopefully towards the three men behind Paula. Their faces had an eager, hungry look and it was clear that they would not intervene to save her. Instead, they were going to enjoy the terrible destruction of her body.

'For God's sake, Paula, you can't be serious.' She would do anything now to save herself, even if it meant pleading with this woman and humiliating herself.

'Oh, I mean it all right.' Paula was exultant. If she could make Marie crawl to her, so much the better.

'Now that my moment has arrived, you don't expect me to stop, do you? However, I'm going to savour it a little longer and give you time to rue the day you crossed me, so we're going to leave you for an hour. During that time you can reflect on your misdeeds and have a last look at that fine body of yours. When we return, your punishment will be carried out. Come, Marcel. Leave the lights on, Gorky.'

Marie heard their footsteps retreating along the passage and getting fainter until she could hear them no more. Then she was alone.

It was perhaps just as well that the pain in her wrists was so great, for she was now in a sheer panic and with nothing else to take her attention she might well have become hysterical and lost her reason.

She wondered what Mark would do when he arrived at her flat and found her gone. There was absolutely no hope of him rescuing her, since he would not have the faintest idea where she was. In fact rescue or escape were so far beyond the bounds of possibility that the very thought of them made her predicament seem the more acute.

There was no way by which she could gauge the passage of time. They might have been gone only a few minutes, or perhaps they were already on their way back. Was it her imagination, or did she hear something near the door of the cellar? She heard it again, unmistakable this time, and then in the mirror she saw a figure glide up behind her. It was Paula, and she still had that ugly maniacal smile on her otherwise lovely face. She came round in front of Marie and gazed silently at her for a moment.

'Making the most of your last hour?' she asked. 'You've got twenty minutes left before . . . well let's not get ahead of ourselves. I came down to speak to you alone before the men come back because I wanted to tell you one or two little things. Afterwards, you may not be in a fit state to understand what I say.'

Paula looked furtively around her before going on.

'I didn't really mean what I said about Mark. I still love him and I intend to have him.'

She placed her hands on her hips and posed before Marie.

'Would you care to bet who he will want now? Will it be my lovely smooth body or your horribly charred remains?'

'What about your new boyfriend, Marcel?' Marie asked in a

low voice loaded with terror. She did not really care, but she had to say something. Perhaps by talking she might induce some sanity into the other girl's warped mind before it was too late.

'Are you kidding? I'm only using him and those two horrors with him to put my plan for you into effect. After tonight, I'll not be seeing him again.'

She shuddered.

'Ugh, he's a slimy character. I cringe every time he touches me.'

'That's most interesting, my dear Paula. One always likes to know who one can really trust.'

Marcel's voice from the doorway struck like a whiplash.

'Marcel!' Paula cried. 'I didn't hear you.'

Her dominating manner had evaporated in a flash and she looked very frightened.

'So I gather.'

Marcel sauntered into the room, his ever-present escort close behind him.

'Have you been standing there long?' Paula asked fearfully.

'Long enough.'

From the tone of his voice, there was no doubt that he had heard everything. Without warning he lashed out and struck her savagely across the face. The force of the blow made her stagger back.

'So I make you cringe, do I?'

He turned his head in the direction of his two shadows.

'I think we've strung up the wrong girl. Swap them.'

The last two words were fired like pistol shots and the two men moved swiftly into action. While Gorky gripped Paula from behind by her arms, his companion reached above Marie and, with a quick flash of his knife, cut her down.

The sudden relaxation of the weight on her arms almost caused Marie to crumple to the floor. She retained her balance, however, and backed carefully away from the centre of the room towards the open door. She had not yet fully comprehended the dramatic turn of events. All she knew was that she would fight with every last ounce of her strength if they tried to drag her back again.

But the three men appeared to have forgotten her. All their attention was now centred on Paula, and in spite of her dread of this appalling place, and the overwhelming desire to flee from it, Marie paused at the door. Drawn by a fascination even stronger than her personal terror, she stared back into the room and watched the awful scene being enacted there in the centre.

Although she struggled like a mad thing, Marcel's men quickly bound Paula's wrists and hung her from the pulley in Marie's place. The economy of effort with which they handled her, suggested that this was not the first time they had subdued an unwilling victim. Their efficiency was further demonstrated when they proceeded to strip the girl. Since her wrists were tied, the thin man had to cut away much of her clothing while Gorky pulled away the tattered remnants with obvious relish.

Marcel had watched the struggle in silence, but when Paula was quite naked, he rapped out a further command.

'The gag.'

'No, Marcel, please . . .' Paula screamed, but her words became a mumble as a rubber muzzle was forced roughly between her teeth and over her mouth and secured.

She stopped struggling momentarily and there was an unnatural silence as Marcel stepped forward.

'Soon, my dear Paula, it will be you who will make others cringe when they touch or even look at you. You should have known better than to have thought that you could play me for such a fool.'

At the doorway, Marie watched the girl's pale, nude body swivel helplessly and heard the plaintive whines from behind the cruel gag. But for a few unguarded words, she knew that Paula would have had her hanging there and yet she felt a deep pity for the wretched girl. Helpless to intervene, she still could not tear herself away from this cellar of horror.

Marcel reached out and ran his hand slowly down the length of Paula's body. She tried to arch away from it and then began to struggle furiously once more.

'Let's not waste any more time,' Marcel commanded sharply at last.

Like two robots the two men moved in on their victim.

Rubber plugs were thrust into Paula's ears, the metal manhole cover drawn aside and she was pulled along until she hung above the gaping hole.

'Quickly.' Marcel snapped, and while the thin man started to lower her, Gorky pushed two more plugs up her nose.

As her body descended towards the hole, Paula's legs threshed furiously in an effort to push herself away from its gaping embrace. It took the concerted strength of the two men to force her in, but once her legs were below ground level, it was a simple matter to lower her until she was out of sight.

Apart from a faint splashing sound from the hole, there was complete silence in the cellar for almost a minute. The two thugs stood back a little breathless, Marcel closely studied his watch and Marie shivered, but remained rooted to the spot. It was impossible to even comprehend the terrible agony which Paula was suffering as the acid ate into her face and body, disfiguring her beyond recognition.

'Right, get her out and into the other tank,' Marcel rapped at last.

The thin man hauled on the rope and the hideous, writhing creature that only seconds before had been a beautiful woman, was drawn up. A faint sizzling came from the red, raw flesh and the sounds from behind her gag were not human.

She was almost clear of the hole when the rope snapped and, with a splash, she fell back out of sight. The thin man staggered back, cursing, as the tension on his end of the rope was released.

'The acid must have eaten into the rope as well, boss!' he exclaimed.

Marcel made up his mind quickly.

'We'll never get her out now,' he snapped. 'Throw her clothes in and put back the cover and let's get out of here.'

Marie was already on her way. The splash of Paula's falling body had broken the spell which had compelled her to watch. She scrambled up the stairs and, oblivious of her nakedness, fled screaming into the night.

SOMETHING IN THE CELLAR

By A. G. J. Rough

CHARLIE TALBOT was, by nature, an extremely possessive and almost insanely jealous man. Consequently, when he found his wife, Stella, in what could only be politely described as an extremely compromising situation with his business partner, Clive Ratcliffe, one might naturally have expected him to explode in a fit of emotional fury and physical violence.

Surprisingly, Charlie did neither of these things. He just stood stock still in the bedroom doorway while his face darkened from red to purple as he stared at them, wide-eyed. His tightly compressed lips turned down in a white line that suggested both disgust and contempt. Every now and then his short, fat frame shook with an uncontrollable spasm of rage, but he said and did nothing.

Stella and Clive clung to each other, prepared for the on-slaught that never came. When it became obvious that Charlie didn't intend to kill them there and then, they were under-standably relieved. As soon as Clive managed to shake off the paralysing grip of fear he rolled off the bed, grabbed his trousers, dashed out of the house, and within the space of a few minutes was several miles away.

Stella didn't move. She lay naked on the bed, exposed and vulnerable, until Charlie turned on his heel and stormed out of the room, slamming the door behind him. Then she got dressed.

Stella was surprised when Charlie made no further reference to the incident. During the weeks that followed he hardly spoke to her at all, but there was nothing strange about that because Charlie had always been a man of very few words. Once upon a time Stella had admired him for his strong silence, but now she hated it as she did almost everything else about him. The trouble was that Stella needed plenty of physical love and attention. Charlie had long since ceased to give her either, so she had looked elsewhere for the physical pleasures that Charlie had failed to provide. Stella had serious doubts as to whether she would ever see Clive again. She was already compiling a list of young men who she thought might possibly jump at the chance of filling the space he had left vacant.

Charlie had different ideas. Now that his fears with regard to Stella's extra-marital behaviour had been confirmed, he kept her on a much tighter rein. He seldom let her out of his sight and even took to doing most of his work at home, instead of at the office. He was determined that Stella would never get a chance to make a fool of him again.

When the time came for Charlie's annual business conference he took great pains in devising a plan to ensure Stella's fidelity during his absence. He couldn't take Stella with him because her presence would seriously interfere with his own private arrangements. His secretary was, after all, very attractive. No, Stella would stay where she was. Very much so, in fact. Stella was overjoyed at the prospect of having three weeks to herself. With Charlie hundreds of miles away in Austria she would have ample opportunity to rid herself of some of her pent-up frustration. She was so busy making plans that she didn't notice the sound that Charlie made as he worked in the cellar.

The night before he was due to leave, Charlie walked up to Stella, gave her a friendly smile, and then hit her so hard with his large meaty fist that she didn't wake up until he had carried her deep down into the dark, damp cellar.

When she finally regained her senses Stella was able to examine Charlie's work at first hand. He had removed a great deal of masonry from the cellar wall and had dug out a small cave, about six feet square, in the tightly packed earth behind it. Charlie had driven a large wooden post into the floor of the cave and had chained Stella to it by her left wrist. She shook her head and looked up to see Charlie, still smiling, mixing cement out in the cellar, jaundicedly illuminated by a single, naked electric bulb.

Although she fully realized her position Stella didn't panic.

Her senses were still numbed by the crushing blow she had received.

'What are you doing, Charlie?' she asked in a small, shaky voice, nervously fingering the chain on her wrist.

'This, my love,' chuckled Charlie, vigorously turning and patting the cement with his shovel, 'is the modern man's answer to the chastity belt!' Stella said nothing. Her head was still spinning. She gave an involuntary start as a rat scuffled past her in the darkness.

Charlie laughed.

'Just a rat. I would've thought that you'd be used to them by now! Anyway, if not, you should be after spending three weeks with them!'

Stella still said nothing, but just stared at him. She believed him all right. Charlie was capable of anything.

Charlie was inwardly annoyed by the fact that she was taking it all so calmly. He wanted her to scream, he wanted her to suffer, the deceitful bitch. He was comforted by the thought that she was sure to be screaming before the three weeks were up.

He dropped the shovel, stooped down, and started to cement the bricks into place.

'Don't worry – you won't starve,' he muttered, pointing to a pile of cardboard boxes and several plastic containers that stood in one corner of the cave.

'Plenty of food and water, but it'll be bloody dark. But there again, you always were at your best in the dark, weren't you, Stella? Anyway, love, be good and don't do anything I wouldn't!' He laughed loudly at his own joke and slapped another brick into place.

Stella watched him slowly disappear as the wall grew higher. It took him over two hours to finish the job of walling her up. He left out one brick so that she would be able to breathe, and then sat down on the cellar floor and waited for the cement to dry. Stella knew he was still there because the yellow light shone into the cave through the hole in the wall. Finally the light went out and Stella sat in total darkness, knowing that Charlie had gone.

Charlie wasn't as happy as he should have been. Stella still wasn't screaming.

Charlie intended to make a holiday of the trip. Instead of flying to Austria direct he decided to make the journey by road. In this way he hoped to be able to admire the scenery and to appreciate more fully the pleasure of Miss Taylor's company.

They took the air-ferry from Southend Airport to Ostend and from there drove through Belgium and Germany and on towards Austria.

It was late at night when the accident happened. Charlie's mind wasn't on driving. His thoughts were divided between those concerning the delightful Miss Taylor who was curled up on the seat beside him, her head resting lightly on his shoulder, and those about Stella who was walled-up in a cellar, many miles away, with only rats and worms for company. Charlie was almost asleep at the wheel when the car slewed off the greasy ribbon of mountain road, splintered through the white safety railings and slowly somersaulted down towards the floor of the valley below. Charlie glimpsed the headlights insanely illuminating first the wall of the cliff, then the scudding clouds in the night sky above, and finally the jagged rocks, towards which they were plunging.

As the car tumbled Charlie was thrown about like a helpless rag doll. He could hear Miss Taylor screaming a long, drawn-out, and terrified scream. He had the ridiculous thought that it was Stella who should have been screaming. It was the only thought he had time for before pain came at him from every direction as the car ploughed into the rocks. Metal warped and twisted as if in the crushing grip of a giant hand, and then everything was suddenly silent.

The staff at the hospital did their best. They straightened Charlie's broken bones, amputated two of his fingers, stitched him up, and left him lying in a coma. Their best wasn't good enough for Miss Taylor. They could probably have saved her life if they had been able to find all the pieces. As it was she was dead within an hour of her arrival at the hospital.

Charlie lay in a coma for nine months before he returned to the conscious world of the living. As soon as he was able to think for himself his first thoughts were of Stella. He was scared, because the sole responsibility for what he assumed had resulted in his wife's death rested on him. He didn't voice his fears for that very same reason. He hadn't intended to kill her, but he had become, nevertheless, a murderer.

Charlie's remaining months at the hospital passed with agonizing slowness. He slept very little, but when he did his dreams were haunted by ghastly visions of Stella's rotting corpse lying deep beneath the earth, covered in dust and cobwebs, with white-glazed eyes staring blindly at the rodents that gnawed away at her mouldering flesh. The dreams became so bad that he didn't sleep at all during his last week at the hospital. He just lay quietly in his bed, forcing his eyes to stay open until the coming of dawn.

It was a full year before Charlie's doctors pronounced him fit enough to return home. They warned him that he was still very weak and instructed him to take things easy for a few months, avoiding all unnecessary excitement. They were totally unaware of the tension and the fevered excitement that he felt, even as he left the hospital.

The house was exactly as he had left it. Before leaving the German hospital he had telephoned his office so that they would get somebody to clean out the house in preparation for his return home. He deposited his suitcases in the hall-way and wandered from room to room, all the while trying to resist the compulsion to go straight down into the cellar. He wanted time to prepare himself for what he might find there.

Charlie was both relieved and surprised by the fact that nobody, so far anyway, had questioned Stella's disappearance. He assumed that this was probably due to the extremely limited social life that he and Stella had led. They had very few friends and those same friends were probably under the impression that Stella had gone to Germany to attend him during his stay in hospital. It was reasonable to assume, therefore, that they would expect her to return home with him. It would probably prove necessary to fabricate a story of some sort to explain her absence, but that was a bridge he would cross when he came to it.

Charlie didn't want to go into the cellar, but he found himself drawn irresistibly towards it. His eyes rested on the heavy wooden door that stood before him, slightly ajar. He reached forward to close it, but as he did so he could have sworn he heard the metallic rattle of a chain from somewhere down below. For a moment he stood frozen with terror. It was impossible even to think that Stella might still be alive. Her supply of food and water would barely have lasted four weeks. He refused to believe his ears. Then he heard it again.

Charlie's hand was shaking as he pulled open the door, switched on the light, and made his way slowly down the stairs. Now the only sound he could hear was that of his own harsh breathing and the creak of the staircase as he took each hesitant step downward. Beads of perspiration stood out on his forehead and, as he reached the cellar floor he licked his lips nervously before going over and placing his ear against the cold, damp wall. For a few moments he heard nothing, but then, very faintly, came the sound of a low moan followed by a further, louder, rattling of the chain. There was silence for a short while, and then came the noise of something sharp scraping at the inside of the wall, very close to his ear. Then the scraping stopped and Charlie nearly collapsed with fright when he heard a feeble, cracked voice speaking to him.

'Is that you, Charlie?' wheezed the voice.

Charlie pulled his ear sharply away from the brickwork and stood, mouth agape, staring at the wall in disbelief. Stella was still alive. It seemed impossible, yet he had heard her voice. This sudden realization snapped him into action.

'Hang on, Stella! I'll get you out!' he shouted, frantically looking for something suitable with which to break through the wall.

He snatched up the shovel and swung it violently against the brickwork. The recoil of the blow sent the shovel spinning out of his hands and it clattered to the floor. The wall was undamaged.

Charlie searched elsewhere and eventually found a sledge-hammer, lying with an assortment of rusty gardening implements, under some sacking in a dark corner. He dragged the formidable hammer out of the darkness, swung it on to his shoulder and approached the wall. With his first thudding blow the brickwork began to crumble. He worked in a frenzy, swinging the hammer harder and faster as the hole in the wall became larger. His breath came in short, laboured gasps and the frantic pounding of his heart hammered in his ears. When his strength began to fail him he dropped the hammer and began to tear the loosened bricks out of the wall with his bare hands. Finally the job was finished and Charlie sank to his knees, exhausted, with blood dripping from his raw fingers. Through the darkness and the settling dust he could make out a dim figure, crouched in a black corner of the cave. Charlie coughed as the irritating dust found its way into his lungs and, as he did so, the crouching figure stirred. The figure dragged itself, slowly and deliberately, out into the yellow light of the cellar, and Charlie saw her clearly for the first time in over a year.

Charlie stopped coughing as suddenly as he had begun. He tried to scream, but all he could manage was a strangled croak. Stella's face was only two feet from his own and what he saw wasn't at all like the Stella that he remembered.

A green fungoid growth had sprouted from her left eye socket and had eaten its way through the flesh of her cheek, exposing the bleached white bone beneath. Large patches of her hair had fallen out, leaving moist red sores in their place. The bottom lip of her slack, shapeless mouth hung down to reveal a jagged row of pointed yellow teeth. A trickle of blood dribbled down over her chin and in one gnarled claw she clutched a half-devoured rat. She stared at Charlie with one white, sightless, sunken eye, set in a pillow of bloated grey flesh and then, groping out of her personal darkness, she stretched a horny hand towards him.

'I knew you wouldn't forget me, Charlie!' She dragged herself closer to him.

'Kiss me, Charlie, kiss me!'

Charlie was nearly sick. He found the strength to pull himself to his feet and would probably have fled from the cellar if it hadn't been for the sharp stabbing pain that he suddenly felt, deep in his chest. He staggered to the far wall and leaned against it for support. He knew that he had nothing to fear while Stella was chained to the wooden post.

When the pain had hit him Charlie had instinctively clenched his teeth and closed his eyes. However, when he heard a shuffling noise he looked up to see the grotesque figure of Stella tottering towards him. Somehow she had managed to unfasten the chain and he watched with terror as she came closer and closer. He pressed himself tightly against the wall and managed to raise one arm to defend himself before the pain in his chest exploded in an all-consuming fire and he crumpled to the floor. The beating of his heart ceased to thunder in his ears and the silence was broken only by the rattling gurgle that died in his throat. Charlie twitched a few times and then everything was still.

Stella carefully removed her elaborate make-up and then made a telephone call. They came in an ambulance and took Charlie away in it. The doctor was very kind, but he did say that Charlie should never have been knocking walls down in his condition. Anyway, he was dead and nothing they could do or say would change that.

Stella was pleased with the way that things had worked out. She wasn't too scared when Charlie walled her up in the cellar because she knew something that he didn't. Clive, naturally enough, had been aware of Charlie's impending business trip and had phoned her beforehand in order to arrange a meeting for as soon as possible after Charlie left home. Fortunately Charlie had been in the bathroom when the phone rang, so he knew nothing about the conversation.

Clive had turned up only a few hours after Charlie's departure and had let himself into the house with a key that Stella had given to him some months previously. Stella had been able to hear Clive's car drive up to the house because the driveway passed directly over the portion of the cellar in which she was imprisoned. As soon as she knew that Clive was in the house she had shouted and rattled her chain for all she was worth. Fortunately Clive had heard her and had come to the rescue.

After that it had been easy for them to keep tabs on Charlie while he lay in a hospital bed somewhere in Germany. Charlie had played right into their hands when he had phoned the office to let them know that he was coming home. It had given them plenty of time to make their plans.

Going back into the cellar had been Stella's own idea. She had done a good deal of theatrical work before she married Charlie, so she had been well prepared for the part that she intended to play. She had spent hours preparing her face and when she was ready, Clive had obligingly walled her up in the cellar again. Then she had sat patiently in the darkness and waited for Charlie.

Stella was pleased both with her performance and its outcome. Now she had Clive and Charlie's half of the business. Of course, she wouldn't work at the office the way Charlie had done. Clive would have to find another man to do that. Somehow Stella couldn't help wondering who the man would be, and hoping that she would find him attractive.

RINGING TONE

By John Christopher

HE WAS a quiet ordinary man of about fifty, his voice educated and well modulated, his blue-grey suit of good cloth and cut, his manner pleasant, at times almost apologetic. He had put up at a small country hotel in the north of England, and had one drink in the bar before dinner, and was now sitting in the lounge over his coffee.

The manageress of the hotel thought he might have been a military man: his carriage was erect and his small moustache neatly clipped. But if so, he did not use his title. He registered simply as J. F. Hall, nationality British, home address: The Pines, Burdock, Devon. He had booked for one night only, and asked for an early breakfast the next morning.

She wondered briefly if he were married. He did not have a married look. She saw him as a bachelor, or perhaps a widower, returning to a small house in the country.

She glanced in on him as she passed the lounge. He had taken the local telephone directory from its place in the hall, and was leafing through it.

A traveller, looking for possible contacts. The manageress nodded to herself, and moved on. Had she stayed, she would have seen him browse on through the directory, and note down half a dozen other numbers. But not, although she was right about his being a traveller, the numbers of commercial firms. Each number had a girl's, or woman's, name beside it.

She had been right about his background, too. Burdock was a village south of Exeter, The Pines a small cottage on its outskirts. A simple country place, where he was known and liked. It was about seven o'clock, on a still bright summer evening. He put the car away, in the garage behind the cottage, and carried his bag and his briefcase to the house. Inside he found a note from Mrs Williams, his daily help. It told him that she had picked both broad beans and raspberries and they were in bowls in the fridge.

He unpacked, putting his dirty clothes in the laundry basket for Mrs Williams to take away next day. He moved about the house, seeing that everything was in order and properly dusted. Then he went down to the kitchen and made supper for himself.

Mrs Williams had left him a piece of rump steak, and washed and scraped new potatoes. He grilled the steak, boiled the potatoes lightly with a little mint, cooked some of the broad beans from his garden, and tossed them in melted butter. He worked well and deftly, leaving no mess. He did not eat in the kitchen, but took things through to his small but nicely furnished dining room, with water-colours of the Middle East round the walls. He brought a bottle of beer from the fridge, too, and drank it out of a silver tankard with an inscription on one side. The inscription ran:

Captain J. F. Hall
42nd Lancers
Middleweight Boxing Champion
1939

He had raspberries and cream after the steak, and put a kettle on for coffee while he washed and dried the plates and pots.

He took the coffee with him into his parlour. There was a radio and a television set, but he did not switch either of them on. There was also a case on the wall, full of books, but he did not take one out. He stirred his coffee, relaxed and contemplating pleasure. When he had sipped it, and found it still too hot, he took his diary out of his pocket and went through it.

There were several pages covered with his meticulous hand-writing, more than fifty names and numbers culled from directories ranging from Newcastle to Bristol. The first was Jennifer Gillott. He sipped his coffee again, and pulled the telephone towards him. Picking up the handpiece, he dialled the number. At the end there was a brief silence and then, with the familiar lift of excitement, he heard it ringing out. His mouth dried as he waited, and he was forced to swallow. A click, and a voice said: 'Hello.'

'Is that Miss Gillott?'

'Yes. Yes, it is. Who's that?'

A young warm voice, no older than late twenties, with a touch of the North in the vowels. Self possessed, though. A secretary, perhaps. He said: 'Jennifer, are you listening carefully?'

'Who *is* that?'

'Listen.'

He began to talk in his quiet, well modulated voice, at first only touching on the outrageous, more innuendo than anything else, a careful slow assault on modesty. She allowed him to go on for quite a long time before she broke in: 'Who are you? You're disgusting!'

Then the obscenities began to flow, slowly at first, spaced out, but more torrentially as excitement quickened. When she interrupted, he allowed her to do so, relishing her shock and nausea. It was quite a good one; several minutes before she hung up. He put down his own telephone and sat back.

Gradually his pulse subsided. Against the name in the diary he put a small tick.

He made three other contacts that evening. The first hung up on him very quickly. The third listened readily. He sensed rather than heard the other person in the room, the hand over the receiver, the quick instruction to go next door and telephone the police. He hung up and sat back, wiping his brow.

Besides, he had the memory of the second one to dwell on. The best of the evening. A soft-voiced girl, whose genuine horror and disgust were tinctured with fascination; innocence surrendering itself to be corrupted.

Against her name, he put a cross. He would come back to her.

He was, as always after the calls, tired, drained of energy but relaxed. He made himself a cup of hot milk.

The following evening he was asked out to supper by a

couple, a retired bank manager and his wife, who lived in the next village and who seemed to like his company. They were nice people, but depressingly concerned with social distinctions. He had a notion that a lot of their interest in him was due to his accent and his old school tie. He found this pitiable, but tolerated them; and although he quite enjoyed preparing his own meals, it made a pleasant change not to have to do so.

The evening after that, he walked into the village, had a couple of pints, in halves, at the Spread Eagle, and came back to eat bread and cheese and watch television. It was during the next day that he felt the restlessness beginning to stir in him. A couple of times he went into the parlour for no particular purpose, and found himself gazing at the telephone where it sat, black and anonymous.

The feeling had returned earlier than usual. His need – the tension building up, to be followed by the release – came at intervals that varied between a fortnight and six weeks, averaging rather less than a month. But he understood a lot about himself, and could find a reason for its swift return this time. That last call had been a mistake; he should have ended on the soft-voiced girl, on the delicious note of half-response. The one after that, the woman who had tried to keep him on the line so as to trap him, had unsettled him.

He made himself China tea at four o'clock, and nibbled a chocolate biscuit while he drank it. He stared at the telephone, but did not lift it. He did not make calls until the cheap period. Sunday morning, perhaps? He had never done that. They would be lying in bed, some of them, drowsy and vulnerable. It was a tempting speculation, but he did not pursue it. Sunday morning was wrong. On Sunday morning he went to church, as he had done since he was a boy. Just before six he switched on the television for the News. Words and pictures washed meaninglessly across his mind. The News began at five minutes to the hour. At six o'clock ... He felt for the diary in his pocket and then, with his unhurried military gait, walked across the room to turn the television off. There was silence, with no sound except birds outside. Silence, and the telephone.

He drew three blanks in succession, and the fourth hung up on him before he had the chance to say more than a word or two.

He did not dial the next number on his list, but put on his jacket, and walked down to the village.

He had a few half pints at the Spread Eagle. He knew all the people in the bar, and one or two of them spoke to him. But the tension was still in him; he heard, like a whisper of delight, the thin clamour of imagined voices. He refused the offer of another drink, thanking the man politely, and set off for home.

He got through right away. It was as though she had been standing by the telephone, waiting for him.

'Miss Spalding?' he said.

'Yes,' she said. 'Speaking.'

The voice was slightly breathless, young. He began to talk, weaving his way forward into the suburbs of pleasure. She did not interrupt him. When he paused, she said: 'Go on.'

It happened sometimes, though rarely, that he chanced on a woman whose need matched his own. Those occasions, when they occurred, were exquisitely enjoyable, though he felt unhappy afterwards and never telephoned them again. But this one was not like that. There was a strangeness in her voice, but it was not sensual response.

She said: 'Go on. Talk to me.'

He tried, and thought he was succeeding, but the situation confused and disturbed him. He broke off again, and she said swiftly: 'Don't stop. Say anything. Anything you like. I don't mind. But please don't stop talking.'

It had gone wrong. There was nothing he could say, and the sensible thing was to put the telephone down, to try another. But he was held by what he had recognized in her voice. It was desperation.

She said: 'I have to talk to someone. I don't mind ... anything. I have to ... Listen, do you want to know about me? I'm twenty-one, but people say I look even younger. Men say. And pretty. They say that, too. And sexy. You want to talk about that, don't you? I'll listen. I promise.'

He did not speak.

'I'm dark,' she said. 'And I have a good figure. Thirty-six bust. Thirty-six hips. Twenty-four waist, but I can pull it in even smaller. Do you want to know what I'm wearing? Well, practically nothing. Just a housecoat and slippers. And scent. It's called *Femme*, and that means *woman*. I've been told it's very seductive. I've been told.'

He heard her draw breath.

'Do you want more? Do you want to talk about my love life? I'm not a virgin. Does that matter? There were . . . two or three. Unimportant ones. And then one more serious. Do you want to know about him? I don't mind telling you. His name was Tony. Tony Phillips. He used to make love to me. Do you want to know the details? Where and when, how many times? I don't care. Honestly. I just want to believe that the world isn't all emptiness – that there is someone there, anyone.'

He said: 'I don't think . . .'

'Don't go! Please don't go. It's such an old story, a tale out of a cheap fiction magazine. I can't help wondering – am I a cheap fiction character myself? Is everyone? No, you're not, are you? You're real. You have to be. But you see – he was married, and he and his wife didn't get on, and he was going to leave her – get a divorce and marry me. You've read about that, haven't you? And seen it on films and television. So perhaps it didn't happen at all. Perhaps it was just something I read, or saw, and dreamed about. A bad dream. People don't die of bad dreams.'

He moved slowly to put the receiver down, hearing her voice get smaller, more tinny, as the handpiece approached its rest. But, as though she sensed what was happening, he heard her cry: 'Please! Please stay!' and almost unwillingly brought it back.

'You're there, aren't you?' she said. 'You are there?'

He said: 'Yes. I'm here.'

'You know what happens, don't you? The girl finds she's going to have a baby. And is happy at first, because she wants that. She wants his child. His wife is bound to divorce him, isn't she? But then the girl realizes he isn't happy. He's worried. It would cause a scandal, and would hurt him in his job.

'And there's the daughter he already has. She's away at school, and he hasn't talked about her much, and the girl hasn't realized how much he loves her. And it would hurt her, too, you see. He doesn't say anything, not at first. But it's enough that she can tell he's worried. And so instead of loving the thing that's growing inside her, she begins to hate it, for his sake, because it might hurt him. In the end, it's she who talks about abortion. He looks so much happier when she does. He says she's not to worry. He'll find out everything, pay for everything. And it isn't like a person when you don't see it. And there will be time to have children, later, when things can be done tidily, properly, with no scandal and no fuss.'

She paused, and he thought she might be going to weep. But she went on: 'He did all he said, he found the place and he paid the bill. And he came in to see me. He brought me flowers and liqueur chocolates, and he'd forgotten that I don't like cherries, but you can't remember everything, can you? And probably he was pre-occupied, thinking about the note he was going to write to me. How to put it tactfully. He didn't send the note until I came out of the nursing home place. It was very well written . . .

'He put it very well. That a crisis like this makes one realize things. That an affair like this wasn't right for me, but that he had been living in a fool's paradise in thinking it could ever be any different. Because Helen, that's his wife, Helen, would never let him go. And Jane, that's his daughter, the next few years were vital for her. She was taking her O-levels. So it wasn't fair to me, and therefore it had to end so that I wouldn't be hurt any more than I had been. It was thoughtful of him, wasn't it?'

He did not answer.

She said: 'That was yesterday. I wrote back to him. I begged him to come and see me today, at least telephone me if he could not manage that. I told him I would wait in. And then this morning I thought that they might have gone away for the weekend, so I telephoned his house. His wife answered: Helen. I met her once, at one of the firm's parties. I didn't say anything, just held my hand over the telephone. And I heard her call to him: "*Tony, there's someone here, but they're not answering.*" And him saying, very far off: "*It's probably only a joke. Hang up.*" I've been sitting here since then, waiting for him to come, or to ring me.

'It's a funny thing, I used to be afraid of heights, but today I'm not. I've always avoided looking out of windows, but today I've kept going back to them. Everything below looks so small, so unimportant. As he is, as I am. I told myself I would give him till six o'clock to ring, and then I gave him another hour, and another. And at last I gave him half an hour, and my mind was quite made up, and I was glad about it, and then, on the very last minute of the half hour, the telephone rang, and I picked it up. It was you.'

He said: 'I'm sorry.'

'Don't be sorry. Talk to me. Or listen. I don't mind what we talk about. Because everything's so small and far away, and I've left the window open, and I think I am a little frightened, but there's nothing else that makes sense, because I can't live like this. Don't you see? There has to be someone else, apart from myself. Do you want to know what happened, the last time we were together? I made a meal for him, a risotto because he liked risotto, and he brought a bottle of Chianti, and afterwards we put the record player on, and we . . .'

With a sudden movement, he hammered the receiver down. There was a metallic clang.

Dusk was falling. The air was calm and warm, and the scent of stocks and roses came through the open window.

He often walked in the garden, after telephoning. It gave him reassurance, and a kind of peace. But tonight peace evaded him. His mind was prey to another's agony. He attempted to dismiss it: an hysterical girl, no more than that. The world was full of them. It did not concern him. None of those he telephoned concerned him. They were not people, but voices. She was alone, and trapped, but who wasn't? There was nothing, anyway, that he could do for her.

Early stars winked in the sky. The earth was rolling on eastwards into the night.

He walked back into the house. For several moments he stood by the telephone, staring at it. Then he dialled her number.

It rang, and went on ringing, with no reply.

THE NECKLACE

By Dulcie Gray

LITTLE BERNARD STUBBS wasn't like other boys. His head was enormous, his body was small, and one leg was crippled. When he talked which was seldom, he talked with a lisp, and he had a bad stutter. His personality was as unattractive as his appearance. He was cruel and bad tempered, and totally unloving.

His parents did their best with him, but they found the going tough. The local social worker had suggested that he should be 'taken care of', but his mother had refused on the grounds that a family upbringing was better for the boy; that parents, however inadequate, were better than strangers, however skilled. The social worker had retired, dubiously.

Bernard Stubbs loved sewing. Though mentally extremely backward, he was fairly clever with his hands, and he especially enjoyed threading large china beads, to make necklaces and bracelets. He would adorn himself with these, and then stare for hours at himself in the mirror. He seemed to find the spectacle delightful.

He also liked pulling the wings off flies and attempting to set fire to the tail of the next-door neighbour's cat. On very rare occasions, as a 't-t-tweet' he would give his mother 'a prethy' in the form of one of his bead necklaces, and for the following few days, as long as she was in his sight, she was forced to wear it. If she didn't, he flew into such an ungovernable rage that it seemed as if he'd start a fit.

Life was hard for Bernard's parents.

Looking on the bright side, however, this creative urge did have the merit of keeping him happy for hours at a time, while he was actually employed. It also kept him from trying to catch the tamer sparrows and robins that frequented the garden, and wringing their necks.

On Bernard's eighth birthday he was given a trout for lunch. For the first time, he was allowed to have the whole fish on his plate, and to wrestle with the bones himself. Until now, he had only been given the flesh of a fish, carefully filleted, and since he was seldom allowed in the kitchen (where his mother felt he might come to harm) he had never seen a whole dead fish before. The trout enchanted him. 'Fith! Fith!' he chanted. 'Lubbly fith!' 'Yes, darling,' said his mother. 'Eat it up.' 'Eythe. Eythe!' he went on rapturously. 'Lubberly eythe. Fith eythe. Fith eythe. Beautiful.' 'Lovely fish eyes,' cooed his mother comfortingly.

Bernard ate his fish in absorbed silence, skilfully avoiding the bones, but making a hell of a mess round his plate. Both his father and mother tried not to look at it, and they both did their best to signal gay smiles of encouragement at him – it was after all the boy's birthday; but when lunch was over, his father went thankfully into the garden to do a bit of pruning, and his mother began equally thankfully to clear the table. Bernard, his face smothered in fish, cabbage, and ice-cream, remained in his place, deep in what appeared to be some sort of trance.

The telephone rang and Mrs Stubbs went to answer it. Bernard got down from the table and went thoughtfully out of the room.

At half past three it was finished; a neat little bracelet of china beads and trouts' eyes. 'Lubberly. Lubberly. Fith eythe. Prethy,' said Bernard, handing the bracelet to his mother. 'For you, M-m-mammy.'

'How nice!', exclaimed Mrs Stubbs, revolted. 'Thank you, darling. How kind.' She wore the bracelet unhappily for two days, until the eyes mercifully disintegrated.

From this time on, Bernard became obsessed by eyes. He would stare at his own in the mirror; at his parents' eyes; at the eyes of the birds in the garden, of the neighbour's long-suffering cat, of the cows in the fields which surrounded the cottage, of the strangers he met, and best of all, at the eyes of the dead fish on the marble slabs in the fishmonger's, when his mother took him shopping in the village. 'Eythe, eythe. Lubberly eythe,' he would chant. And at home he went on making his bracelets of beads.

As he grew older, his fits of rage became so frightening that his parents called in the social worker once again. Bernard had considerable strength when he was in a temper. Though his body was still undeveloped and his leg was still crippled he could set about him, when he was angry, in such a way, that even his father couldn't control him. And at sixteen, he was even more unfortunate to look at, than he had been as a child. The social worker was delighted to be of assistance. 'He'll be far happier with us,' she said. 'We'll know how to deal with him. Our staff is dedicated, and he'll be with lots of boys just like himself.'

Bernard's parents looked at each other in amazement.

The days before Bernard went to the home were anxious days. His first reaction to the plan was violently antagonistic. When he was calmer, his mother explained how exciting the future was going to be. 'There'll be lots of other boys just like you,' she said, quoting the social worker. His father said heartily, 'It's a kind of school, old chap. All boys have to go to school, you know.' Bernard only stared at them thoughtfully and said, 'Will they let me make necklaces?'

'Of course!' cried the parents simultaneously.

'And how many boys will there be?' asked Bernard.

'Thirty-four I believe,' replied his mother anxiously.

'And will they all have eythe?' asked Bernard.

'Of course.'

Bernard smiled happily.

A look of relief passed between the parents. Apparently he was reconciled to the idea.

The next two years passed uneventfully. Bernard did well at the home, and his parents flourished guiltily in his absence. So well did Bernard behave, in fact, that it was decided that he could spend a weekend at his own home on trial. His mother had heart palpitations before his arrival and had to take sedatives. His father went on a drinking spree.

Bernard wore a new blue suit with a green satin tie, for the occasion. His hair was plastered down over his enormous head, and his stutter was even more pronounced. He had asked for trout as a special treat for supper, and he seemed pleased to see his parents and his old home. He was taken up to this own room before the meal, where he found several old bead necklaces, which he wore festooned round his neck while he ate. He didn't offer his mother one.

He was particularly silent while he was eating, and to his parents' surprise he went to bed quite early. Emotionally exhausted they followed suit shortly.

Soon after midnight Bernard crept down the front stairs, and out to the gardening hut, where he found a hatchet. With this he hacked his mother and father to death, and for good measure he went next door and did the same for the neighbour, the neighbour's wife, and their cat.

When the police came, he was sitting calmly on the floor of the living room, making a necklace for the matron of the home, from eight human eyes, six trouts' eyes, two cat's eyes, and assorted coloured beads.

SELF-EMPLOYED

By Walter Winward

SOMETIMES IT could be a very rewarding job. Like all jobs, of course, it had its awkward, irritating moments, but in the last analysis it was better to be one's own boss than work for someone else. He'd tried being an employee when he was younger, but it hadn't been a successful experiment. Whether he was employed by a shipping company or an insurance company or even a bank, there was always someone with a little power who'd make life hell. Mainly, they'd make life hell for him, never anyone else. 'Chalmers, do this. Chalmers, do that. Chalmers, these figures are incorrect. Chalmers, when will you learn that it's only by constant endeavour, by studying and mastering your profession, that you will get on?'

The trouble was, they were right. He'd always know that. But they were not right for Fred Chalmers. They were right for the others, for the slaves, for those who would always be employees – but not for him. He was an individual. He couldn't work for others. He had to be his own master, make his own decisions. Sometimes he'd be right and sometimes he'd be wrong, but they were *his* decisions. And that was what life was all about: making decisions and standing by them. Weighing up the various factors involved and then taking action. Always that. Always taking action. Never clock-watching or wishing to God it were Saturday or planning next summer's holiday.

He sipped his coffee and glanced down at the newspaper by his elbow. It was three days old, but that didn't matter. Three days old or three months old, the same tales of woe were always bannered across the front page. War, famine, rape, murder, robbery, accident, eviction. Why in God's name was it that newspapers concentrated on such things? Wasn't anything pleasant happening in the world?

Yes, of course it was. Outside it was spring, and the daffodils in the park were yellow and fluffy. On the lake, the drakes would be squabbling with each other over a mate. Children would be laughing and dancing and skipping, and their parents would be keeping an anxious eye on them, scolding them when they went too near the water. The trees were in bud, and soon the buds would become leaves and winter just a memory. Of course pleasant things were happening in the world. It was only unpleasant people who made the opposite seem the norm.

A man learned a lot about people when he worked for himself. It was not like being a member of a vast corporation, where, if something went wrong, there was always someone else to carry the can. A man who was self-employed *had* to know about people, otherwise he rapidly went out of business. He learned to tell the difference between the bad and the good, the fortunate and the unfortunate, the avaricious and the meek, the go-getters and the hell-benters, and the placid let's-do-something-unusual-and-watch-the-television-ers. He learned, by studying their eyes and their hands and how they stood, to tell whether they were going to try to put one over on him.

It was a lonely life, naturally, when one was managing director, travelling salesman, chief clerk, and all the etceteras of one's own firm. His solitary assistant showed promise, but it would be years before he could say to the lad: 'Okay, it's all yours. I'm pensioning myself off.'

One assistant.

All right, so it was a small organization, but it was unique in its field. And who else of the slaves he'd left behind him twenty years ago could say that they had their own firm, small or not?

Anyway, lonely life or no lonely life, it had been a damn good and interesting one. For almost half of his fifty-three years he'd been happy, doing what he wanted to do, doing, he was certain, what he's been born to do. He'd made very few mistakes in those years. In fact, the single major mistake of his life had been made before he set up on his own ...

He was twenty-nine and she was twenty-four when they met. Her name was Mary, and he'd fallen for her immediately. She was a beauty; dark hair and darker eyes and so small and light he could have picked her up in one arm. The lads around the office where he then worked used to tease him, saying that shy Freddie Chalmers stood no chance at all with a girl like Mary. She had a reputation for being fast and flighty, and her tastes were in the expensive-dinner and sports-car league. He'd plucked up enough courage to ask her out on two occasions, and he'd been refused twice. But he persevered, and the fourth time he asked her out, she said yes.

It had been a wonderful evening. They'd had a simple meal and a bottle of wine, and he'd listened while she chatted about everything she'd done and all the things she wanted to do. He hardly spoke at all. There was no need. He loved to listen and she loved to talk. Later, when he took her home, she seemed very surprised that he made no attempt to kiss her goodnight.

He took her out again, and then a third time. The lads in the office were amazed. What the hell did Freddie Chalmers have that none of the others had? Perhaps they'd misjudged him. Perhaps old Freddie had something tucked down his trousers that none of them knew about. Perhaps he was giving Mary a slice of the cake she'd always been looking for but never found.

He didn't understand it, either. He liked to think it was because he was gentle with her, because he gave her a good, relaxing time without demanding anything in return. He liked to think it was because of the flowers he sent her or the fact that, in some way, she knew he secretly took dancing lessons in order to be able to please her the more. But really he didn't understand it. The one thing he did understand was that he was fascinated by her.

He proposed within a month, and she accepted. He walked on clouds. The lads in the office shook their heads and gave the marriage a year at most. Whatever it was that made flighty Mary want to marry a dullard like Freddie, sooner or later she would again show her true colours. The she-leopard did not change her spots *that* easily. One day, Freddie would be sorry he'd taken her on. A quick bang in the hay was one thing; marriage was a different ladleful of soup.

He knew about the gossip and it didn't bother him. Where all the others had failed, he had succeeded. He had his Mary and she was happy. To be exact, she was happy for just under a year.

Looking back, it was difficult for him to pinpoint the precise moment she started to complain they didn't get out enough. He was working during the day and studying in the evening. It was against his nature to study for advancement in this particular job, but he was doing it for her. He wanted to give her more and more and more. He wanted her to have a house of her own and not just furnished rooms. He wanted to be able to buy a car and take her out for spins on a Sunday. He wanted her to have a new dress whenever she needed one. And so he studied.

One night she announced that she was going out.

'Where to?' he asked.

'Oh, just to see some friends. You stick with your books, love; I won't be long.'

She was away an hour. And then it was two hours. And then it was two hours three times a week. And then it was every night.

He heard talk around the neighbourhood and in the office that Mrs Chalmers had been seen going into a dance hall with a man. He ignored it. There was more talk. Mrs Chalmers had been seen here, there, and everywhere with one man, another man, a third man. Poor Mr Chalmers, the talk said. He married a tart.

The lads in the office nodded wisely.

The day he decided to go home early had been a bad one for him. He had a splitting headache and it seemed that everyone in the department had the name Mary Chalmers on their lips. Or his name.

Poor Freddie, didn't know what he was letting himself in for . . . Had it on the best authority that she was seen getting the business in an alley off Praed Street ... Well, I can name you a dozen blokes who've been there ... She's quite a lay, though, Mary ... She throws it around a bit ... Who's complaining? ... I haven't had my share yet ... Just call her up, she's available ... Listen, she does one of the greatest turns this side of the Thames ... Poor Freddie ...

The headache grew worse. Poor Freddie ... She's quite a lay ... Throws it around a bit ... Just call her up ... Poor Freddie ... Poor Freddie ... Poor Freddie ...

It couldn't be, he told himself on his way home. It couldn't be. It was another Mary. Not his Mary. She wouldn't do it. Every penny he earned was for her. He'd do anything for her. Die for her. Not his Mary. Not his ...

But it was his Mary they were all talking about; he knew it, so he didn't call when he got inside the front door. He walked straight into the bedroom. And there she was – naked, thighs wide, moaning, whispering dirty, unbelievable things to the man on top of her.

The whore. The filthy, dirty, spew-ridden whore.

He tore into the man and then into his wife. He beat her until his arm ached, until she was crying and sobbing and begging him to stop. But he kept on and on until she bled.

The divorce was a simple matter. The judge didn't blame him for beating her and she did not defend. It was impossible for her to defend. Now that it was all out in the open a dozen witnesses came forward to testify that they had seen her with this man or that man or another man. The list seemed endless. Everybody was sorry for poor Freddie, and everybody was getting a tight little vicarious thrill out of denouncing another man's wife as a whore and seeing him squirm.

The judge, he thought, summed it all up very succinctly:

'My sympathies are with you, Mr Chalmers. Although your wife is not in court – and I wish she were, as I'd like to say this directly to her – it seems likely to me that she will come to a very unpleasant end unless she mends her ways. She will not always be a young woman. If she is by nature licentious, she will one day find that her looks have gone and that she has no weapons left with which to gratify her desires.'

She had left the district after that and changed her name. And he had not seen her again ...

The newspaper fell off the table and startled him. He picked it up.

But he'd been lucky, he thought. If she'd been the ideal wife he might have studied for ever and finished up as a minor employee. As it was, her departure had left him nothing to live for – except himself. And so he had set up on his own. Yes, one way or another, things had turned out for the best.

There was a knock on the door and his assistant came in.

'It's time, sir.'

He nodded and got up from the table.

He followed his assistant along the whitewashed passage and into the execution chamber. He mounted the scaffold and checked that everything was in order. Not that he had any need to check. His assistant was a bright lad and would have made sure that the trap was functional and the noose just right.

It was a moment before they came through the doorway: the Governor, the chaplain, the warders, and the condemned woman. He kept his back to them and only turned when she was on the trap. He let her see him. He wanted her to take a good look.

'Mary,' he whispered softly, as he put the hood over her head. 'He said your looks would go, and they have. Did he want to leave you, Mary? Is that why you killed him?'

Her knees buckled, but the warders kept her upright. He was very careful about the position of the knot. It had to be just under the ear. He was a perfectionist.

He heard her moan and mumble a prayer, and he knew from past experience that now her insides would be loosening and she would be smelling the foetid smell of her own filth.

He moved towards the lever that would send her to eternity, and waited for the signal. Yes, sometimes it could be a very rewarding job.

SUPPER WITH MARTHA

By Rosemary Timperley

IT WAS FRIDAY night, his usual night for visiting Estelle, his mistress. He gave his wife a different excuse every week and she never asked awkward questions. But then Martha was an ideal wife. She kept the house beautifully clean and tastefully decorated. She entertained his business friends when necessary. She never argued with her husband. She waited on him. She fitted in with any arrangements he made. She wasn't extravagant. She was amenable in bed. She didn't flirt with other men. She was never bad-tempered. She was very quiet and a good listener. And, most important of all, she was a wonderful cook.

So Paul was contented with his marriage and quite envied by his friends, who often had more difficult women on their hands. Why then did he need a mistress? Well – a little variety never did anyone any harm and Martha, for all her virtues, was a bit dull. She lacked humour and gaiety. She smiled sometimes, in her restrained way, but she never laughed.

Estelle was the very opposite. She had all the faults which Martha lacked. She was careless, quick-tempered, talkative, extravagant, flirtatious. But also she was passionate and gay. During their evenings together they would laugh a lot, and drink quantities of gin, and make love a lot. Supper consisted of not much more than a plate of sandwiches, and those not very well made, but Paul was so well fed at home that the scrappiness of Estelle's suppers didn't worry him.

He would have hated to be *married* to an undomesticated firebrand like Estelle, but one evening a week of her company thoroughly cheered him up and even heightened his contentment with Martha's quietness afterwards.

Now, on this Friday night, when in theory he was dining with some business clients, he rang the bell of Estelle's flat.

Usually she came to the door immediately and flung her arms round his neck – the sort of impulsive movement which Martha never made. Then there would be a kiss of passion, wafts of her expensive scent (paid for by him, as also were her pairs of fine stockings and many pretty dresses), laughter, light music, strong drink— his spirits lightened in glad anticipation. Friday night was gaiety night!

But there was no sound now of her quick footsteps approaching the door. Hadn't she heard the bell? He rang again and waited.

He glanced at his watch. Was he early, or late? No. It was exactly eight o'clock, his usual time. He tried the bell a third time. Still she didn't come.

So he bent down and peeped through the letter-box. The little hall was dark and empty. The living-room door was closed. This was unusual: the light should have been on, and that door open in a welcoming way. And there was no sound of music, yet she nearly always had the record-player on when he arrived.

It dawned on him, with angry astonishment, that Estelle had gone out! Gone out! On *his* night! Of all the bloody-minded things to do. If she'd had to go out, the least she could have done was ring him at the office to tell him so. He'd been there all afternoon. He couldn't have missed a message.

Depressed and indignant, he left the block of flats. In the drive, he looked up at the windows of her flat. They were dark and the curtains had not been closed. He wondered where she was and what she was up to.

He decided to go home. There was nothing else to do. Martha might be unexciting, but at least she'd be there, and give him something decent to eat.

Lights from his house shone welcomingly as he came up the garden path and let himself in. He hung his overcoat and hat on the hall-stand, noticed that Martha's coat hung there too, and wondered briefly why it was there, instead of in the bedroom wardrobe where she usually hung it, then went into the living room.

Martha was curled in the big easy-chair by the fire. She was reading, as usual. She was a great reader, of many serious subjects. For a month or so she would be reading everything she could find on, say, astronomy; next month it would be botany, or mathematics, or ballet – all was grist to the mill of her serious, industrious mind. Her present craze was medicine. She was reading everything she could find in the public library about doctors, drugs, anatomy, surgery. Indeed, only the other day he had said to her: 'We shan't need our GP any longer. I'll bet you know as much as he does now.' It had been a mild little joke. She had not laughed. Martha never laughed.

However, she had a pretty smile, and now she looked up and smiled at him. Any other wife, he thought, would have been surprised to see him when he had said previously that he wouldn't be home for supper, but Martha never showed surprise. She accepted events without any emotion. Her smile now conveyed nothing but mild pleasure at seeing him.

'Hello, dear,' she said. 'Was your business appointment cancelled?'

'Yes. They rang up this afternoon to put me off.'

'Oh, well, it won't do you any harm to have an easy night after working all day. I'll get your supper.'

'Sorry about it,' he said. 'I should have let you know I'd be home tonight.'

'No need. There's always plenty of stuff in the fridge. How about liver and bacon – and some very nice kidneys?'

'My favourite,' he said. 'You are a dear!' And he felt a bit ashamed. He was an awful old liar and she was always so straight. She looked extra pretty tonight too.

'Has anything nice happened today?' he asked.

'I *have* had a nice day. Why?'

'You look happy, in your quiet way.'

'I am,' she said. 'I'm very happy tonight.'

Just for a second, he wondered if he were the only partner in this marriage who was having a secret love affair. But he dismissed the thought. Martha would never be unfaithful even in thought, let alone in deed. If she were, she would have 'used' Friday night – the night he was usually out – yet here she had been, sitting by the fire as usual, her nose in a book. Bless her!

'You'd better have a little drink while you're waiting,' she said, and served him with a small glass of medium sherry, the only alcohol they kept in the house unless they had guests. Then she went into the kitchen to prepare his meal.

Sipping his sherry, Paul considered the contrast between this Friday night and his usual Friday nights. It was nearly nine o'clock. By this time he and Estelle would have knocked back several double gins and would have been making love on the white fur rug in front of her electric fire, while the record-player played jazzy music – the sort of music Martha disliked, mildly. All her feelings were mild.

He glanced at the large book she had been reading – one of her current medical tomes. He flipped through its pages and came across a full page illustration of the female figure – but not the sort of female figure that *he* enjoyed looking at. It was an anatomical drawing, showing a cross-section of all the internal organs, and all were neatly labelled for the benefit of the student of anatomy. It put you off women a bit just to look at it! With a touch of distaste he closed the book, tossed it back on the chair, and brought from his jacket pocket his paperback thriller of the moment.

He let his eyes linger on the cover of the book before he began to read. It pictured a voluptuous blonde, standing with her back to him, and clad in nothing but her long golden hair and a silver chain-anklet. The girl looked rather like Estelle, although her fair hair wasn't as long as that. But it acted as a reminder that Estelle had let him down tonight, and he felt another pang of annoyance and humiliation. This was no way to spend a Friday night!

However, when Martha brought his supper he felt more cheerful . . . liver, kidneys, and bacon, all perfectly cooked. He was hungry and ate the lot.

'That was really delicious!' he said, as he took the last succulent mouthful. 'Real *cordon bleu.*'

'Yes, it was rather special.' She smiled.

'You're very good to me. And very trusting,' he said impulsively.

'You're the one who is trusting,' she said.

'Me? In what way?'

'The way you eat everything I give you.'

'Why shouldn't I? You're such a marvellous cook.'

'That would make it all the easier for me to polish you off if I felt like it.'

A joke? But Martha never made jokes. Martha never even laughed. So he didn't know how to take the remark.

'Polish me off?' he said, uneasily. 'You wouldn't know how.'

'But of course I would. I've read all the books in the library about the various poisons. I'm glad you enjoyed your supper, dear. It's the last I shall ever cook for you, and I shall quite miss that. I do so enjoy cooking.'

'Martha, what are you talking about? The last supper—'

'Yes. I shall be leaving tonight.'

'Leaving?'

'Yes. I'm not sure when. It depends how soon anything happens. How are you feeling?'

Paul was feeling frightened. He didn't know what was happening. His heart was beating too fast. The meal he had eaten with such appetite was curdling inside him.

'How are you feeling?' she repeated.

'In – in what way?'

'I was wondering if your supper has agreed with you.'

'Why shouldn't it? It was a lovely supper. Martha, is this some joke?'

'I never make jokes,' said Martha. 'I saw Estelle this afternoon.'

That gave him such a shock that he could have been sick. He said nothing.

Martha smiled.

Paul muttered: 'How did you find out?'

'Quite by chance, dear. You left one of her letters in a trouser pocket. I found it when I was taking the trousers to the cleaners. But that was months ago. It's taken me quite a long time to decide what to do.'

'So that's why she wasn't there tonight,' he said dazedly. 'You went in the afternoon and told her that you knew—'

'Yes,' said Martha. 'How are you feeling?'

'Feeling?'

'I mean – any indigestion – after the supper?'

'I feel sick,' he admitted.

'Poor little sensitive stomach!'

'*Did* you poison my food?' he whispered, sweat on his hands and face.

'That depends on what you mean by poison.'

'You know what I mean! Did you poison my supper tonight!'

'No,' said Martha, smiling.

'Is that true?'

Her smile vanished. 'I have never lied to you, Paul. Never. You have often lied to me. That is the great difference between us. I never lie. I shall not lie about anything now. I carried out a plan, and I shall gladly, truthfully, tell you all about it.'

'Well – go on.'

Then the doorbell rang. Paul jumped. But not Martha.

'Will you answer it, dear?' she said. 'Don't keep whoever it is waiting on the doorstep. It's a cold night.'

Paul went to the door.

Two police officers stood there.

'Mr Paul Ferrow?' said the taller of the two.

'Yes.'

'We'd like a word with you, sir. May we come in?'

They came in. The taller one went, with Paul, into the living room. The other stayed by the front door.

'And this is Mrs Ferrow!' asked the tall policeman.

'Yes. My wife,' said Paul. 'But what—'

'Mr Ferrow, did you visit Miss Estelle Montjoy at 14 Exley Court at any time today?'

'I went there, but I didn't see her. She was out.'

'What time was this?'

'Look, what is all this about?'

'Just answer my questions, please, sir.'

'I called at eight o'clock. No one answered the bell. She must have been out.'

'Mrs Ferrow, what time did your husband come home tonight?'

'Shortly before nine,' answered Martha.

'Has something happened to her?' Paul asked.

'Yes,' said the tall police officer. 'She's dead.'

Paul was shaking badly, and he still felt dreadfully sick. 'Dead? Estelle? But how?'

'We were hoping you might be able to tell us something about that. Your name and address were on this sheet of paper on her bed-table when we found her.'

Paul looked at the name and address on the sheet of paper. They were written in Martha's neat, upright handwriting. He looked at his wife. She smiled. Sweetly. Happily.

'If I'd killed her,' said Paul, 'I'd hardly leave my name and address—'

'That thought did cross our minds,' said the policeman.

'How did you come to find her?' Paul asked.

'We received an anonymous telephone call, shortly before eight o'clock. The caller, a woman, told us to investigate that flat because the occupant had died. It might have been a hoax, but all the same we went along there. No one answered the bell, so the hall porter let us in with his pass-key. Estelle Montjoy was lying on the bed with her throat cut, and there were other—'

He stopped and turned to Martha, who had moved towards the kitchen.

'Where are you going, Mrs Ferrow?' he asked.

'I have something in here to show you,' she said.

He followed her into the kitchen. Paul followed them both. Martha pulled open a drawer where she kept a large range of kitchen knives. She picked out the strongest and sharpest. She handed it to the policeman.

'It was I who telephoned,' she said, 'and this is what I used. The "murder weapon" is the term, I believe. I have nothing to hide. I am quite ready to come with you. My coat is ready in the hall. And there is no need to tell my husband the details of what I did to the fair Estelle. I'd rather tell him myself.'

She turned to Paul.

'I called on the fair Estelle,' she said. 'I told her who I was, and she let me in. We talked about *you*. Something that men never hear, unless they eavesdrop, is two women discussing them. We had a most interesting discussion. I pointed out to her that my great advantage was that I could cook. I have a genius in that direction. I can cook anything, however vile, and make it tasty. After our talk, I told her she really ought to leave you alone, and she agreed. So, to make it easy for her, I fetched that knife' – and she pointed to the kitchen knife which the policeman still held in his hand – 'out of my handbag, and very quickly and neatly cut her throat. There was a lot of blood, of course, but I'm not squeamish. No cook can afford to be squeamish. Every kitchen is, in a sense, an *abattoir*. I carried her, with some effort, into the bedroom, and put her on the bed. I wrote your name and address on the sheet of paper, which you have seen. After all – one must help the police a little in these cases. Then I took off her clothes, folded them neatly, and left them on a chair by her bed. Then I cut out her kidneys.'

'That's enough, madam. Come along with us now.' The policeman, his eyes hard with horror, took Martha's arm and began to lead her towards the hall.

As they crossed the living room, Martha, determinedly, detached herself from the policeman's grip, pointed to the big medical book still laying in the easy chair, and said:

'I made use of my knowledge of anatomy, dear. I was really very skilful. My first operation! I must be a frustrated surgeon really. I did it beautifully. You should have seen me. You'd have been impressed. I just cut out her kidneys—'

'Is it true?' Paul asked the policeman.

'From what we could tell of the body – yes.'

Paul turned to Martha. 'You cut out—'

'Her kidneys, dear. Yes.'

And she laughed. It was a beautiful laugh. Happy. Melodious. Like birdsong in the morning. Paul had never heard her laugh before. The sound made all other laughter pale into insignificance. She was laughing – laughing—

Still laughing, she said: 'It was the happiest moment of my life! I cut out her kidneys! And you ate them for supper!'

PUNISHMENT BY PROXY

By James Connelly

TINA MASON gazed out of the small oval window of the twin-engined executive jet at the blue shimmering waters of the Persian Gulf far below. They were nearing the end of their journey, but she could still scarcely believe her good fortune at getting in on a trip such as this. That she had was due to her brother, Bob, who sat beside her in the aircraft.

He held an executive post with one of Britain's biggest oil companies and when he came home one day and announced that he was going to the Persian Gulf on business for a week, Tina was full of envy.

'How about taking me along?' she had suggested in fun. She was home on holiday before her final term at technical college and rather at a loose end. To her surprise, Bob did not brush off the remark as a joke.

'As a matter of fact I was thinking about that,' he replied. 'I'm entitled to a first-class air fare, so I thought if I travelled tourist, the difference would pay for most of your fare as well. What's more, when I mentioned this to Julius, who's going too, he thought it was a good idea and said he'd travel tourist as well. So we can more than cover your fare and anything over will pay for your hotel.'

Bob had looked serious as he spoke, but there was a twinkle in his eye as he added.

'I warn you, it'll be darned hot at this time of the year, but you can come if you want to.'

If she wanted to? What a question! Tina did not have to think twice. She simply threw herself round Bob's neck and hugged him.

'Knock it off,' he smiled, trying to break free of her embrace. Secretly, though, he was pleased with her response.

He was ten years older than Tina, but they had always been very close, even for a brother and sister. Even now that she was eighteen and had developed into a lovely young woman, in his eyes she was still his little sister and in need of protection.

Tina was still considering her good fortune when Julius Grant looked over his shoulder at them from the seat in front.

'We should be there within half an hour,' he announced.

Grant was a man in his middle forties with thick greying hair and a pencil-thin moustache. He held a senior position with the oil company and had been quick to spot Bob's potential when the young man had joined them nearly eight years ago. He had taught Bob everything he knew about the business and, in the years that followed, they had become a good team and close friends.

'It was nice of the Sheikh to send one of his personal planes to meet us off the scheduled flight at Tehran,' Tina said for the fourth time since they had taken off. She glanced about her at the lavish furnishings.

'This is what I call real luxury.'

'Yes, whatever the outcome of our talks on the oil concessions, I don't think the Sheikh will ever be short of a square meal,' Grant smiled wryly.

'You know, Julius, I've been boning up on Sheikh Abdul Al Hahrid, all powerful ruler of Kahrain,' said Bob seriously. 'Apparently, he has the reputation of being something of a tyrant.'

'Why do you say that, Bob?' asked Tina.

'Unfortunately, when a report comes out of a country like Kahrain, you can never be sure how accurate it is,' Bob replied.

Tina nudged him in the ribs.

'Come on, don't hedge. What have you been reading?'

'Nothing very specific, but I've seen a number of newspaper cuttings which suggested that the country isn't exactly a democratic welfare state. The Sheikh has his own small army and apparently has the absolute power of life and death over his people.'

'There's nothing unique about that, Bob,' Grant pointed

out. 'I could name half a dozen such states in the Middle East, maybe a dozen, where they have the same set-up.'

'Yes, I know, but I've also read the occasional outbreaks of unrest in Kahrain have been put down with exceptional severity,' Bob insisted. 'That is the euphemistic way of saying, "with unnecessary cruelty". It would seem that our Sheikh or at least some of his men, has an unusually nasty streak.'

'As you say, Bob,' Grant reminded him. 'It depends who writes these things, but name me any of the great powers who haven't been subjected to similar accusations, even in recent years, never mind a small Arab Sheikhdom. What about Russia in Hungary and Czechoslovakia, China in Tibet, America in Vietnam, or the French in Algiers? Even the British in Cyprus came in for a similar attack, so I don't think we should be too critical of our friend, Hahrid, on the evidence of a few newspaper cuttings.'

'Perhaps you're right, Julius,' Bob agreed reluctantly. 'But it seems to me that when these things happen in one's own country, it is even more reprehensible. It somehow smacks of Feudalism and the Middle Ages.'

'If they happen.' Grant repeated. 'Anyway, it's none of our business how Kahrain is governed. Our job is to talk them into renewing the oil concessions at the most favourable terms.'

'And I still say it was thoughtful of him to send one of his own private aeroplanes to meet us,' said Tina for the fifth time.

'Yes, and if you had ever experienced this trip in an old Dakota, with no pressurization or air-conditioning, you would appreciate it even more.' Grant assured them.

'I'll bet the Dakota didn't have one of these either,' Bob smiled.

He was referring to the attractive coloured girl who had looked after them and plied them with food and drinks throughout the journey. Now she was approaching from the front of the aircraft, her white teeth gleaming in the same broad smile which she had worn ever since she welcomed them aboard at Tehran.

'We will be landing at Kahrain in a few minutes,' she announced. 'Would you please fasten your safety belts.'

Kahrain is situated halfway down the Persian Gulf. It is a tiny Sheikhdom extending about twenty miles into the huge land mass of Saudi Arabia and with no more than ten miles of coastline. It is also, however, one of the richest two hundred square miles of land on earth, with unlimited deposits of oil beneath its sun-parched sand. The small airport is situated to the west of the capital, which is also called Kahrain, and where nearly four-fifths of the state's entire population live.

A black Mercedes met the three travellers off the aircraft and drove them straight to the Sheikh's palace, without any explanation from the driver. Within half an hour of landing, therefore, they were swinging in through heavily-guarded gates and approaching the huge white building which held a unique position on top of a hill overlooking the grey, dusty city on three sides and the cool waters of the Gulf on the fourth.

Alighting from the car, they were met at the massive porticoed entrance by a man in flowing white robes and traditional kaffiyeh head-dress. As they approached, he bowed low.

'I am Hassan, personal assistant to Sheikh Abdul Al Hahrid. Welcome to Kahrain,' he said in a deep, solemn voice. There was no hint of a smile on his bearded face as he shook hands with the two men. Then turning to Tina, he asked:

'And who is this lovely young lady?'

'May I introduce my sister, Tina,' said Bob.

'Welcome, Miss Tina.' Hassan took her hand gently and bowed low again before looking closely into her face for several seconds with his dark hypnotic eyes.

'Thank you.' Tina smiled shyly. 'Actually, I only came for the ride. I am hoping to see something of your country while Bob and Mr Grant are working.'

'In that case, I trust you will enjoy your visit.'

Hassan addressed the three of them.

'It is the Sheikh's wish that you stay at the palace while you are in Kahrain.'

'But I am only on holiday,' Tina protested. 'I couldn't possibly . . .'

'The Sheikh would be most offended if you were to refuse his hospitality,' Hassan interrupted her, and continued as if the matter was settled. 'Now if you will follow me, I will show you to your quarters. Please do not worry about your luggage, it will arrive there before you.'

The cool lofty interior of the palace reminded Tina of a cathedral. Their footsteps rang out loudly on the polished marble floor as they passed along great echoing corridors which linked an endless succession of huge empty chambers. Vaulted ceilings of intricate mosaic tilework formed a colourful series of canopies high above their heads and priceless tapestries and paintings adorned the walls on all sides.

Their spacious quarters were furnished with a lavish splendour which would have made even the most expensive hotel in the western world seem drab by comparison. It provoked Bob to comment, when they were alone and had gathered in his apartment a little later. 'If these are the visitors' quarters, I wonder how the Sheikh lives?'

'Yes, and in spite of your doubts about our host, I don't think he's given us much cause to question his hospitality so far,' Grant pointed out.

'I'm forced to agree with you there,' Bob acknowledged.

'The thing that's bothering me,' said Tina, 'is what do I wear when we meet him?'

She hugged herself happily.

'Fancy him saying that I was to come along as well when you two are introduced to him! Wait till I tell the girls back at the college.'

'I expect, like most men, he enjoys meeting a pretty girl,' Grant suggested.

'Come off it, Julius.' said Bob. 'If he's anything like the Sheikhs one reads about, he'll have more girls at his beck and call than he knows what to do with.'

'In that case, perhaps he'll put some of them at our disposal while we're here.' Grant smiled.

'Honestly, you men!' Tina protested. 'Remember you're

here on business. I'm the one who is supposed to enjoy herself.'

Sheikh Abdul Al Hahrid was a short, fat little man with a dark pointed beard and close set eyes. The intensity of his gaze made Tina slightly uncomfortable when she was introduced to him and, not knowing the etiquette for such an occasion, she curtsied when he took her hand and placed it to his lips.

'This is indeed an unexpected pleasure, Miss Mason.' He said with the same solemnity that Hassan had shown earlier, and then, to Bob, 'You have a very beautiful sister, Mr Mason.' He gave a little smile as he added, 'I know a lot of tribal chieftains, not too far from here, who would give many goats in exchange for her. I take it, though, that she would not be for sale.'

'I think, sir, that our parents would have something to say to me if I were to return home with a plane-load of goats instead of Tina.' Bob replied with a broad grin.

Hahrid became serious again.

'Yes, I'm afraid the customs of east and west are still centuries apart and in spite of modern communication the two really know nothing of each other. Here, in Kahrain, we try to take advantage of twentieth-century progress, while retaining the best of our old customs and traditions.'

He looked at the three of them in turn.

'Apart from Allah, of course, the most sacred of all our traditions is hospitality to an invited guest and I hope there will be time, while you are here, to demonstrate what I mean.'

'We have already had ample evidence of your generosity and hospitality, sir,' Grant assured him.

'Good, good,' Hahrid approved. 'And now I hope you will excuse me. Tomorrow morning, before you begin your discussions, gentlemen, I would like to show you some of the more interesting parts of my humble palace.'

He looked apologetically at Tina.

'I regret, Miss Tina, that you will be unable to accompany us as custom decrees that much of the palace is forbidden to women.' He smiled. 'You see, female emancipation has not reached the stage that it has in your country. In fact I doubt if it ever will. However, I would be honoured if you would come to the dinner, which I will be giving in honour of your visit, the day after tomorrow. In the meantime, I will put a car at your disposal and please feel free to come and go in our small country as you wish. Now I bid you good day.'

The audience had ended.

The following morning, Tina set off to tour the capital, while Grant and her brother renewed their acquaintance with Sheikh Hahrid. Much to their surprise, he insisted on conducting them personally around the palace, with Hassan close on their heels and palace guards trailing a discreet distance behind.

The palace was a treasure house of art and antiques and the Sheikh was the perfect guide, with a remarkable knowledge of their history. After nearly an hour, they took a concealed lift to the giant dome which towered above all else in Kahrain and from the balcony, which encircled it, they looked down at the teeming life of the city far below. At that height, the morning air felt relatively cool on their perspiring faces and to the two Englishmen it was as if they had stepped into an Eastern fairy tale.

'If you have seen all you wish to up here,' the Sheikh announced at last, 'I will now show you what few western eyes have ever seen.'

They took the lift back to ground level and, leaving the palace, walked out into the extensive grounds at the rear. Part of these, near the palace itself, was sectioned off by a high, shrub-covered wall of local stone, and the only access to whatever lay behind the wall was through massive iron gates, which appeared to be even more heavily guarded than the palace entrance. These were drawn open, as they approached, and they passed through into a beautiful landscaped garden beyond.

'This, gentlemen, is my garden of pets,' the Sheikh announced, when they were inside and the gates had shut behind them.

The two Englishmen just stood and gaped in astonishment at the sight which met them. It was not the exotic flowers and plants, blooming with unnatural splendour, that made them speechless, however, nor the mosaic-tiled pools of crystal-clear water into which cool tinkling fountains sprayed endlessly. Nor was it the many acacias and tall white barked chinar trees which sheltered the garden from the sun's torrid rays, transforming it into a green, shady oasis.

It was the twenty or more girls who strolled or swam or just lay sunning themselves in this paradise. All of them were young and beautiful, but the most surprising thing of all was that every one of them was completely naked.

'I can see from your faces that your initial reaction is favourable,' the Sheikh observed. 'Let us walk round.'

As they sauntered through the garden, each girl in turn stood stiffly to attention, when they approached, and then after they had passed, continued with whatever she had been doing. To the newcomers, it was like inspecting a heavenly guard of honour and they gazed with a mixture of desire and admiration at each bare female body.

'It is strange,' said the Sheikh, with a knowing smile, when they stopped in the centre of the garden. 'But all my guests go completely silent when I bring them through here, as though they had lost the power of speech.'

Bob found his tongue at last.

'I think we are surprised and delighted that you should allow us to look at such beauty, sir.' He admitted.

The Sheikh shrugged indifferently.

'Please do not make the wrong assumption, this is not my harem. That is in another part of the palace, where no one but myself and my special guards are allowed, and they would certainly not be permitted to appear unclothed like these young females. No, gentlemen, these are my prisoners.'

'Your prisoners?' echoed his guests in astonished unison.

'That's right. They are all here because of some misdemeanour against either myself or the State.' Hahrid spread his hands. 'But how am I to judge them? Although I am their ruler, I am only human and so I leave it to Allah to

decree their fate. While he decides, however, I try to make
their captivity as pleasant as possible within certain limits of
confinement.'

The Sheikh looked again at the two men and smiled
strangely.

'Before we go, there is just one more thing. You may each
choose a girl to share your bed with you tonight.'

'Any of them?' asked Bob, unable to believe his good
fortune.

'Any one,' he was assured. 'And perhaps you would like to
choose first, Mr Mason.'

Any of the girls would have attracted a man's attention,
with or without clothes, but Bob was in doubt. Walking
round, he had spotted a dusky-skinned beauty, who had been
swimming in one of the pools when they entered the garden.
She had quickly climbed out, as they passed, and stood erect
with tiny droplets of water streaming down her young athletic
body. She could not have been more than seventeen or
eighteen, but she was fully developed and a superb specimen.
Even in such company, she was head and shoulders above the
others in Bob's eyes.

'All the girls are lovely, but my choice would be that dark
one over there by the pool, sir,' he said without hesitation.

When she was led over to them, she stood staring straight
ahead with her arms at her sides and as still as if she had
been carved from mahogany. Then at a signal from Hassan,
she walked up and down before them, so that they could
examine her from every angle. The rear view was equally
alluring, and the sensuous way her plump round bottom
swayed with every step, made Bob wonder if she was deliberately trying to excite them.

'You have a good eye for a woman, Mr Mason,' the Sheikh
said approvingly at last, while his hand strayed intimately
over her coffee-coloured skin. 'She is a fine choice and
tonight she will be yours, but there is just one more thing I
would like to know. Which part of her body do you find most
attractive?'

'She looks perfect all over to me.' Bob admitted.

'But surely there's a part you particularly like?' the Sheikh insisted.

'Well, with the accent very much on short skirts in our country, I am bound to say that she has the most magnificent legs I have ever seen,' Bob replied.

'Excellent,' Hahrid applauded. 'And now, Mr Grant, would you also like to choose a companion for your bed tonight?'

Tina was full of her day spent touring the capital, but when she tried to relate her adventures to her companions that evening she was disappointed to find that the two men were only half listening to her.

'I don't believe you've heard one word I've said, Bob,' she complained impatiently at last. 'I thought you'd want to know what I've been doing all day, but you don't seem a bit interested, and you're as bad, Julius.'

'Sorry, Tina,' Bob apologized. He looked meaningfully across at Grant. 'I'm afraid we've had rather a heavy day. In fact, if you don't mind, I think I'll turn in.'

'I think I'll do the same, if you'll excuse me, Tina.' Grant added quickly.

'What's wrong with you two?' she protested. 'It's still early and I was hoping you were going to take me out and show me the Kahrainian night life.'

'Please, not tonight, Tina, I really am whacked,' Bob pleaded. 'I don't think I've got fully acclimatized yet. It must be the heat.'

He kissed his sister lightly on the cheek and left her, very conscious of the indignant gaze which followed him out of the door. Grant waited a few minutes longer before making his apologies and retiring as well.

'Honestly,' she grumbled, when she was alone. 'We come all this way and all they want to do is go to bed. I just don't understand it.'

Bob was in his room only a few minutes when the girl arrived. He had been beginning to wonder if the events in the garden that morning had really happened or whether they were just a lovely dream.

She was a lovely dream all right, but she was very real. Dressed in a wispy blue silk shift that hung in loose folds to her feet, she looked even more beautiful than he had remembered her from the morning. Before he could speak, she reached for the clip which fastened the shift at her throat and, with a whisper, it slid from her body to lie in a pool of blue round her feet. Beneath it she was as naked as when he had first seen her.

'I have been told to make you 'appy,' she said simply, in broken English.

The blood throbbed heavily in Bob's veins.

'You are the most lovely creature I have ever seen,' he said softly, taking her hands in his and gazing almost reverently at her nude body. 'It makes me very happy just to look at you.'

She slipped her hands gently out of his and moved into the encircling embrace of his arms. Placing her arms round his neck, she drew his face down and their lips met.

Any lingering feelings Bob might have had that it would be wrong to take this girl, because she was being forced to come to him, vanished at that moment. The effect of her physical presence overcame any moral scruples he might have held up until then and, besides, she appeared to be as eager as he was.

They made violent, passionate love with an intensity and mutual understanding that transcended mere animal attraction. The girl's sexual awareness equalled the exceptional beauty of her velvet-skinned body and when they paused to rest at last, Bob felt that he had discovered the ultimate pleasures of true physical love.

As they lay in each other's arms, her long shapely limbs entwined with his, they talked. She told him that her name was Aisha and she lived all her life in Kahrain, learning English from her father. When he whispered in her ear that he loved her, however, he felt her stiffen against him. Drawing back to look into her face, he saw that her big dark eyes mirrored an infinite sadness tinged with fear.

'You must not say that, Bobby,' she told him.

'Why not?' he asked. 'Even though we have just met, I still know that I am in love with you.'

'I am a prisoner of Sheikh Hahrid and will never see you again after tonight,' she explained sadly.

'But what have you done?'

She shrugged.

'I did nothing, but my father owns a newspaper in Kahrain and 'e printed things which the Sheikh regarded as critical of 'is person.'

'I don't see what that has to do with you.'

'You do not know the Sheikh. 'E is a cruel man and takes 'is revenge in strange ways, where it 'urts most. You see my father is old and there is little they can do to 'im. At the very worst they could kill 'im, but already 'e is a sick man and may soon die anyway, so by punishing me 'e is made to suffer much more. Most of the girls you saw today are innocent, but they were brought to the palace because one of their friends or relatives has broken the law.'

'But what will happen to you now?' asked Bob.

'None of us knows for sure,' Aisha replied. 'But we have 'eard terrible rumours which I dare not even repeat. All we are certain of is that no girl remains here longer than a year. Also, when one of us is chosen to spend the night with a guest of the Sheikh's, she never returns to the garden.'

'I must and will see you again,' said Bob fiercely. 'And please don't be sad or frightened any more. Everything will turn out all right, I promise you.'

They made love several more times that night and Bob finally fell asleep with his head cushioned on the girl's breasts and the wonderful musky scent of her body in his nostrils.

When he awoke in the morning, she had gone.

'It doesn't look as if the early night did you two much good. You both look awful,' Tina said candidly, when she saw Bob and Grant at breakfast.

The two men glanced at each other, but made no comment until they were alone.

'Have you got fully acclimatized yet?' asked Grant. 'If appearances are anything to go by, I take it you had a good night.'

'Unbelievable, and how about you?'

'Me, too.' Grant smiled wanly. 'But I'm not looking forward to a day of hard bargaining with our Kahrainian friends. Anyway, come on, let's get on with it.'

The negotiations were protracted and inconclusive. Snags were reached at an early stage and the way the Kahrainian delegation dug their heels in on relatively minor points suggested to the Englishmen that they did not want to arrive at an early agreement over the oil concessions.

'I reckon they've got someone else on the hook as well,' said Grant at the end of a dispiriting day, when they were back in their apartment.

'Could be,' Bob argued. 'Anyway, we know how far we're prepared to go, so if they won't come to terms before that stage, I suppose we'll have to reconsider our whole position and contact London.'

He had found it a particularly trying day. On an occasion like this when he needed to harness all his knowledge and concentration to help his senior colleague with the negotiations, he had been unable to put Aisha out of his mind. The memory of the previous night, in all its wonderful vivid detail, kept crowding in on his mind and he wondered guiltily if he had done his best for his company. It even crossed his mind that presenting girls to Grant and himself for the night might have been a ploy on the part of the Kahrainians to soften up their business opponents before the talks began. Surely, though, this was too devious, even for these strange impassive people. In any case, his feelings for the girl remained unchanged. He had to see her again no matter what the cost.

It was with this unsettled feeling of frustrated preoccupation that Bob accompanied Tina and Grant that evening to the dinner which the Sheikh was giving in their honour. Apart from Hahrid himself, the dinner party included one of his favourite wives and two of his sons. They were slimmer versions of their father, but not yet capable of growing a respectable beard between them, although one of them was obviously trying hard. Several ministers and other important officials were also present, including two who had taken part in the talks during the day. Hovering on the edge of the party, as well, was the faithful, ever-present Hassan.

The Sheikh was a cheerfully attentive, if somewhat dominant, host. When he talked, everyone listened and he talked incessantly. Nevertheless, with young scantily clad girls serving the food on large silver platters and a small orchestra providing a background of shrill Eastern music, the traditional oriental atmosphere was firmly established.

The food itself was quite sumptuous and though many of the dishes were foreign to a western palate, Tina recognized the caviare, though she was tasting it for the first time in her life. She was not impressed. The skewered sturgeon was much more to her liking and so was the heavily-garnished chicken kebab and the assortment of citrus and other fruits, which adorned the tables in juicy clusters of rich colour. A succession of local and far-travelled wines accompanied each course and clearly no effort had been spared to make the meal a memorable one.

Yet Bob worked his way through it without enthusiasm.

'You have been very quiet this evening, Mr Mason,' remarked Hassan, who had been sitting beside him.

Bob made up his mind there and then to unburden himself.

'Perhaps you can help me, Hassan. Do you remember that girl I chose in the garden yesterday?'

'Of course. She was very beautiful, but then Sheikh Hahrid only keeps beautiful girls in his garden of pets,' Hassan replied. 'I trust she was to your liking.'

'Very much so,' Bob said seriously. 'In fact I want to see her again. Do you think you could arrange it for me with the Sheikh?'

For the first time since they met, Bob noted the suspicion of a smile on the face of the Sheikh's personal aide. It was not a friendly smile, though, but more a curl of the lips.

'I am afraid that would be quite impossible,' he assured

Bob. 'You have already enjoyed the girl as no man will ever enjoy her again. That is how Allah wished it and with that you must be satisfied. There is nothing I, or even Sheikh Hahrid, could do for you, even if we wished to.'

Hassan turned away and the conversation was obviously closed as far as he was concerned.

Bob was far from satisfied, however, and much later when the dinner was over and he was back in his apartment, Hassan's words went through his mind over and over again. They left him strangely disturbed but even more determined to see the girl again.

At last he made his mind up and, on soft rubber soles, he left his room and crept down a back stairway to the ground floor of the palace. It was getting late and the lights had been dimmed in the great silent chambers and corridors. Keeping to the shadows, he glided towards the rear of the massive building, only stopping to get his bearings or to dodge for cover when any unsuspecting servant or guard came his way. He found the door which led out to the grounds and followed the inside wall, coming finally to a more enclosed part of the palace. Here, the corridors were narrower and long lines of closed doors, as in an hotel, were in marked contrast to the wide open spaces of the rest of the palace which he had known up until now.

It was like searching for the proverbial needle, but he was determined. Anything was better than the yearning uncertainty which had gnawed at his thoughts all day. He tried each of the doors in turn. Some were locked, while others gave access to empty bedrooms. Then, as he approached the end of one of the corridors and had almost given up hope, he heard a low moan close at hand. It came from behind the very last door which opened when he tried the handle.

A clinical antiseptic smell met him as he slipped inside, closing the door behind him. The room was in semi-darkness, but he could still make out the low couch against the far wall. Another soft moan came from it, much louder now that he was inside the room and, moving towards the couch, his heart leapt when he saw who lay there.

It was Aisha. Her eyes were closed and, as he put his face down to hers, another little moan escaped her lips.

'Aisha,' he whispered, placing his hand gently on her feverish brow.

'It's me, Bob. I said I would see you again.'

The girl's eyes opened and stared unseeingly for a few moments before focusing on his face.

'Bobby,' she whispered through parched lips. 'Oh, Bobby, why did you 'ave to come?'

She appeared to have been heavily sedated and her eyes kept flickering as if the lids were too heavy for her to keep open.

'I had to see you again,' he repeated. 'But what's the matter, are you in pain?'

He sank to his knees beside the couch and held one of her small hot hands in his. As his other hand rested lightly on the blanket over her thigh, however, an icy finger of horror ruffled the nerves at the nape of his neck. Then it sped down his spine when he drew back and looked down at the length of her.

The bulge made by her body under the blanket ended halfway down the couch.

He flicked back the bedclothes so that his eyes could confirm the ghastly evidence of his hand. The girl was still naked, but it was not her sun-kissed shoulders or golden breasts that held his gaze. Instead, he stared unbelievingly at the white bandages which swathed her hips. Below these there was nothing. Her legs had been amputated high up at the hip bone!

'Oh my God,' he breathed.

She opened her eyes again and tried to raise her head. Even in her drugged state, she knew that he knew.

'I did not want you to see me like this, Bobby,' she murmured weakly. 'They took off my legs to punish my father.'

Her head sank wearily back on to the pillow and Bob gently drew the blanket back over her mutilated body. He knelt for several minutes looking down at her lovely features, now composed in merciful sleep before finally rising to his feet and tiptoeing out of the room, closing the door behind him. His heart was sick with disgust and despair, but over-riding all his other feelings was an intense anger and hatred for the people who could have done such a thing to an innocent girl. He stumbled blindly through the silent build-ing and, though he no longer made any attempt to move un-seen, no one crossed his path.

Somehow he found his way back to Grant's apartment and hammered on the door until his friend let him in. In a few garbled sentences, he explained what he had just seen.

'How could anyone do such a thing?' he sobbed. 'I told you there was something wrong with this country before we even got here.'

Grant tried to console him, but he too felt sickened and even a little frightened by what Bob had told him.

'Tina!' Bob gasped suddenly. 'We must get her out of here. There's no telling what these swine might do if they have the notion.'

In spite of his friend's assurances that nothing could possibly happen to his sister, a British subject, Bob insisted that she must leave at once and so in the end Grant agreed.

When she was awakened and told to pack, Tina protested bitterly at first, especially since neither her brother nor Grant would give her an explanation. The haunted look on Bob's face, however, convinced her that something serious had happened and so she finally obeyed.

In a matter of minutes she was gliding down the stairs and out of the palace between the two men who carried her luggage. They reached the car, which had been put at her disposal by the Sheikh, without meeting anyone and Bob almost pushed her behind the wheel.

'Look, Tina,' he said to her through the window. 'If you drive north up the coast road you will reach the Kahrainian border after about six or seven miles. On the other side is Basira. The capital, Anam, is only about ten miles farther on, so you'll be there in less than an hour. Go straight to the British Consulate and stay there till you hear from us. We'll be in touch within the next day or two.'

'But what are you going to do?' she protested. 'And what will the Kahrainians say when they discover that I've gone?'

'More to the point is what will I say to them,' Bob replied fiercely. 'Anyway, I don't want you to be around to get any of the backlash, so off you go and don't stop for anything.'

The car roared into life and a reluctant Tina drove out through the palace gates and out of their sight.

The two men walked slowly back into the palace, each deeply engrossed in his own thoughts.

'What are you going to tell Hahrid about Tina?' asked Grant, when they had reached his apartment and were discussing the situation over a drink. 'Remember we've still a lot of negotiating to do over those oil concessions.'

'To hell with the oil concessions,' Bob snapped vehemently. 'I'm thinking about that poor girl down there whose life has been completely ruined, for nothing. What about her?'

He glanced at his watch and felt a wave of relief. It was half an hour since Tina had left and she would be over the border by now and completely out of any danger, real or imaginary.

'I'm going down again to see Aisha,' he announced. 'Are you coming with me, Julius?'

Knowing that nothing he could say would dissuade his young friend, Grant agreed to accompany him and so, once more, they groped their way through the dimly lit building.

It was easier this time, since Bob knew the way, and they duly arrived at the door of the room where Aisha lay. They were surprised to find it ajar, but when they pushed it open and looked inside, they saw why. Hassan was standing by the couch, contemplating the still form of the girl and two armed guards stood behind him with their backs to the door.

'You brutes,' Bob spat at them. 'Why did you do it?'

Hassan and the guards whirled round, but relaxed when they saw who it was.

'You should not be here,' warned Hassan. 'How did you find this room?'

'Is that all you've got to say?' Bob screamed at him. 'Look what you've done!' He pointed to the girl on the couch.

'You have exceeded your position as guests of Sheikh Hahrid,' Hassan said coldly. 'That is most regrettable. Now you will return to your rooms at once.'

Bob stood his ground.

'Not until you explain this atrocity,' he gritted through thin hard lips.

'I am not obliged to explain anything to you, but since you insist I will,' Hassan said coldly. 'Then you must go. This girl's father wrote traitorous words against the person of Sheikh Hahrid and so to punish him and make him and others think before they do such a thing again, his daughter was arrested.'

'But why this?' asked Grant.

'It was Allah's wish,' Hassan replied simply. 'The Sheikh is a humble man and in such matters he does not feel that he alone can prescribe a suitable punishment. Therefore, he lets Allah decide. This girl and others, whose families or friends have committed crimes, are kept in his garden of pets. Many of them are set free after a year, quite unharmed, but those chosen by Sheikh Hahrid's guests during that year are dealt with. Having made his choice of a bed partner, each guest is asked which parts of the girl's body he likes most. Those parts are then surgically removed after she has spent the night with that guest. When the girl has recovered sufficiently she is returned to her home as a living example of Allah's judgement.' He went on: 'You Mr Mason, chose this girl, not Sheikh Hahrid. You spoke of her fine legs and so it was you, as the mouthpiece of Allah, who decreed her fate.'

'You cruel bastards,' Bob shouted, unable to contain himself any longer. 'You play these monstrous games with young girls' lives for your amusement and then blame it on your God. You'll pay for this.'

Hassan actually smiled, a cruel mocking smile which served only to inflame Bob's fury.

'The Sheikh will be made aware of your accusations and they will not improve your chances of gaining the oil concessions for your company,' he sneered. 'I know you western capitalists. When it becomes a matter of money and profit, you swallow your pride quickly enough. However, if you make a full apology to me now for your rash words, I may be persuaded not to let it go any farther.'

The man's arrogance and complete indifference were the final straws as far as Bob was concerned. His sorely tried restraint snapped and, with a roar of anger, he leapt at one of the unsuspecting guards and hauled his revolver from its holster. Before he could raise it, though, Hassan closed on him and the two men grappled for possession of the gun. Suddenly there was a shot and the expression on the Kahrainian's face turned to surprise and then pain as he sank slowly to the floor and lay still.

'Now you've done it,' said Grant.

'I didn't mean to shoot him, but the rat deserved it anyway.' said Bob, keeping the two guards covered. Although he had regained control of himself, he felt no regrets.

'I only wish it had been his master.'

'We've got to get out of here,' Grant insisted.

'What about Aisha?'

'We won't be able to help her if we get caught. Come on, we've no time to argue.'

Bob saw the sense of his friend's words and the two of them backed out of the door, locking it on the outside before racing down the corridor. Shouts and the sound of many running feet were gathering momentum as they found an outside door which led out to the palace gardens. A breathless gallop across the open ground brought them to the high perimeter wall which they scaled with an agility shared only by wild beasts and hunted men.

Keeping to the shadows, they raced through narrow streets, heading downhill towards the harbour. Once they had got clear of the palace, however, they heard no sound of pursuit and reached the water without difficulty.

'Our best way out of here is by sea,' gasped Grant, looking over the long lines of small craft that bobbed under a full moon.

Bob nodded in agreement and they selected a small sailing dinghy. When they cast off, a light off-shore breeze filled the single white wedge of sail and pushed them silently out into the bay and the open Gulf beyond.

Their escape had been incredibly easy, or lucky, and soon they were well clear of land and able to look back at the many pinpricks of light, which were all that remained for them of Kahrain. Perhaps they imagined it, but they both thought they could see brighter moving lights up on the hill above the town, where the palace stood. The few distant sounds that reached them from the shore gradually receded and they were left in a vacuum of smooth moon-drenched sea.

Their objective was to sail northwards up the coast until Kahrain had been left behind and then they hoped to be able to go ashore in safety. The Shamal had other ideas, however, and this local prevailing north-west wind drove them south, during the night, and out of sight of land. A day and a night later, they were picked up, parched, burnt, and exhausted, by a Panamanian tanker and taken to Abadan.

By the time they reached Basira, three whole days had elapsed. They went straight to the British Consulate building only to find that Tina had never arrived there.

Tina never even got out of Kahrain on the night she left her two anxious companions.

She cleared the city without difficulty, but about four miles farther on, the steering got heavy and the car started to pull to one side. An ominous bumping sound confirmed that she had picked up a puncture and having no idea how to change the wheel, she sat disconsolately for the next half hour, before an increasing glow in the night sky heralded the approach of another vehicle.

When she flagged it down, it turned out to be a police car, and two policemen climbed from it. They walked round her car eyeing it suspiciously, before one of them returned to his and put out a radio call. When he returned, he told Tina that she was to accompany them back to the city and, despite her protests, she was bundled into their car. When she had been returned to the palace, she was locked in a bare, uncomfortable room, far removed from the luxury which she had enjoyed since her arrival in Kahrain.

The next day was the most bewildering and frightening of Tina's young life. The Sheikh visited her in the morning, but displayed none of the friendliness of their previous meetings. He told her in harsh tones that her brother had committed a very serious crime and if she wanted to help him, she must do exactly as she was told without question.

When he had left, Tina was made to strip completely and was bathed and perfumed by palace servants. Still naked, she was then led out into a beautiful garden at the rear of the palace and there, for the next two days, she was left in the company of another twenty or so girls, each of whom was as naked as herself.

Late on the second day, the Sheikh came into the garden, accompanied by two middle-aged men in white western-styled suits and followed by one of his personal servants. They walked slowly round and each girl stood up straight and silent as they passed. Tina had been warned about the procedure and stood like the rest, feeling her face redden when they approached and gazed for what seemed ages at her exposed charms. Worse was to follow when she was summoned across to them afterwards and made to parade up and down while they examined her body from every side.

'I applaud your choice, Signor Romani,' the Sheikh said approvingly at last, as he stroked Tina's soft vibrant flesh. 'And now tell me, which part of her lovely body do you find most attractive?'

'Everything about her is quite beautiful,' replied Hahrid's guest in halting English. 'But above all, I think that she has the most exquisite breasts and . . .'

He paused.

'Yes?' prompted the Sheikh.

'And I also think she has wonderful blue eyes.'

THE END OF THE LINE

By Frances Stephens

I SHAN'T COME back to Alder Lea again. Maybe it was once a pleasant little station, but now there's nothing except dirt and decay. The weeds seem to have taken over, and the grass in between the tracks has grown far too long. I stumbled twice today.

It wouldn't matter nearly so much if it wasn't for the rats in the waiting room. They don't scuttle away under the broken boards any more. They take no notice, as though they're not afraid; as though they remember me, and recognize me as a friend.

Nobody knows I come here. Not my aunt. *She* doesn't care where I am, as long as I'm out of her sight. Maybe she thinks I'm watching the children in the school playground again, or going down to Out Patients' for those useless pills. But I fool her there. I fool them all. I toss the pills in the nearest drain, and they never know, just as they don't know I come here.

She's cunning, that aunt of mine. She'd stop me coming here if she could. She'd say it was too lonely. Why don't you mix with more people, Mary? Why don't you take a little job? For heaven's sake girl, don't sit there rocking that ragged doll. It should be in the dustbin. Pull yourself together, Mary. Pull yourself together.

Listen to her yapping, the cunning vixen. She pretended to be so kind, offering me a home when mother went away, but I see through her. I know what she did to mother – having her locked up in that dreadful place. She hated mother. She hated her like poison. Just because I hadn't a father, and everybody knew that mother liked to have some fun.

She's as bad. My aunt is worse than mother ever was. *She* goes away for weeks on end with those friends of hers. I dread being shut up in that house on my own. The walls come down and down on me until they are suffocating me, and the silence is so loud I shriek and shriek to break it.

So I come here. I've never seen anyone else. Except, of course, for Steve. Even when I used to come with Steve, the tracks were rusty, and the panes of glass were broken in the signal box. How long ago was that? One year? Three? I don't know. I don't know. Oh, God, why is it I can't remember?

But I've had to keep coming back. I couldn't stop myself. All the time I've prayed and prayed it would be like it was before. That Steve would be waiting, and that we'd climb over the fence, and run down the fields with the long grass pulling at our ankles. Then Steve would be pulling at me, and I'd be panting 'No, not again, Steve. Please, please, not again.'

But he took no notice. He never heard me, or perhaps I never said it, or maybe it never really happened, and it's all part of that oozing greyness that won't let me think.

There's a rat watching me now. It has mean greedy eyes. I wonder if it's hungry. Sometimes I wonder if there are rats in the tunnel down the line. There must be, because it's so dark, with water dripping down the walls, and the smell of soil and decay.

I wonder what they eat, those rats in the tunnel. They must eat something, but I'll try not to think of that.

This one's coming nearer. I shall hunch my head on my knees and take no notice. If it touches me with those filthy teeth I shall scream. Scream and scream, like I do in the house when my aunt is away. Till I'm laughing and crying together, because nobody will come. Not to the house. Not here. I'm all alone. This station has been closed down for years, and nobody ever comes. Except Steve and me. Now only me.

Where are you, Steve? Why aren't you waiting when I come? I won't say no again, Steve. I won't cry, because I know you don't like me to cry. Don't leave me here on my own. It's the only place I've got.

I feel so cold and frightened when it starts to grow dark. I shan't stay here as long today. Maybe if I go back, I can watch those children playing at the end of the lane. There's one little tot – she's far too young to be allowed out. Perhaps I can stand by her, and maybe even coax her hand into mine. Just to feel her little fingers – the livingness of them, the warm flesh and blood.

Or maybe that woman in the end house would let me hold her baby again. If I went and stood by the gate, the pram might be in the garden. I wouldn't hurt the baby. I wouldn't hurt it. I *wouldn't*. I wouldn't squeeze it too hard, like that time when the woman came running out before. Shouting to me to stop. I didn't mean any harm. I love babies. Don't you love babies, Steve? They're so small and soft in your hands. They should be sung to, and loved, not called filthy spawn and unwanted brats.

That was a wicked thing to say, Steve. When I think of the way you said those words, I have to stand up and walk about. My heart starts banging louder and louder, and I can feel the sweat pouring under my clothes. You didn't want a baby, did you, Steve? Was that why you were so angry? Shouting at me, and pushing and hitting. That was the last time I saw you. How can I ever forget about that?

I hate you, Steve. Please come back to me. Please give me my baby back. Don't leave me here, because all the time I feel something pulling me down to that dreadful tunnel. I've never been there again since that night.

Did I stay there one night? Or two? Or a week? I don't know. It's another of those things I can't remember, like how long it is since you went away, or how long since I spoke to anyone else at all.

But I'm cunning. That's a joke, isn't it? I said my aunt was cunning, so perhaps I'm like her, just a little bit. She didn't find out about you, or the baby, or the way we used to come here. When I knew you'd gone away, and I'd be all on my own, I made sure she didn't find out. I strapped myself up until I was dizzy with pain. She never pays any attention to me anyway. I'd have stood and died rather than let her see me cry.

It worked out in the end, only this red darkness comes back when I turn my mind to that. It was one of those times when my aunt was away. A month or more, I don't know. I'd been here at Alder Lea all day, wandering about, looking for you, Steve, hoping you would come. Then I heard someone shouting across the field, and I started running, faster and faster, in case you went away. But it wasn't you. I saw that then. Only a boy disappearing with a dog.

I lay there on the ground where I fell. When I came round, I knew I had to be on my own. I dragged myself back towards the tunnel where it was dark and hidden. I didn't kill that baby, Steve. I didn't kill it, did I? It was too little and pulpy and it never cried at all. It's fingers, Steve – they were too soft and blunt. I know because I held it, Steve. I sat there and I rocked it backwards and forwards, crying and singing, backwards and forwards, and tasting the blood on my lips.

But what could I do? I couldn't take it away. It was dead anyway. There was rubble and soil enough to bury it so that no one would ever see.

That's why I dread going down there again. But if I come here any more, I shan't be able to help myself. My feet move as though a magnet draws them. Help me, Steve. For God's sake, give me my baby back. I want my baby, Steve. I haven't got anyone else.

My legs and arms are so cold that I can't feel the use in them unless I pinch and rub. But I *must* go. I'm not staying here another minute. I shan't come back to Alder Lea. I mean it. I shan't come back ever again.

There's something I've remembered. This afternoon a man spoke to me. He was outside that cottage a mile or two up the hill. He said they were tearing up the lines soon, demolishing everything, sealing off the tunnel because it was in a dangerous state. There won't be any more point in coming back, will there, Steve?

So I'm leaving. Do you hear me? Do I have to shout? The

rats can gnaw away where they like. It couldn't make any difference now.

Perhaps if I hurry I can be back in town before the shops are closed. One or two often stay open late. If I can find some money I can buy a ball of wool. Then when I'm on my own in the house I can start to knit a little coat.

THE FAT THING

By Martin Waddell

> *Old Mother Hubbard,*
> *Caught in the cupboard,*
> *Thought she was in for some fun,*
> *The Fat Thing was there,*
> *All flab and no hair,*
> *And Old Mother Hubbard got done.*

SOMETHING ... SOME Fat Thing ... minced her and munched her, chewed her and champed her, inwardly digested, and spat out her bones like pips all over the clean tiles and the electric toaster. It made ever such a nasty mess in the kitchen, and didn't bother to eat her at the table, or use a knife and fork. Some Fat Things have no manners.

That was the way Fred saw it, and he was the one who saw most of it, poor man. Fred Hubbard was her brother-in-law. Fred it was who came into the property, and Fred it was who had to clear what was left of Minnie Hubbard out of the cupboard, not to mention the scullery and the bits that were choking up the backyard grating. He could have called in the GLC Cleansing Department, but he felt he owed at least a spot of Ajax to her memory. The sentiment was noble, but he regretted it when he got down to the job. He didn't *much* mind the gore sticking to the cauliflower, or the way spare bits of intestine had got mixed up with the tapioca pudding ... Fred was rather partial to tapioca himself, and, intrigued by the new mixture he ... anyway, he could have put up with these horrors; it was the trail of bloody entrails down the hallway to the front door that gave Fred the quivers. It ran down the street outside for a few yards, and then disappeared abruptly, at the edge of a manhole cover.

Obviously, some Fat Thing had gone underground.

Some Fat Mrs-Minnie-Hubbard-Eating Thing had eaten Mrs Minnie Hubbard and got clean away with it, if clean is the word for a Fat Thing which drags its blood-and-entrail soiled self through a sewer in the lunch hour. Mind you, Fred had nothing against the Fat Thing. He was glad to be rid of Minnie. The Fat Thing was welcome to her, as far as Fred was concerned.

Mrs Minnie Hubbard, you see, wasn't all that enticing in life, and when life had departed she must have left a lot to be desired, even from a gastronomic point of view. In her prime, she'd have been a meal fit for a . . . fit for a . . . she'd have been all right to eat in her prime, I expect, although she was inordinately fat, for she ate too many free steakburgers in the Wimpy where she worked. But when her prime had by-passed her, poor Minnie went right off . . . not the bulk, there was still a lot of her, but the quality. She swept around in black tights, a purple smock and a bandelero, squeezing herself through the motions of a life she had quite outgrown, a gross elephant on the floor of the over-forties club and a danger to traffic down the Mile End Road on Saturday nights. She was, in essence, a jelly filled balloon of flesh, liberally coated inside with grease from her steakburger obsession. Greasy she was, horribly greasy; grease wound up in driblets of fat when the Fat Thing was through with her. It chewed her up quite happily.

That is what happened to Minnie Hubbard, and the end of the Minnie Hubbard bit of this story. Despite keeping a twenty-four-hour watch on manholes all over London, the police were unable to catch the Fat Mrs-Minnie-Hubbard-Eating Thing, or the Mrs-Minnie-Hubbard-Eating Fat Thing . . . put it whatever way you like, it adds up to the same Fat Thing.

In the heart of a brooding city the police waited, their best brains glued to the ground, eager for a whisper of evil, or the rattle of a manhole cover in the night.

When would the Fat Thing strike again?

Only the Fat Thing knew.

Alone in a dark steamy lair somewhere in the central London

sewage system, cleverly disguised as central London sewage, the Fat thing poured over a book of nursery rhymes, illustrated by Mabel Lucie Atwell . . . you may remember she drew fat little girls, did Mabel Lucie, and the Fat Thing was partial to fat.

*   *   *

> *Little Bo-Peep*
> *Had lost her sleep,*
> *The Fat Thing came oozing behind her.*
> *It followed her home,*
> *Where she lived all alone,*
> *And proceeded to mash and to grind her.*

Barbara, Bo or Peek-a-Bo to her friends, depending on their gender, lived in a tenement block in Wapping. She was a pub-cum-club singer. She liked to sing *Roses of Picardy*, *Yes, We Have No Bananas*, and *God Save The Queen*, though when she sang them they all sounded much the same. She had a great big belly, purple knickers, a piano accordion, and a little moustache.

It was the belly which first attracted the Fat Thing as it oozed through the night-life of Wapping. It was the belly, and perhaps something about the way she walked. She had a cumbersome gait which allowed mottled flesh to slurp over the tops of her thigh-high black leather boots with the Lone Ranger Studs; to slurp over the top and slap against her mini-skirt . . . in effect almost a rhumba rhythm.

The Fat Thing approved of her appearance from the blonde hair to the faint speckling of cigarette ash which turned her little black outfit silver grey. The Fat Thing, I can only suppose, wasn't all that discerning. It was been too long in its sewer. It felt like some fresh air and a good square meal . . . and you can't get much squarer than *Yes, We Have No Bananas*, can you?

As she hurried through the dimly lit streets of Wapping, Bo

somehow sensed that something incredibly old, something
from the foul primeval swamps of pre-history lurked in the
darkness watching her, furtively slurping betimes. She can
scarcely have heard the Fat Thing, for though it made sloppy
slippy noises as it oozed along, it did its level best to ooze
quietly, being well aware that sloppy slurpy slippyness is often
defined as anti-social by people who have ordinary legs. Bo
turned her head now and then, anxiously, but she could see
nothing peculiar.

As we know, the Fat Thing was oozing right behind her, but
she couldn't see it. She had been in a lot of B pictures and
several pantomimes.

'Slurp,' it went, and oozed over a milk bottle that happened
to be in the way. It didn't *say* 'slurp', that was the noise it
made when it slopped down on to the pavement.

She turned quickly, all a-quiver. In the distance she could
see a milk float and two charwomen in their fur coats. Closer
still was a large man with a rubbery face, all wrapped up in
an overcoat, but there was nothing about him to suggest
slurping, beyond a faint air of acquaintance with primeval
swamps.

'It cannot be him,' she said. 'He.'

How wrong she was!

It could be him, he, and it was.

She would have seen the truth about the rubber-faced man
immediately if she had been walking behind him for, instead of
footprints in the snow . . . there was snow, I left that bit out in
the first graphic bit of scene setting, but there was snow . . .
instead of footprints in the snow the rubber-faced man left
behind him a trail of slime and ooze which was later to lead the
police to a manhole cover in Lighterman's Entry, where it
ended abruptly . . . with, I think it is safe to assume, a
splash . . . or should it be slop? These sound effects are very
difficult to convey.

Why did the man with the rubber face leave a trail of slime
and ooze and other unmentionables behind him, instead of
footprints in the snow?

Because he was no ordinary rubber-faced man, but that very

incredibly old something from the foul primeval swamps of pre-history which she had expected to see when first she heard him slopping about.

Bo almost guessed it, but not quite.

Coincidence being what it is, at that very moment Fred went by in a stolen motor car. If this were real life, Fred would have spotted the foul trail of slime and ooze the rubber-faced man left behind him and made straight for the police station. But Fred was driving a stolen car and had no wish to have Minnie regurgitated all over his clean tiles, so he drove on whistling and never said a word.

It started as a bad smell in the drains opposite Nos 224 to 386 in the flats. Then the drains became blocked, and little bits of Bo came bubbling up the Gents Convenience in Flotilla Street.

Whatever bit of Bo it was that they uncovered, when at last the courtyard flags were lifted, it was certainly disgusting. Something like papiermâché blended here and there with porridge, with just a dash of sarsaparilla.

There was a lot more of it in flat 248, blocking up the plug hole.

Every flat these days should have the basic amenities, indoor lavatory, larder, and bath. Bo's flat . . . 248 . . . had the larder and lavatory, but not the bath. Bo took a bath every second Thursday in a wooden tub she'd brought up from her mum's house in Brixton. She liked to put it by the fire, so she could watch television and soap herself at the same time.

The Fat Thing had made a mistake. It had put Bo's wooden tub on top of her gas cooker, with what was left of Bo in it, presumably with Bo broth in mind. But the tub, being wooden, had caught fire, and the Fat Thing's broth was spoilt. So it put a little of the unburnt Bo in a pot with spices and flour, a little garlic and some well-whipped eggs and produced a sort of a stew . . . it had an over-all sickly red stickiness, and a great deal of body.

The curious thing about it all was that the neighbours didn't take the stew for Bo at first. They were downtrodden and very short of food, so that when they discovered that Bo had gone off on her holidays leaving a good stew to go to waste they sent their little ones round in relays with plastic buckets to fetch it.

There were some splendid meals in Honigmann's Tenement that night. Many a pale child savoured little bits of stewed Bo before Mr Feldman found the ... the ... the piece of Bo's anatomy that he found. It was very wet and not at all firm, set in a wedge of egg and sausage meat, and ever so faintly toasted ... it must have been in the original Bo broth to begin with ... it was ever so faintly toasted, but it was still a ... a ... well, it was.

He finished up his stew, wiping round the plate with a piece of bread, and rang the police afterwards. After all, he was hungry, and he was a Chinese, despite being called Feldman. He could remember the bad old days in the old country.

The news unglued the police brains pretty quickly, I can tell you. They took away what was left of the Bo broth and the Bo stew and tried to put the bits they could identify together again, but it proved to be a quite impossible task.

The Fat Thing had oozed again. All of London rose in horror, terror stalked the nightlong streets, lit up only by purple prose. Men with the merest primeval swamp look about them were stoned in Madame Tussaud's.

Through the darkness of the sewers, the Fat Thing oozed on with a contented belly ... if you can call it a belly. We are fast approaching a difficulty in the story of the fearful Fat Thing, a difficulty which can best be explained away by the revelations contained in part three of this tale ... the Fat Thing Eats Jack Horner.

*   *   *

> *Little Jack Horner*
> *Sat in a corner*
> *Watching his guest on the sly.*
> *The Fat Thing betrayed him,*
> *It stuffed him and spayed him,*
> *And put what was left in a pie.*

Jack Horner was a rotten no-good layabout from Harrow and King's College, Cambridge. He had been brought up by a loving old auntie and given every opportunity, but he had gone to the bad. This is a bit of character stuff put in to provoke sympathy for the Fat Thing, who was also an orphan. Jack had lost his parents in 1929 when they fell off the gold standard and, on the day he met his death, had a damn good job as a bus inspector with London Transport which was more than he deserved.

At half past eight that fateful evening Jack was in his front room counting the matchbox labels he had stolen from his blind twin sister Mabel when he heard a soft oozy knock at the door. He should have been suspicious about soft oozy knocks after what had happened to other gross people with nursery-rhyme names, but he was not. Jack refused to pay for newspapers and his television had been taken back by the finance company, so he knew nothing of the rhyme in crime.

'Good evening,' said the man with the rubber face, when Jack answered the door. 'I believe you let furnished apartments.'

Jack didn't, but he was always glad to be in on a good thing. 'Sixteen guineas a week and no questions asked,' he snapped, his treble chin quivering with emotion. It may have been Coronation week, but sixteen guineas was still overcharging.

'Done,' said the rubber-faced man, feeling Jack's flabby forearm with his fingers.

'Come upstairs,' said Jack, his chubby face beaming. 'I'll show you to your room.'

The rubber-faced man followed him upstairs, carrying only a large suitcase which contained flour, vanilla flavouring, sausage meat and raspberries, mingled with some dodgy things from the sewer.

'This will suit splendidly,' said the rubber-faced man, easing himself down on to the rickety bed with only the faintest of 'slurp' sounds.

'Give me my money,' said Jack, and the rubber-faced man did.

When Jack had gone, the rubber-faced man pulled the curtains and switched off the light. Then he felt for the zip on his body stocking, and tugged it down.

As the rubber skin of the rubber-faced man slipped off the Fat Thing stood revealed in its awful corsets.

Corsets? Why corsets?

It needed corsets because it wasn't man-shaped in the least, it was thing-shaped, *shapeless*. When the corsets came off it collapsed quivering on the floor, a mound of pale hairless breathing flesh, all stale and pulpy, sweating and oozing as its suckers sucked the carpet, drawing it across the floor to the doorway which it oozed through, before welling down the stairs, slurping from step to step with the suitcase full of cooking ingredients contained in a handy sac in its intestines.

'No pets allowed,' cried Jack, who was sitting by his one-bar electric fire.

They were his last words. The fat thing oozed over his arm-chair, formed a Jack-shaped hump over him, flopped across his nostrils, swelled over his mouth and eyes, flesh to flesh, pale sticky flesh to flesh, sucked and scraped, oozed and embraced, drowned and smothered him before it dragged him in a fleshy bundle to the floor and set off for the back kitchen where it . . .

There can really be no excuse for continuing any further with this story, which is most objectionable.

Jack went the way of the rest, amid incredible slime and gore. The only reason for including Jack at all was to explain the bit about the belly. In a sense, you see, the Fat Thing was *all* belly, inside and out, greasy all-embracing hungry belly, a belly with no mouth, but infinite flexibility. Whatever it slithered around was suddenly inside it, all sucked up in its digestive juices.

*   *   *

Isn't it wonderful how, when I've got this corset on and my rubber body stocking over it, I can get my fingers . . . fingers . . . sufficiently firm to type out this manuscript and send it to a publisher.

They say there's a book in everyone, even primeval Fat Things.

Don't think too badly of me. Fat Things have to live you know.

Fat doesn't grow on trees.

It grows on people.

THE FLATMATE

By B. Lynn Barber

September 9th

I am very lucky to have got this flat. It is large and cheap and convenient, and I think I will settle down here. To think I might never have got round to moving from the grotty basement if I hadn't bumped into Simon. I got it on a plate really, it was all so quick and easy. I must remember to write to Simon and thank him. I wonder why he was in such a hurry to move from such a gorgeous pad? Bloody lucky for me, anyway.

There are hundreds of things here – all the wardrobes and cupboards are full. Simon promised to move it out later this week, but some of it goes with the flat. I hope the saucepans and things do, otherwise I won't be able to cook. But I will be glad when he takes his clothes out of my wardrobe, and that stinking basket of dirty linen. I can't really settle until he does, and I so much want to settle, be homely for a change – please God may I never have to share a flat with another girl again ever in my life.

September 11th

Simon came today and moved his things out. He also dropped a major bombshell in his quiet way. He had collected lots of things together and packed them in his car, then he wandered round a bit, and said, 'Well, that's all my stuff, I think.'

'*What?*' I screeched, seeing as how most of the cupboards were still full.

'Lots of things go with the flat,' he muttered.

'Not bloody suits of clothes' – and I flung open a wardrobe door to show him.

'Ah yes.' He sat down on the bed, and looked even more

embarrassed. 'I'm sorry, Laura, I should have told you before, but I was so anxious to get that lease off my hands.'

I sat down too, shocked. What ghastly revelations was he going to make now? What was wrong with the flat? Rats? Coloured neighbours? Ceilings falling in? 'What do you mean?'

'Well. You see there was someone else living here with me. Tom. Those are his clothes and things. I hope someone from his family will come and take them away soon, but they're all abroad. They live in Thailand. But he's got a cousin somewhere in England, and they wrote and said he'd come.'

'Why can't Tom come?'

'Oh. Because, because he's dead.'

'Dead?' I said, then, 'How?'

'Suicide. Here. I was away, I stayed away that night. He killed himself here. I couldn't live here any more.' Simon slumped down and put his head in his hands. I thought he was crying, and I was desperately embarrassed. I shouldn't have been so beastly to him, especially since he'd given me the flat. Besides, I was rather relieved. It wasn't nearly as bad as rats or falling ceilings. It didn't matter to me what his mouldy old flatmate had done, though I must say my morbid curiosity was champing at the bit, dying to ask more questions. Simon looked so shattered, though, that I couldn't, and so I took him off to his car and watched him drive off. He promised to try and get in touch with the cousin, to collect Tom's belongings, but I said it wasn't urgent.

So here I am, in a flat full of a corpse's clutter. I shall sort it out tomorrow, and put it all in one cupboard. Then I can settle in properly.

September 12th

Today I went through the place and emptied all the drawers. Tom had masses of stuff. I put all his clothes in the spare-room wardrobe, and threw the dirty washing away. One whole chest of drawers is crammed with his papers, and I daren't really burn them, so I have left it as it is and moved it into the spare room too. He seems to have used the spare room as a painting studio: there are masses of brushes and pots of paint and about twenty canvasses, some unfinished still. His paintings are rather good. There is one portrait of a girl who looks like me, but it isn't finished. It never will be, I suppose. Then there is one that might be a self portrait, a three-quarters head, very handsome, dark hair, dark violent eyes. All the paintings are signed T.T. I know what the second T stands for – Traherne. I know that because *The Listener* came today in the mail, addressed to Thomas Traherne. I opened it and read it – it seems pointless to keep old magazines and newspapers for his cousin to collect. Maybe he subscribed to lots of papers – that will be useful.

September 13th

This evening a man rang up, he sounded nice, and asked to speak to Tom. I didn't know what to say. I paused for about a hundred years, and then said, 'He isn't here any more.'

'Has he moved?'

'Mm. No.' Another ghastly long silence. The man was making impatient noises. 'Are you a close friend of his?' I asked.

'I suppose so, inasmuch as he has any close friends apart from Simon . . . is Simon there?'

'No. He's moved.'

'Oh, well, I . . .'

'Tom's dead.' There, I'd done it. There was a silence, and then the nice voice said very softly, 'I suppose he killed himself.'

'Yes.'

'It must have been a fortnight ago.' I did some mental arithmetic and worked out that it probably was – I had been in the flat five days, and Simon had moved out pretty quickly. Christ, so recently. Somehow I had thought of it as months ago, but the man confirmed it by saying 'I spoke to him only the weekend before last.'

'Oh.'

Then he rang off very suddenly, and I thought of all the questions I would have liked to have asked him, and felt very annoyed.

September 14th

I have found a pile of records; Tom's, I suppose, and the record-player works. There was a record actually on the turntable and I played that first – César Franck's Symphony in D Minor, very romantic and very sad. I have been playing it all evening. Tom seems to have gone in for the heavy romantic stuff. All the records are like that, Brahms, Wagner, Berlioz, and his paintings are too. The books are more varied, because there's so many of them, but there's a high proportion of poetry and things like *The Sorrows of Young Werther* and *A Hero of Our Time*. I am beginning to build up quite a clear picture of Tom – dark, romantic, introspective. I am sure I would have liked him if I had met him: we share the same tastes. I wonder why he killed himself.

September 16th

Well, now I have been here a week and discovered that Tom subscribes to *The Listener*, *The Gramophone*, *Newsweek*, and the *New Statesman*. Not bad at all. Perhaps there will be some monthlies too. If he paid his subscription at the beginning of the year, I shall go on getting them free for over three months – isn't that nice? There are lots of other nice things too, and it seems pointless to lock them all away for the possible arrival of this possible cousin. For instance, I found a very gorgeous genuine Arab caftan, and I don't see why I shouldn't wear it to a party, just once. Also some mules, about a hundred sizes too big, but it saves me having to buy some boring slippers. I put them on to go to the bathroom and I suddenly thought 'stepping into a dead man's shoes' and it was all a bit shuddery for a minute. I must stop this morbid tendency. Last night when I got into bed, it suddenly occured to me – 'Perhaps Tom died in this bed'. That was ghastly, but then I thought of it a different way round – 'Perhaps Tom *slept* in this bed' and it gave me almost a cosy feeling. The idea of having a man about the place is somehow reassuring. I slept particularly well last night.

September 17th

Damn, damn, damn. Someone has rung up again for Tom and I didn't ask any of the questions I meant to. This was an older man, and he started off like the other one, asking to speak to Tom. I decided not to beat about the bush this time, and said straight out 'He's dead.'

He didn't seem at all surprised, and asked, 'Was it suicide?' as cool as anything. Isn't it odd – both he and the other man seem to have expected him to kill himself. Just to rub it in, this man said 'We should have known all along', and then rang off. Damn. If all his bosom pallies were so sure he was going to do himself in, why the hell didn't they do something about it? Then I remembered what the first man had said – 'inasmuch as he had any close friends except Simon'. Simon must know all about it. Shall I phone him and ask him? I feel almost a sisterly interest in Tom now.

September 18th

How did he kill himself? This is what is obsessing me now. The other night I thought 'Perhaps in this bed' – that would have to be with pills – and then today, even more grisly, as I was taking my dinner out of the oven, it suddenly hit me – perhaps he gassed himself here, in my oven. It was so awful I just threw the food away and didn't eat anything at all. I can't go cooking in someone's death chamber. But now I am being ludicrously melodramatic – he probable didn't gas himself at all.

This morning I got all worked up and decided it must have been in the bathroom, with a razor, and I spent over an hour looking round for bloodstains. Thank God there weren't any. Not that that proves anything. I am really getting into a state about it. I must stop myself. I must go and see people. I haven't visited any of my friends since I moved in here. I suppose I should invite Stan and Rose to dinner – oh, God, the gas oven again. No one has been in this flat except me, and Simon once, since I moved in here. Tom and I live here alone, un-visited.

September 19th

I am behaving very oddly. The fact that I know I am behaving oddly proves I am not going mad, anyway. Mad people don't know they're behaving oddly. Besides, I'm perfectly sane. It's just that I'm beginning to feel rather affectionate, possessive almost, towards Tom. I sleep between his sheets (they have the laundry mark Traherne) in what I am sure is his bed. Last night I said 'Goodnight, Tom' when I put out the light. Then this morning I went into the spare room and dug out the two canvasses – the one that looks like me and the one that might be a self portrait of Tom. I hung them on either side of the mantelshelf and they looked very nice. The one of me isn't a terribly good likeness, though. The eyes are right, and the smile, but the hairstyle's hopeless and the wrong colour. I could alter it easily. I could just do it longer and darker. Would that be wrong? I don't think so. After all, portraits are meant to look like the person. I will go and mix the paints and do it now – I'm not tired.

There. The picture's done and it looks just like me. I am very pleased with it. I wonder whether the one of Tom is such a good likeness. If only I had a photograph. If *only* I had a photograph. How ghastly if it wasn't a self-portrait at all. Tom might be short and pink and gingery. No, I can't believe that. It *is* him, I'm sure. But tomorrow I am going to go through all his papers and find a photograph. He must have one somewhere.

September 20th

Oh Tom, Tom. Your letters have upset me dreadfully, and there was no photograph, not one. Your parents in Thailand are monsters – do you realize that? From your father, typed on Embassy paper, signed by his secretary pp Thornton Traherne – 'Thank you for your letter of the 5th. I am glad to hear you are fit and well. Your mother and I are also enjoying good health. Do you realize that you are living off your capital? This painting nonsense cannot continue. I look forward to hearing that you have found yourself a decent job. Affectionately—'.

And his mother, drivelling on about her cocktail parties and dinner parties, and how hard it is finding honest servants. And at the end – 'Do you ever see the Crowthers' daughter, Sally, I think? She is awfully nice. I do wish you would find yourself a nice girlfriend.' How dare she? What about *me*?

But there is also this girl Anne. She writes to him a lot, mainly boring drivel about her own boring activities and incredibly banal thoughts. How she enjoyed the concert, how Chopin almost moves her to tears, why she loves Keats – what piss! I can just picture her, the prissy, mousy little creep. I can't see what Tom sees in her at all. There's one consolation, anyway – all her letters are over four years' old. She wrote every week for about eighteen months and then they just stop. I wonder what happened? Anyway, they're not really love letters, though they're signed 'All my love'. She never seems to have seen him much, otherwise she wouldn't have had to write so often, and there's nothing romantic. The high point of passion is one in April 1963 where she says 'It was so nice to see you last week, after so long. I really did enjoy that evening so much.' I wonder what they did? I'm absolutely certain they didn't go to bed together. I'm positive of that.

Those are the only letters from a girl. The others are all from relatives and male friends, one called Nigel writes a lot and it's very odd stuff. His address is Ambleside in the Lake District and he goes on and on about how glad he is to have got away from 'the temptations' of London, though he keeps saying how much he misses Tom. It is all in a rather unhealthy, self-dramatizing vein, and there are bits about religion. He has the nerve to tell Tom he ought to seek the consolation of the Church. Puke! Thank God there are no signs that Tom ever did this – not one Bible among all his books. I think Nigel is a very bad friend for Tom to have. Luckily his letters get more and more infrequent, only two in the past year. If any more arrive, I shall write to him to stop pestering Tom.

On the whole, the letters are not very interesting at all. What is much more interesting is Tom's own writing. There are some poems, and they seem very good though I can't really understand them. One *To Shakespeare* goes:

> *Your dark lady*
> *Did you love*
> *As I*
> *Love*

and then there's just a row of dots. Who did he love? Surely not Anne? I found the dots so irritating that I wrote in my own name, Laura. It sounds better now—

> *Your dark lady*
> *Did you love*
> *As I*
> *Love*
> *LAURA?*

I will keep it under my pillow. I will treasure it.

The other thing is his diary but, like everything I find, it is more frustrating than illuminating. It is written in French. I could curse. Everyone except me speaks French – if only I had listened to Mme Volnay at school. There are some bits I can do – '*Ce matin je me suis lévé à onze heures*' means 'This morning I got up at eleven' – which isn't exactly devastating news. But there are pages where it goes on and on, overflowing the printed dates at the top of the page, and the writing gets looser and looser, impossible to read, even if it were in English. You can see those were the bits where he was getting excited, and I can't believe it is all 'This morning I got up at eleven'. Lots of my friends speak French, but could I show them the diary? No. Definitely not. It would be an intrusion on Tom's privacy, to have a stranger reading his inmost thoughts. But I would give anything to be able to read the last entry, dated September 2nd. After pages of sprawl, the last sentence is clearly written in capitals. JE ME SUIS DECIDE. I have decided. From that and from the date, I know for certain that this is his decision to kill himself, and the pages and pages before it must explain his reasons. I am going to learn French.

September 26th

All this week I have been working on those pages of his last
entry with a French dictionary and a French grammar. I have
gone over every line, trying to decipher it with a magnifying
glass, and then translating the words, but even so I can only
get scattered phrases here and there. The writing is just hopelessly illegible. The name Simon occurs over and over, but I
suppose that is only to be expected. *Nul espoir* – no hope – is
written three times, large, at the end of a page. There are no
names mentioned apart from Simon's, as far as I can make out.
It seems clear that Simon was with Tom earlier that same
evening he wrote the last entry, and the evening he committed
suicide. So Simon must know what was on his mind. There is
nothing else for it – I must talk to Simon. *Je me suis décidé.*

September 27th

I have phoned Simon and he has agreed to come round tomorrow. I didn't tell him it was to talk about Tom. I made out
it was just a social call. After all, we are supposed to be friends,
though I must say I really can't stand him. He is always so
creepy and hangdog and shifty-looking. I know him vaguely
because in the bad old days when I thought I ought to have a
job, he was in the same office for a while. I think he was sacked
in the end, or maybe I just left, I can't remember. I would
probably never have seen him again in my life, if I hadn't
bumped into him in the street that day and mentioned that I
was looking for a flat. What luck – or perhaps it wasn't just
luck. I feel I was fated to meet Tom, otherwise why should he
have painted my portrait and written a poem about me? He
knew so much, of course, he must have known about me.

I resent Simon's having lived with Tom before me. I don't
know how Tom could have stood having that drip around the
place. I suppose it was just to help with the rent, while he
painted and his capital dwindled. Anyway, I shall be nice to
Simon for Tom's sake, but when he has given me all the information I want, I won't see him again. I want to forget all
about Tom's past, when I have cleared up the details. Once

we have got the old hang-ups, the letters and the diary, out of the way, we can start living properly together in the present. I hate Simon.

September 28th
There. I have cleared up all the mess, and washed the glasses, and dealt with Simon. Now I can forget he ever intruded into our lives. He was a loathsome man, Tom, and we are well rid of him, you even more than me. We won't see him again now.

I can't forgive the way he talked about you – no wonder he was reluctant to get on to the subject. I built up to it gradually, and wasted about half an hour on idle chit-chat about all the boring jobs he'd done since leaving that publishers. He kept saying 'Do you remember so-and-so at the office?' as if I could possibly be interested in any of those deadly deadbeat drips. I thought he would go driveling on for ever, but then there was a pause and I said, 'I've hung up two of Tom's pictures'.

'So I see,' he said, looking embarrassed in his usual fishy way.

'They're good likenesses, aren't they?'

He looked puzzled and didn't reply.

'It's a good self portrait of Tom, isn't it. *Isn't it?*' I said.

He turned his head very slowly and looked at it for ages before he muttered, 'Yes, it is a good portrait. How he liked to see himself.' He shuddered, I noticed, as he said it.

'Did you know Tom a long time?' I asked.

'About two years, I suppose. I only lived with him for six months though.' Then he had the nerve to try and change the subject – 'Do you have a job, Laura?'

'No I don't. Did Tom have many friends?'

'Mm. No. Not really. None at all in fact. He belonged to some societies, and had plenty of acquaintances, but nobody knew him well.'

'Didn't *you*?'

'I – I don't think so. Only in the last few weeks. Up to that we hardly spoke to each other, even though we were living together, but gradually I got to know him, and he liked to talk about his paintings.'

'What did he say about them?'

'Oh, nothing much. He thought he was improving, but still not good enough. He wondered if he ought to go to art school.'

'What did you say?'

'I said I thought it would be a good idea. It would get him out of the flat a bit.'

'Why on earth did you want to get him out of the flat?'

Simon looked even more shifty, and twisted his horrible white bony hands.

'He was going out less and less. In the last few weeks he hadn't been out at all, except to the shops. He stopped going to his societies, he never saw anyone. I thought it would do him good to see other people.'

'I suppose you mean see some girls, like his bloody mother.'

Simon looked really amazed, and sat upright.

'What on earth do you mean, Laura?'

I realized then that he might not be too pleased about my reading Tom's letters, not that it was any of his business, so I just muttered 'Oh, nothing. He didn't have a girlfriend, did he?'

'No he didn't.' Simon retreated with his head in his hands again. After a while I got bored with this display of phoney sentimentality and said, 'How did he do it?'

'With a razor. He lay down on the bed and cut his – cut his – it was horrible.' Simon was crying again.

'This bed? My bed?'

'Yes. Maybe he didn't mean actually to kill himself, but he bled to death. He – he looked awful. I had to identify the body. He was all twisted, and that – mess – between his legs.' Simon was mumbling into his hands, and choking. I could see the tears coming down through his fingers and dripping on to his hideous mohair sweater. What a creep!

'Were you here when it happened?'

'No. No, not when it happened. I left earlier in the evening. I stayed away that night.'

'Why?'

'I didn't want to see him. We had had – we had not been getting on very well. I couldn't stand him going on at me any more, so I spent the night at a friend's.'

'So you knew he was depressed, and you got bored with being sympathetic, and you walked out on him. You knew he was likely to kill himself. All his friends knew it. You were so goddam selfish you were prepared to let this – to let Tom – you knew he was a hundred times better than you, more intelligent, more talented and you were jealous – he would have been such a great artist – and you were prepared to let him kill himself rather than waste one minute of your precious time.'

My voice rose higher and higher, and I was shouting by the end. Simon was silent for a while and then, with a deep sigh, he took his hands from his face and stood up. His expression was strange, feverish, and he had lost his hangdog look. I felt almost afraid of him at that moment. He stood over me where I was sitting, and started talking very quietly and urgently:

'No, Laura. Laura, you fool, you bitch. It wasn't like that at all. You're so wrong, so totally wrong, and I'm going to tell you the truth. I intended to keep it secret for Tom's sake, but you deserve to hear the truth. You really deserve to hear it. Tom was a despicable man. Anyone who knew him will tell you that. He whined, he dramatized himself, he sponged off everyone he met, he thought he was Shelley and Van Gogh rolled into one. He believed he was the best goddam artist in creation and everyone ought to realize that and fall at his feet.

'I knew all that, when I moved in here, but I felt sorry for him in a way, because I knew he couldn't be too happy in his fool's paradise. There were already signs that his great faith in himself was cracking. He actually asked me whether I thought his paintings were any good. A few months before, he would have hit anyone who said he wasn't da Vinci. I said I thought they were promising and he must work at them. He began to ask my opinion of everything he did, not just his painting, but his poems, and his ghastly self-castigating diary. I had to see everything he did.

'And I had to see him, too. That was when I began to realize. He was forever wandering around the flat naked. He never shut the bathroom door. He always asked me to come in and talk to him when he was in the bath. And then he took to coming into my bedroom when I was undressing. One night he got into bed beside me. He thought I was asleep, but I wasn't, and I said "What the hell do you think you're doing?" He sniffled a bit and then he said "I'm so lonely, so miserable. Let me just lie here, Simon." So I let him stay for a bit, but then I felt his hand on my cock and I threw him out. I was furious and shouted at him. But next day I calmed down a bit, and talked to him as kindly as I could, and said I thought he ought to go out more, meet some girls perhaps. He burst into tears, but he said he'd try.

'A few nights later he came into my room again, wearing his infernal caftan, with his long hair down to his shoulders, and flowers – he had put flowers in his hair! And he stood at the end of my bed and smiled and simpered like a girl, and then he said in a silly put-on girl's voice, "Don't you find me attractive, Simon – other men do." And as he said it he moved towards me, and I shouted out and hit him and pulled the flowers out of his hair. I said I would leave the next day. Then he broke down, and cried, pawing at me with his clammy hands, begging me to stay. He said if I didn't, he would kill himself, and I was frightened he might mean it, so I calmed him down and sat him in the armchair. He began to talk more sensibly, and I promised I would stay, so long as he didn't try to – try anything – again. And he agreed and went back to his own room.

'It was all right the next day, and I think for four days after that. It was September 2nd that it happened. I came home from work and found him in my room, lying on the bed, wearing that caftan thing again but pulled up so that I could see his legs – I had never noticed before but they were quite hairless. And he started saying things again, begging me, half flirting like a woman, half pleading. He kept saying "Come to bed, darling. Think of me as a woman. I'll look after you." It was obscene. It was foul. And then when I didn't come, he got up and started following me around the room, pawing me, clinging to me, crawling around on the floor after me. Then I shouted at him. I can't remember what I said. I shouted and went on at him, and then I left the flat. Later that night he took the razor – and killed himself. It was the window cleaner who found him the following afternoon.'

So that was Simon's story. He put his head in his hands again when he had finished. I was so furious, Tom, you can imagine, so wrought up with hatred for him – his lies, his horrible tissue of lying self-justifications – and I looked at his repulsive bony body there – and he had had the nerve to pretend you found him attractive. Flattering himself. And my anger just boiled and boiled inside me, and I couldn't say anything because I was so furious. But suddenly I saw what I must do and everything was clear and sensible. I went into the kitchen and found the carving knife and whetted it in the machine. Then I went back into the room with it and Simon looked up at me – that phoney expression of what – sympathy? apology? – on his ugly face, and I walked right up to him, and he didn't see the knife, not until the last moment, not until I raised it above my head, and brought it down as hard as I could into his shoulders. But it was difficult to do, much more difficult than it should have been. He put his arms up to protect himself and even when I got the knife in, I had to pull it out again, and it was stiff, to do it again, and again, and again. And he started making noises, not real screams, but nasty bubbling noises, and we kept falling over on to the bed, and it was so messy, I got his blood on my dress. It must have been half an hour at least before I could get him finally to shut up. To stop the filth that was coming out of his mouth, stop his blabbering. So I was very tired, physically exhausted, by the time he was lying still, and then I had to take his trousers off, and his underpants before I could really finish it – that'll teach him to invent lies about you.

So I hope you appreciate it properly, Tom, what I've done for you. I hope you are truly grateful. I had to avenge your death, and stop him telling those lies about you, desecrating you. He murdered you with his dirty-mouthed insinuations, and so I murdered him.

I am coming to bed now, Tom. Our bed. I am coming to lie beside you. Wait for me, Tom.

THE SKI-LIFT

By Diana Buttenshaw

WERNER AND KLAUS came up from Innsbruck together to stay for two nights in the mountain village of Durach, and to go ski-ing in Hoch Durach two thousand feet higher. They had been friends once, inseparable boyhood friends. Sometimes, even now, this friendship broke through again and they could be happy in each other's company; but for most of the time they were bitter rivals and hatred between them flowed in sudden spurts. They were rivals because of the beauty, the quite devastating beauty, of Brigitte Zach. They had both fallen in love with her the moment they saw her, when she first came to live in their Innsbruck street, and their friendship had fallen apart as though split by an axe.

They had only come up to Durach together because, although they both wanted to spend the weekend ski-ing, neither trusted the other to stay away from Innsbruck and Brigitte once out of sight. They had agreed to stay in the same Gasthaus in Durach: to go up ski-ing together to the snowfields of Hoch Durach, and to return by the same bus to Innsbruck.

After the months of rivalry and suspicion there was a feeling of mutual relief now they were out of Brigitte's sphere of influence. They even began to feel their way back to friendship as it had once been, to talk naturally and serenely together. They were happier than they had been for some months.

There are two ways of getting from Durach, in the valley, to Hoch Durach, high above in the mountains. One is by a track which winds and writhes its way up the slopes, twisting among the trees lower down, clinging to the bare shoulders higher up, for some three miles. Cars can get up or down this track one at a time, very slowly. The other way is by chair-lift, a giant cable carrying dozens of swaying chairs over the tops of the trees, from pylon to pylon, two-thousand feet up the face of the mountain. Sometimes the chairs are not far from the ground: sometimes they are thirty or forty feet up. There is something rather terrible about this chair-lift when seen from below, but once in the chairs the peace and the silence take over from the fear.

Werner and Klaus arrived on Friday night and slept well in their plain, scrubbed bedroom in the Krone. In the morning they joined the queue at the foot of the chair-lift, and waited their turn. When it came, the attendant wrapped a rug swiftly round Werner and swung the chair under him as it swept round the wheel and towards him. He sat back with a jerk, clutching his skis in one arm, and rose swaying away from the engine-house and up towards the woods on the slope above. Turning, with a sudden, jealous doubt, he saw Klaus behind him, and settled back, relieved. Klaus was not such a bad fellow after all. It was a pity he had to get this infatuation for Brigitte. Especially when he wasn't at all her type. Brigitte liked tall, dark men like himself; not small bouncing blond ones like Klaus. Much wiser if he acknowledged defeat and left the field clear. They could have got on so well then, Klaus could even have been best man.

The chair clattered quietly over the arms of a pylon and jerked a little, and he looked down to see the blue-shadowed snow piled on the rocks below. Now they were going over the woods, over a clearing cut between the trees to allow the chairs to pass up and down the endless cable. He could see one of the ski-runs down from Hoch Durach winding between the pines, the corners banked by the turning skiers. The first people were coming down already: lone experts ahead of the crowds, and the advanced classes led by instructors. Werner watched as a girl shot down a straight and swung into a perfect parallel turn beneath him, her body slim and supple. Brigitte ski-ed like that. What a shame she could not come up this weekend, held in Innsbruck by some dull relation or other down from Vienna.

The cable ran over a quarry, buried now in the snow, but deep and hollow below. Then it dipped into the trees again, so that they were dark on either side. The sun did not reach the valley except at midday, and Werner clutched the rug against his stomach, feeling the chill creep into him.

Behind him Klaus regarded his back with complacency. No risk of Werner stealing a march on him, no chance of finding that he had slipped off to see Brigitte alone as he had that day last month when they had gone with a crowd to watch ski-jumping on the great Olympic jump. Werner had been a good chap once: a true friend. But one couldn't trust him any more. Not that he had a chance with Brigitte, he was too dour, not gay and carefree as he was himself.

The chairs ran suddenly into sunlight, out over the snow slopes above the trees. Above them lay the scattered chalets and hotels of Hoch Durach and the vast, white spread of glittering snow flowing up to the peaks of the mountains, tremendous against a blue sky. There were people everywhere already, flashing like swallows round the humps and curves of snow, or stumbling slowly in line in classes on the nursery slopes.

The attendant at the top whisked away the blankets as they stepped out of the chairs and clear of them, and the chairs swung round the wheel and downwards again towards Durach.

Werner waited for Klaus, and they walked together along the track towards a shorter lift which took them even higher up the huge snowslopes. Then they ski-ed swiftly downwards together, laughing in the wine-clear air, their skis hissing in the soft, new snow, the sun warming their faces.

They stayed up on the slopes all morning, speeding down to Hoch Durach and travelling up on the short lift several times to keep in the sun. They found themselves more and more in accord, and when they raced it was amicably, without bitter rivalry. As the sun warmed their glowing bodies so their hearts warmed too, and they forgot the arid months which lay immediately behind them, and remembered the gleaming years before, when their friendship had been a most splendid thing. They even forgot Brigitte.

They had lunch at the Alpenblick, with tall glasses of beer, sitting out in the sun on the terrace. There was every sort of people there: Dutch and English, French and German, Belgian and American.

'Even some Austrians!' laughed Klaus.

There were a few people they knew from former times, but no one who knew them well enough to join them, and they were glad, enjoying being alone together again.

After lunch they ran down the fast run into Durach, and came up on the giant ski-lift again to have another. No time to waste sitting about when there were only two days in which to ski! This time they ran down the Green Run, longer than the fast run and less exacting. It was full of classes in various stages, and Werner grumbled at the delays which they imposed.

'One can never get a good free run. These beginners stand about all over the track, and bunch up at the corners. If one goes through them at all fast, the instructors curse one.'

'Well, I suppose we should have stuck to the Red and the Yellow Runs, where they don't learn,' remarked Klaus peaceably.

'Yes, but you get down them too fast. You do get more skiing in this one.'

'We shan't have time for another tonight. The lift stops in under ten minutes,' said Klaus.

'Gottdamm! We should have just made it without all these learners.'

They swung round a corner together, making plans for the evening. They decided on the bar of the Golden Rose, and perhaps an hour at the dance in the Eidelweiss before bed. They were very contented in spite of the slowness of the run. Then they saw a girl ahead of them they both knew, an old schoolfriend from Innsbruck.

'Hello Anne-Lise! We didn't know you were here!'

'Of course you didn't, with Brigitte about,' she answered wrily.

'Brigitte? She isn't up here, she couldn't come,' said Klaus.

'She could. She has. She came up this afternoon in her cousin's Mercedes.'

'Her cousin? The old man from Vienna?' asked Werner, astonished.

'*Old* man? This isn't an old man! A pretty distant cousin, too, I should think. Although not all that distant as a man.'

Anne-Lise was fed up with Brigitte. She already had Werner and Klaus as her slobbering slaves, and now here was this so-called cousin, infinitely more desirable, and with a Mercedes too.

'She isn't—'

'She doesn't—'

Werner and Klaus both shouted at once.

'I should think she is and she does,' snapped Anne-Lise, and ski-ed on.

'Stop a minute! Where is she now?' shouted Werner.

'At the Berg, I should think. They were stopping there the night. They *said* in separate rooms.'

'The Berg? That's in Hoch Durach,' muttered Klaus. 'And the lift will stop in another minute or two.'

Werner suddenly saw him through hostile eyes. He was thinking of going up there, was he? Up there to cut out this cousin. Well, why not? Only it wouldn't be Klaus who would cut him out, but he, Werner. The lift would be closed by the time they reached the bottom, the gates shut while the chairs did their last run round until all were empty. The only way would be up the three mile track. Well, that wouldn't take all that long, and his legs were longer than Klaus'.

Klaus was thinking the same as they sped in silence down the darkening track. Werner could stride faster on the flat, but he was heavier. He would tire much quicker.

We shall get there almost together anyway, thought Werner furiously. What fools we shall look, panting in, one behind the other!

It was then that they came upon one of the pylons carrying the chair-lift cable, looming out of the gathering dusk like the ghost of a skeleton. The chairs were still moving, they would go on empty for some time yet. Klaus was the first to realize its possibility. He remembered that Werner hated heights, he had never been a climber, as Klaus was. Klaus skidded to a violent halt at the foot of the pylon, flicked off his skis in one movement, and started to climb the pylon.

'Klaus! What the hell—?' As he shouted, Werner stopped too in a flurry of snow, and then came leaping back. He was trying to steal a march, was he? Werner, too, kicked off his skis and climbed upwards, his fear of heights forgotten in his fury. Before he could reach him Klaus had leaned outwards and caught the bar of a chair as it passed, leaping outwards and jerking himself into the seat. It swung wildly beneath him, then was clear of the pylon and on its way upwards. The sweat burst suddenly out on Werner's face, then he climbed still higher, leant out on one arm, and prepared to seize the following chair as it came past. Klaus knew he was afraid of heights: he had planned to do this to leave him behind. Well, damn him, he was only one chair behind.

Werner landed in the swaying chair in a heap and nearly slipped out again. Then he got a firmer grip and pulled himself properly up in the seat. Ahead of him Klaus turned round and stared at him through the twilight. It was too dark to see his expression, but in the great silence of the snow Werner heard him swear aloud.

It was eerie up there, travelling alone among the trees, with no other human but each other. They must have been almost the last skiers on the slopes: no one now slipped past on the run which shone dimly through the pines: no one came past them on the downwards line of chairs.

The darkness was falling almost visibly upon them; only the snow gleamed white below them, the trees were mingling together into shadow.

The chairs rose on the cable away from the ground a little, riding over a dell between two pylons.

Then they slowed down, and stopped.

For a moment both Klaus and Werner waited for them to start again, assuming some hitch, some temporary fault. Then as the chairs hung motionless in the silence they realized that they had misjudged the time. The lift had stopped for the night.

'Damn!' thought Klaus. 'We shall have to shout.' Then he remembered that neither the road nor the ski-run came near this section of the lift.

'There'll be some instructors coming down after the classes,' thought Werner. They wouldn't be too pleased at having to start up the lift again. There was a heavy fine for getting on illegally. It was all Klaus' fault. Then he, too, remembered that the run was some way off.

'They'll hear if we shout,' he called to Klaus, hating having to communicate with him. 'If we both shout together.'

They called in unison, yodelling at intervals as well. But with the darkness a light wind had got up, and their shouts did not carry to the distant ski-run, if, indeed, anyone were on it so late. Both the top and bottom stations were too far away, and the curves of the mountains hid them.

Werner looked back to see how near the pylon behind him was, but it was quite a distance.

'Are you near the next pylon?' he called, forgetting for a moment his anger.

'Yards away, and all uphill. Can you reach yours?'

Werner looked up at the slender tube that held the chair to the cable. It would be slippery, and icy cold. The cable itself was thin: it would cut into one's hands, even if he had the courage to dangle there above the depths.

'Not a hope!' he answered.

They sat there in silence, listening and listening. There was nothing moving, nothing in all the great emptiness of sky and mountain and snow. The wind stirred again in the trees, moaning through them and whispering round the cables, cutting into their bodies. Then it went, leaving only the still, cold air and the silence again.

'Shout now!'

Their voices rang out, shattering the peace, but there was no one to hear, no answer.

Even with the blankets normally wrapped round one, this lift was always a cold one, travelling so high, and for so long. Without the blankets the cold crept into their bellies and ran down their spines, chilling their arms and legs.

Colder and colder. More and more silent. Silent and still and cold.

Klaus looked down. The slope could not be very far away, and there would be two or three feet of snow. If he made a rope of his anorak and jersey the ground would be even nearer. Without them he would be bitterly cold, but he would warm up moving. Not easy to move in deep snow without skis. But better than sitting up here, waiting for help that was unlikely to come, and freezing. He took off his anorak and knotted one sleeve round the stanchion of the chair, then removed his jersey and tied an arm to the other arm of the anorak. Would they hold? Would one material slide out of the other? He pulled; they seemed firm enough. Without them his body was chilling so rapidly that his heart gave a lurch of fear.

From behind him Werner watched the movements in the darkness, silhouetted against the snow of the slope. What was Klaus doing? The shadow elongated as Klaus slid down off the seat, fumbling his way down the straining garments.

'Damn him!' breathed Werner. 'He's getting a start on me again! He'll get to Brigitte first!' He watched, holding his breath.

Klaus felt his way down, the material stretching and awkward in his grasp. He could feel the knot beginning to give way. He would have to jump now; to let go as he reached the end of his rope before it broke. The ground couldn't be all that far.

He let go, falling, falling, far farther than he had expected. The rocks hit him in a blinding, smashing, flaming sheet of pain which engulfed him and tore away his senses.

Werner saw him fall, heard the crackling thud as he hit the rocks beneath the snow.

There was no sound for five minutes. Nothing. Then the moaning began, high and thin, inhuman in the still air.

As Klaus regained consciousness he knew that both legs were broken; utterly smashed and useless. They were not numb, he could feel them, feel them and hear the bones grating when he tried to move out of his agonizing position. He could hear the same high keening that Werner heard, not understanding at first that it was his own voice. As his mind cleared he cried louder, shouting to Werner to help him, to stop this fearful pain that beat and hammered at him, drowning him in wave after wave.

'Werner! Werner! Help me! Help me!' but Werner sat immobile with horror and hate and fear, staring at the shadow which lay dark against the white snow, his teeth chattering together.

It was Klaus' fault! He had tried to get down first and up to Brigitte. It was he who had led the way up the pylon into this frightful lift. It was all his fault, and now he, Werner, was stuck up here, and no one to help him. Why couldn't Klaus fetch help? Why couldn't he pull himself through the trees to the road?

The moaning rose and fell, wailing through the silence, ghostly and thin.

'Shut up! Shut up!'

Klaus did not hear him. The cold was driving into him through the thinness of his shirt, up the shattered bones of his legs. Already the blood that ran down them had clotted and frozen, no longer running away. Already the pain that engulfed him was changing, eating into his spine and through his entrails, up into his chest. He could hear the wailing still, but thinner, fainter. Whoever was crying was moving farther away. Farther and farther.

When he had lain there for an hour the thin sound faded away altogether. The silence returned to the snow and the waiting trees.

When it had utterly ceased Werner longed for its return.

He was alone now. Klaus had left him alone. With the silence he remembered that he and Klaus had been friends. Only a few hours ago they had been friends again. They had done so much together. Now Klaus had gone away and left him, and he was alone.

No rival for Brigitte now, he thought suddenly. Only the cousin.

All the same, he would rather Klaus had not left him alone.

He sat there, stiffening in the silent cold, watching the still shadow in the snow. He would have to move soon: no use waiting much longer. No one would come now.

Once or twice he looked up at the support above him, measuring the distance to the cable. Then it would be hand over hand down the wire to the pylon. Must get his hands warm first, or he would never hold on. Fall, like Klaus. Keep his hands very still, warmer that way. Not move them on the cold wood of the chair. Keep very still, warm patch between his legs. No, not warm, but not so cold as the rest of him. Move his hands in between his legs. No – keep still. Moving made things colder. Lost heat that way. Keep very still.

He stared at the shadow that had been Klaus. No use going down that way. Must go upwards. Someone might come quite soon. The chairs might start again, moving up and away from the shadow in the snow. Getting colder and colder, right down in the belly, all through. No good moving. Stay very still and get warm.

Poor Klaus.

Rather have Klaus than Brigitte.

The stars coming closer now, right down among the mountains, down among the waiting trees. Pressing down the cold, and the peaks of the mountains leaning over, closing in the cold.

Keep still. Keep still. Keep still.

Werner did get to the top first. When the lift started moving in the morning the attendant at Hoch Durach was surprised to see the first passenger of the day arriving some ten minutes sooner than he expected anyone. He was even more surprised when, as this first passenger drew nearer, he stared clean through him with wide, blue eyes. But his greatest shock came when he seized one arm to help him get out of the chair. The arm was as stiff and as rigid as wood.

Brigitte married the cousin. She had never intended doing anything else.

MAGICAL MYSTERY TRIP

By C. A. Cooper

THAT MORNING, when he woke, his bedroom was two feet deep in blood.

He blinked at it, propped up on one elbow in his narrow single bed. There was no reason at all why blood, even in small quantities, should be present in his room, and yet, without any doubt at all, this smooth, square red lake all round him was pure, fresh blood. He could see it as plainly as he had ever seen anything, and, what was worse, he could smell it. Tremulously, disbelieving, he stretched out a hand to touch it, but the blood was almost exactly level with the top of his mattress, and his movement caused some of it to spill over into the bed, where it ran down round his thighs; so that even before his fingertips could touch it the blood's cold stickiness had registered on his body. Instantly, and irresistably, an unutterable revulsion and bewilderment came welling up in him from the depths of his being, and down in those same living depths he seemed to draw breath for a cry, a scream.

But no sound came from his lips.

He lay, as if placidly, his breathing steady, struggling to scream, and unable to understand.

The door opened and his mother came in with his morning cup of tea. She opened the door easily against the pressure and weight of blood, and it poured out past her on to the landing in a noisy, gurgling torrent. But she took not the slightest notice of it. She waded through it towards him, her movements unimpeded as if it had not been there, and her lined, square face was as it always was when she came in to wake him; drowsy, expressionless, mask-like. And then he glimpsed his own face in the mirror of his dressing-table, and it too appeared exactly as it always did, sleepy and calm.

His mother offered him his tea and he watched, incredulous, as his hands reached out and took it.

'You're awake, then,' said his mother. 'Wonders'll never cease.'

He tried and tried and tried to scream, to tell her about the blood, the awful, impossible blood.

But his face smiled, and a voice proceeding apparently of its own accord from his throat said jokingly, 'I'm quite often awake. I wake up just about every day, in fact.'

And he sipped his tea, though now there was a large black spider floating dead in the middle of it, and this creature's legs touched his lips as he drank.

'Well you'll have to wake up a bit earlier next week, any-way,' said his mother grumblingly. 'It's back to the Uni-versity for you then, my boy, and high time too if you ask me. You've done nothing the whole holiday except lie about in your bed half the day.'

He stared at her, frowning.

As he did so, her face and body crumbled, the flesh falling away till the bones showed, and it was a skeleton in a blue dressing gown that stood and grumbled at him and then turned and walked out of the door through the sea of blood.

His mind collapsed, shocked beyond bearing, and he seemed to exist in swirling darkness, in coloured, exploding mists. But when he came to himself he was sitting on the edge of his bed, half-dressed. The blood was gone, and now a beautiful, dark-haired young girl stood near him, smiling on him softly. She was wearing a pair of black jeans and a blue bikini-top. He gazed despairingly into her brown, gleaming eyes, and then he said, 'You're not real, are you?'

'No,' said the girl. 'I'm not real at all.' She leaned towards him, hands on hips, laughing into his face. 'In fact,' she said, 'I'm just an hallucination. You're mad, you see. Mad!'

And she raised her arms into the air like one crucified, and became a wrinkled old man, and vanished.

Behind him where she had stood, the wall of his bedroom

opened on to an enormous heaving ocean, aflame with the sun, and a great white galleon went swooping and plunging in ecstasy through the burning, thundering waves.

He hid his face in his hands. He could not understand or even credit what was happening to him. 'I'm dreaming,' he thought. 'All I have to do is wake up.' So he pinched himself, and shook his head violently. But he knew it was useless; he knew he was awake already; awake, and mad. He knew this, but the knowledge was unendurable, and again he tried to cry out, to cry out with the whole force of his lungs, so that his parents downstairs would come running to help him and save him. But his chest was a like a log, unresponsive, breathing steadily, refusing to react to the terror in his mind.

Wearily, bewildered almost past caring, he finished dressing and went downstairs to the dining room.

An enormous Zulu warrior, naked, hung upside-down from the centre of the ceiling, and he was singing the National Anthem in the voice of a little girl.

The day passed, outwardly uneventful. Over breakfast he talked politics with his father, who worked in a bank, knew nothing about anything except accounting, and had strong opinions about most things. His mother sat, resigned, as the discussion grew heated, and he listened dully to the sound of his own voice as it produced cogent, sarcastic replies to his father's ignorant dogmatizing. Sometimes, distracted by some new vision, he lost all track of what was being said, but each time when he returned to himself the discussion was continuing with unaltered vigour, and he had only to listen for a few moments to regain the thread of it. Later, when the meal was over, he would have gone out in search of a doctor, but his body refused to obey him; he found himself saying to his parents 'I'm going into the lounge to study,' and so he did. And so it went on, all that day, and for several days after as well. He lived in a state of shock and stupor, which prevented thought, and he was visited continually by fresh hallucinations. As often as not, people appeared to him as walking corpses, hideously decomposed; but even when they were so far gone that he was unable consciously to recognize them, he could hear himself talking to them normally, calling them by name even. Quite frequently, too, he saw ghosts and demons which he knew had no real existence. Dreadful accidents involving people both real and imaginary took place before his eyes on the roads around his home, and a building opposite burned to the ground, then suddenly reared up and was whole again. A speedboat roared down the hall through a sea of rose-petals, the afternoon sky turned a livid shade of green, and cold, moist hands caressed his body while voices whispered obscenities in his ear. Once, at sunset, an immense purple crab sat snapping its pincers in the Western sky, and persistently, at mealtimes, he was haunted by the large black spider which had first appeared dead in his morning cup of tea. But sometimes it was not dead, and once it opened tiny red eyes and watched him as he ate. He saw, too, fantastic, exotic flowers, several feet across sometimes, which writhed as if with conscious life, grew faces, breasts, and limbs, and then, changing their form, became snakes, or dragons, or naked, voluptuous, distorted human bodies. Often these visions were on fire with pulsating, changing colours, and sometimes they dissolved, kaleidoscopically, melting away into whirling luminous rings, into clouds of hurtling sparks, into shifting, iridescent, rainbow-like sheets of light and colour.

He struggled almost ceaselessly to communicate to others what was happening to him, but without success. The horror of this was worse than even the worst of his visions, and robbed him almost completely of sleep; and in an odd kind of way he did thus seem to achieve a degree of communication, for on the fourth day his mother suddenly said to him 'You look a bit pale, you know. Haven't you been sleeping?' But all he could reply was 'No – it's those blasted exams worrying me, I think. But tonight I'll take a couple of pills.' And when night came he did just that, or rather, his body did, and his trapped mind eventually sank, protesting, into oblivion.

When he woke there was a Bengal tiger, with a horn like a unicorn's, noisily devouring a dead child at the end of his bed, so he knew he was still mad. He turned away, sickened. It was late – past ten o'clock – but he still felt drowsy from the pills he had taken, and in this artificial calm he began for the first time trying to think coherently about his bizarre plight. And at once he was jolted fully awake by a realization of what it meant that he was able to think at all. He sat up in bed, resting his chin on his knees while the bright June sunshine beat in on him through the window, and he thought excitedly 'If I can still reason about things then I can't be really mad. Not in the usual sense. And if I'm not mad, then I *must* be able to work out some way of telling other people what's wrong with me.'

But at once he encountered a check. Contact with others could only be made physically, through the use of his body, of his hands or his voice; and he knew already that his body was beyong his control. 'It's hopeless,' he thought despairingly. 'A complete dead end. I'm just a passenger in my own body. Perhaps this is some kind of demon-possession. Perhaps I should go to a priest and ask to be exorcized. But I can't. I can't even do that for myself.'

At the end of his bed, the horned tiger suddenly turned and looked at him, then silently exploded, flower-like, into a whirl of huge crimson droplets. These hung, the size of pears, but gleaming like jewels, on the walls and furniture and ceiling, and the dead child came to life and began trying to take hold of them in its tiny hands. But the droplets kept melting away only to appear elsewhere a moment later, and the child pursued them, laughing happily.

Wearily he closed his eyes, and pressed his hands tight over his ears, struggling desperately for concentration.

He was nineteen, a slight and rather pallid youth with delicate, finely-wrought features, and the hair on his bowed head glowed yellow as butter in the vivid morning sunshine.

Soon, he was able to think again.

'My body is beyond my control,' he repeated. But was it? Suddenly he realized that during the previous few moments he had made many movements which seemed perfectly voluntary. Cautiously, but again excited, he began to experiment. He raised an arm, then both arms, and he swung his legs out of bed so that he was sitting on the edge of it; then he said out loud 'There's something wrong with my brain, I've begun seeing things all the time.' The words came easily, and, hope overwhelming reason and the memory of all that had gone before, he made as if to jump up and run downstairs to his parents. But nothing happened. He sat on the edge of his bed, helpless, in the neat, sunny little room. And slowly, understanding came to him. 'I can do whatever I like,' he thought, 'except tell anyone else what's wrong with me.' The absurd, impossible truth tormented him, like a goad savagely used; he struck his knees with his fists, and, as he did so, he noticed that each of his toes had become like a tiny fire-engine He raised one of his feet, and felt with his fingers where the cold, knobbly metal grew from his flesh, and now an almost unbearable feeling of loneliness and humiliation swept over him. His eyes filled with tears, and a moment later, looking up, he found himself seeing once again the young girl who had spoken to him on the very first morning of his sickness.

She smiled at him, cruelly, then said with glee, 'There's no escape, you see. Not now, not ever. You're on your own with us.'

'Us?' It felt strange, questioning what he knew was non-existent, and his voice was hardly more than a whisper. 'And who are "us", then?'

'I am you as he is you as he is me and we are all together,' said the girl.

'That doesn't make sense,' he said. 'That's just a lot of stupid words.'

But the words reminded him of something, something he had heard quite recently; a song, perhaps.

'Nothing that's true ever does make sense,' said the girl. 'But if you want to know who we are, we're the devils of Hell and the angels of Heaven. We are your Unconscious.'

She sat down beside him on the bed, and draped one arm round his neck, and gently kissed him on the cheek. The fire-engines attached to his feet had extended their ladders, and tiny firemen stood waving and shouting at the end of them, spraying his ankles with their hoses; he could just feel the tickle of water on his skin, and the firemen's shouts were wordless squeaks, like the sound of bats.

'I don't understand,' he said. 'I don't understand why this should have happened to me.'

The girl kissed him again, more intimately, on the side of his mouth.

'He who sups with the devil,' she said, 'needs a very long spoon.' She laid one of her hands on his knee, and he felt the heat of her palm through his pyjamas.

'I don't understand that, either,' he muttered. A feeling of lust was beginning to arise in him in response to the girl's provocation, and this frightened him horribly; in his mind's eye he saw a picture of himself in the act of trying to make love to an hallucination.

But suddenly the girl let him go, and stood up.

'Where were you, the night before we first came to you?' she asked.

He thought, desperately, not looking at her.

'I was round at John's place,' he said at last. 'We were watching that film on television, Magical—'

But the girl interrupted him.

'John takes drugs,' she said. 'He gave you coffee.'

An appalling suspicion leapt into his mind, and he turned to look her in the face. But her eyes had become two large white golf-balls, which suddenly fell out on to the floor with a noise like the smash of glass, and a moment later she vanished altogether, leaving only a tiny blue spark, bright as a star and whistling vibrantly, hovering in the air in the place where she had been. As he watched, this spark started whizzing round the room, resting in this place or that for a moment before hurtling away elsewhere.

It was still visible to him when a few minutes later his mother appeared with his morning cup of tea.

He dressed, breaking the firemen's ladders with his shoes, scattering tiny men over the carpet, and deliberately crushing them with his heel. Then after breakfast he went to see John at the shabby little flat where he lived. The young man seemed surprised to see him, and kept shooting him anxious, puzzled glances as they talked. 'If John did give me anything,' he thought, 'he must have expected it to work before I left. And in that case he must have been terrified when I went before anything happened. That would be why he kept on delaying me, playing me all those records.

'I must ask him outright,' he thought. 'I must ask him outright whether he gave me anything.'

But of course, he could not. To do so would have been tantamount to confessing his condition. Instead, he found himself talking about the film they had watched on television, and they both agreed that it was a bold and thoughtful and important experiment, and not nearly so dismal a failure as its critics had claimed.

While they were discussing this, John's head detached itself from his shoulders and went floating round the room like a balloon. It spoke to him for some time from a corner of the ceiling. Then at last it floated back down and re-settled itself on John's shoulders, but upside-down, and a fountain of sparkling green water began issuing from the severed vertebrae.

Soon it was time to return home for dinner. At the door John several times seemed about to ask him something, but never did, so that he had to go away without finding out whether his suspicion was justified.

He walked in misery through streets full of monsters, and as he ate his dinner he was watched by the red-eyed spider. But now it had grown many times larger; it filled half the table, and sometimes it spoke to him in a deep, gruff voice, telling him meaningless stories that began, 'Once upon a time . . .' His food, too, was strange, in that each of his fried tomatoes looked and felt like a human ear. He ate, sickened, but unable to stop himself, and as soon as the meal was over he went upstairs to his room. A feeling of panic, a very much deeper panic than that which had assailed him at first, was starting to overwhelm him, and he had made up his mind, during dinner, that if he could not find any other way to end his misery he would that night kill himself by taking all his remaining sleeping-pills.

Quietly, he shut his bedroom door behind him, longing for peace; but when he turned round it was to see yet again the girl who had spoken to him earlier. But now she was naked, and every inch of her flesh was on fire, and dense black smoke streamed upwards from the thin, oily red flames that covered her.

He stared at her, aghast.

The flames that burned in her hair crackled loudly as she stared back at him out of her eyes of fire.

At last she said 'You can't kill yourself. If you could you would kill us as well. But we are eternal.'

'You can't stop me,' he said dully. 'This has to end, you see. And if killing myself means killing you as well,' he burst out savagely, 'then so much the better.'

But the girl laughed. Sparks flew out from her mouth as she did so.

'There is a Word, you know, that could save you,' she said mockingly. 'You have only to speak it, to be saved. We would all be different then, and our strength would be in you, and for you – not against you. But you don't know the Word. Do you?'

He racked his brains, but he could not understand what she meant. So he stood in silence, watching her. He could not see into her eyes because of the flames that rose out of them.

'Everyone must face us, in the end,' said the girl. 'And if they don't know the Word, they are lost.' Suddenly, she dropped down on to her knees in front of him, and the terrible, burning features that she raised towards him were no longer mocking. They pleaded, they beseeched, they prayed to him as from the pit of Hell. 'Say the Word!' she screamed. 'Say the Word, and save us! Say the Word, and become our master!'

But he continued to stare at her, utterly bewildered.

'This is crazy,' he snarled at last. 'There is no Word. You're just trying to stop me from killing myself. But I shall, I shall kill myself, and you with me!'

The girl lowered her face, then slowly raised it again, and now the expression of gloating triumph had returned to it.

'You will live for ever,' she said flatly. 'And we shall be your masters.'

And still kneeling she extended towards him hands shaped like burning claws, and before his startled eyes the fingernails began to grow, writhing and stretching upwards in the direction of his body. Rage and terror together overwhelmed him, and looking round for a weapon he saw what seemed to be a great shining sword standing near the door. He caught hold of it, and, turning, heaved it diagonally, with all his might, at the girl's face. It struck home, with a jolt that nearly broke his arm, and the girl was flung sideways against his bed, which cannoned into the wall. He lost his balance, reeled, and fell across the dressing table, breaking the mirror with his forehead; but he got up quickly, and turned to look at the girl. Her head was split almost in two where his sword had struck it, exactly across her eyes, and blood, smoke, and fire gushed out. But she still lived, and her arms were still outstretched towards him, and now her growing fingernails had reached his body, and were starting to twine round him. The sword was still in his hand, and he tried to raise it. But his arms were pinioned in a web of rubbery nails, and he could not. He threw himself forward, sideways, backwards, struggling to get free, but with every movement he was the more hopelessly entangled. And then he was aware that his mother and father had come bursting into the room, and it seemed to him that at last he was shouting out to them, over and over 'I am mad, I am mad, I am mad, please help me.' But to his horror his parents just stood, laughing, and they too were on fire; and suddenly, he understood. He understood that from the very beginning it had been others, the whole world, who had been against him. It was others, and not just the phantoms of his own mind, who were his deadly enemies; for the whole world was united in a gigantic and horrible conspiracy aimed at overpowering him.

And now, the world had succeeded.

He seemed to lie, struggling but helpless, as they all advanced on him, with skulls for faces, with tusks, with great red eyes that dripped blood and fire. They were trying, it seemed, to crucify him. But somehow he had grown twenty each of arms and legs, so they got a thing like a wheel with planks for spokes, and they nailed him to it through his many hands and feet. Then, shrieking and dancing, and striking his body with whips, they turned the wheel over and hung him face downwards over a bed of hot coals.

The pain, the physical agony, was absolute, unbelievable, excruciating.

He was screaming, and it seemed to him that he screamed for days, for months, for years, for ever.

But his parents, who knew none of these things which he never ceased to experience were soon reassured about him. They were, of course, a good deal alarmed when they found him semi-conscious by his dressing-table, with his forehead cut and bits of the broken mirror in his hair, but he soon recovered, explaining with a rueful grin 'I tripped on that blasted mat again.' The doctor examined him carefully, and declared him to be all right, and a few days later he returned to the University as planned. He studied hard, and in due course got his degree, with first-class honours; and a few years after that he married. His wife loved him dearly, and so did his children, and he seemed to love them in return. But every now and then his wife would smile, tenderly, and say to one or other of her friends 'He's an awful dreamer, you know. Sometimes I wonder whether he's really with the rest of us at all, in fact.'

PUSSY CAT, PUSSY CAT

By Frances Stephens

THE STORM did not start until evening, but Lorna Matthews had been restless all afternoon. Her eyes strayed again and again to the cottage window, with its bleak landscape of empty fields. The sullen clouds pressed down on her, like some vengeance from which there was no escape.

Then it came; demoniac wind that howled in the chimney and tore at the trees. Flurries of sleet obscured the glass panes, making her hurry to close the curtains. Her hand was trembling as she turned away.

'Fool,' she told herself. 'What is there to fear?'

The boy was home from school, and the baby slept upstairs. Her month-old daughter, fragile and perfect. A child who would grow up proud and beautiful, as lovely as a summer rose.

Lorna went out into the porch and shot the bolt on the heavy back door. Bending down, she wedged a strip of sacking against the bottom, where the rain was already driving through.

Her heart was racing as she straightened up; the aftermath of childbirth; a climax to months of waiting, and the strain of coping alone.

'What's that for, Mom?'

Gooseflesh prickled Lorna's neck. Nine-year-old Benny had crept up alongside, stealthy as a cat in the dark. He stood, legs planted solidly apart, on the wet floor tiles. His squat body swayed backwards and forwards as he peered at her intently through his crusty lashes.

'I said what's—?'

'To keep us safe and dry,' said Lorna firmly.

With a shriek of glee, Benny was down on the tiles, prodding at the rough canvas with stubby fingers, scrabbling it in an untidy heap.

'That's enough, Benny,' said Lorna firmly, and kicked the sacking back in place.

Benny grunted and took her proffered hand. They went back to the kitchen, where the coal fire gave at least the illusion of warmth and content.

But Lorna's sense of foreboding was as real as an unwelcome stranger in the room. Nights like this made her wish the house was not so isolated; that her husband was not abroad on construction work, with no prospect of an early return.

She shivered, dragged down for a moment by the millstone of complete responsibility for one subnormal boy, and a baby the father had yet to see. The storm made them prisoners here. No escape. No escape.

Then, over the sound of the wind, came the thin yet anguished wailing of a child. Urgent. Allowing no delay. Primitive fear made Lorna's heart begin another mad race. She checked that the fireguard was in position, and hurried upstairs.

But even as her hand hovered on the bedroom light-switch, she sensed that the baby was still sleeping soundly as before. The crib, with its nylon frills and flounces, stood by her own bed. The room was a haven of stillness and calm.

Lorna returned to the kitchen. Benny, playing an endless game, did not look up.

Uncertainly, she folded a baby gown. Imagination played queer tricks on a night like this. Yet every quivering nerve strained to catch the sound again. Ah! There it was. Only this time it was a harsh imperative cry that set her teeth on edge, her scalp shivering.

Benny stood up.

'Pussy cat, Mom. Let the pussy cat in.'

Mewling, caterwauling, more like the devil at the door.

Benny was panting as he pulled at her arm.

'Let it in, Mom. It wants to come in with us.'

Lorna's fingers fumbled with the iron bolt. The cold gust of air was a slap in the face. But already the cat was past her, streaking into the cosy kitchen.

It was a gaunt, ill-looking creature, with bony haunches and yellow hostile eyes, that watched her at every step. Rain and mud had matted its fur, which was probably a nondescript black and white.

Benny was down on his knees in an ecstasy of delight.

'Pussy cat, poor wet pussy cat.'

To please the boy, Laura brought a saucer of milk. The animal lapped it frantically, then cleaned its coat with a rasping tongue. Benny crouched alongside, crooning his pleasure and concern. One podgy hand hovered possessively over the animal's fur.

Already these two had formed an alliance against her, welded in some way she could only suspect, not understand. She must be firm.

'We can't keep a full-grown cat,' said Lorna. 'It must already have a home.'

The boy was seconds before he gathered the implication of her words. Then he howled like a beast with a terrible hurt.

'But it's mine, Mom. It found me here.'

'No, Benny. We can't have a cat in the house. There's the baby to think about.'

Benny stood up, yanking the cat into his arms. The cat's legs dangled grotesquely, but it made no protest. Benny's pale eyes blazed.

'Baby! Baby! You've got your baby. I want my pussy cat.'

For a long moment, Lorna was silent.

'All right,' she said at last. 'But it sleeps in the porch. I don't want it roaming the house.'

She hunted out a piece of old blanket and a cardboard box. Benny fussed around the cat, then finally went upstairs. Swiftly, Lorna locked the glass panelled door that closed the kitchen off from the porch at the back.

When she put out the light to go upstairs, she was compelled to look over her shoulder. Glittering eyes followed her as she moved. Even through the glass, the malevolence of that glance cut like a stiletto going straight through the heart.

Morning was calmer, and Lorna walked Benny along the lane to catch the school bus. The cat disappeared. It stayed away all day, and only returned, with some uncanny instinct, when Benny came back.

The boy was snuffling, showing signs of an incipient cold. He pushed his plate away, then knelt on the rug, chuckling as he fed the cat with morsels of food. Already the mangy stray was sleeker.

Lorna nursed the baby, nestling her daughter's downy head against her swollen breast. Trickles of milk ran down the infant's chin.

Hypnotized, Lorna looked over at the crouching cat. Smoky sulphur eyes bored into her, through her. She turned away. When she glanced again, the gaze was still as intent as before.

She settled the baby for the night, and for the first time, closed the bedroom door. Benny was sent to bed early because of his cold.

Alone in the kitchen, Lorna warily watched the shabby intruder. Once again, the yellow eyes held her own. Brilliant hatred flashed like a searing electric charge.

Enough of this nonsense. She wrenched open the porch door and ordered the animal through. The tone of her voice was a sure command, and the cat understood it well enough. It arched away, despising her for her lack of softness and submission.

Lorna lunged forward. With a sharp hiss, the cat drew away, teeth bared, eyes darting evil.

Lorna vacillated. The cat must be locked in the porch. It must. It must. Now the beast was stalking her, as though she was some half-mesmerized mouse.

'Come here, pussy cat.'

Scarcely comprehending, she stretched forward an arm. Vicious claws shot out, tearing the back of her hand in cruel red lines that beaded with bright drops of blood. Tears stung Lorna's eyes as she gasped with shock and pain.

But the hurt cut through her indecision. She seized a long-handled sweeping brush, and struck out at the cat, which fled to the porch. Lorna bolted the door and went upstairs.

From then, the cat kept out of her way. It disappeared for

long periods. Lorna worried as to whether it was lurking near the house, or stalking the fields. It came back only when Benny was there. The boy gave it protection, unquestioning love.

His cold grew worse, so Lorna kept him home from school. Benny spent his time petting the cat, teasing it with a length of string.

The cat looked rounder, plumper. Lorna frowned, chasing suspicion from her mind. Nonsense. The creature couldn't be pregnant. It was trouble enough, without the extra worry of a squirming litter.

That night, when Lorna looked in on Benny, he was asleep with the cat against his body. One arm pinioned the animal where it lay.

Lorna leaned over to shake the boy, but he snuffled, choking for breath, and she left him alone. She went to her bedroom and closed the door.

Dozing uneasily, she jerked back to consciousness, drenched in sweat, bewildered by the din that was jangling her nerves. Benny! Shouting, gibbering, almost screaming his terror and despair.

Lorna seized her robe. The boy was tossing about in the throes of a nightmare. Soothingly she spoke to him, held the threshing arms. In a few moments, he quietened. Lorna straightened the cover and returned to her rumpled bed.

Her own room was in darkness, but evil met her like a choking blanket of chloroform. As she flicked on the light, the cat arched its back. Legs rigid, its ears lay flat along the bony skull. The nylon flounces trailed disconsolately from the crib, tattered, torn. The satin-edged blanket was snarled and looped with the marks of angry talons.

Fury poured through Lorna's blood. Looking round for a weapon, she saw only the umbrella hanging on the cupboard door. But already the cat was down the stairs. It crouched away from her in a corner of the kitchen, while she went out through the porch to the heavy back door. Her fingers fumbled on the bolt. Moments later, the cat streaked into the blackness outside.

All next day she watched from the cottage window, but the cat held off, basking in the sunshine at the end of the ragged lawn.

In the afternoon, Lorna heard the frantic twittering of a bird. With diabolical glee, the cat worried a bedraggled brown thrush, lay it down to watch it panting, then pounced again. The air was full of wet feathers, cruelty, and death.

Startled by the noise, the baby set up a wail of terror from her pram.

'No more,' shouted Lorna. 'No more,' and rushed outside, picking up a sharp-edged stone. She flung it wildly, but caught the cat a blow that made it spring away yelping, dropping the mangled bird. Then it was off across the fields, moving like the wind.

Lorna was shaking as she put the kettle on to make herself a cup of tea. But she had won. The cat would be no more trouble. It would scarcely come back after that.

Every night, Benny stood by the cottage door, calling in a mournful voice. He prowled on the grass, he peered along the lane.

The days stretched out, and the daylight lengthened. Lorna began to sleep nights, better than before.

One afternoon she took the garden shears to trim the hedge on the far side of the cottage. The day was still and warm, and she pulled the baby's pram into a corner shaded from the sun.

Then she fastened the cat-net over the hood, securing it to the metal clasps. It was old and fraying, a relic of Benny's infant days, but it was better than none.

Lorna picked up the shears and wandered round the other side of the house.

Insects droned in the hedgerow; the sun was pleasant on her bare head. Presently she swung into a rhythm, watching the twigs and leaves as they tumbled to the ground.

A cloud of young birds swooped out of the bushes, surprising her with their shrill and unexpected noise. Fear stalked the quiet lane. Dropping the shears, Lorna ran like someone possessed, back to the corner where she had left the pram.

The cat-net straggled down towards the ground, a dingy dish-cloth torn aside. With panic fingers, Lorna pulled the macintosh apron away.

Four whimpering kittens blundered sightlessly on the flat and sodden bedding. The baby lay silent, a waxy, lifeless doll.

Sounds along the lane made Lorna wrench her eyes away. It was Benny coming home, only this time, he was carrying something, shouting his pleasure and surprise.

'Mom. Mom. My pussy came back, so everything's all right now.'

LONG SILENCE, OLD MAN

By David Lewis

THEY CAME upon it at evening, just as Manello had known they would. In the evening when grey white sand seeped orange under the tangerine sky and sharp shafts of light spat their defiance like arrows from the cover of distant hills. Ten miles back he had turned from the straight highway. The straight ribbon of concrete which uncurled through the nothingness of the desert. Occasionally they had passed another car, dust-filmed, heading in the other direction for the tourist season was over and now for six months only lumbering trucks would burn down the road. Manello knew ... and he hated that knowledge like serpent venom searing his veins.

'Why have we come?' she asked.

Manello took one hand from the wheel, feeling the big car fight him as it slewed over the holed, rubble-strewn track. 'Why have you brought me here?'

Manello rested his free hand on the girl's knee and she laid her own slender hands on his, sandwiching it between cool layers of her body, guiding it up her firm thigh.

Manello looked away from the darkening road, watching the girl. They were riding sideways to the sunset and by some trick of light her black hair, blowing in the slipstream of dry air, seemed tailed with a firy gold. He felt his hand steadily drawn into the soft warmth between her thighs.

The car hit a boulder and slewed a little from the track. Not enough to put them at risk. Not enough to demand the violence with which Manello snatched back his hand to grasp the wheel. He clicked on the headlamps and their beams sprayed like small-arms fire across the strange mystery of the desert and destroyed its magic utterly.

As the bleached desert cooled, a wind stirred, as it always did, and rattled the dry bones of the scrub. It caught up a ball of parched twigs and bowled it along the track beside them, then darted it across their path. She cried out, seeing it flash, bone white with dust, into their lamps and then plunge beneath the tyres.

'It's only dry brush,' he said.

'I think it was a dog.' The girl put her arm around his shoulder, pressed herself to him, trembling.

'No dogs here ... not now.' He felt his hands close on the wheel as though it were a chicken neck to be snapped. He said: 'When I was ten I went out prospecting with a man called Drager and his friend. What his friend was called I forget, it doesn't matter. They were a little crazy, for no gold had been found in the hills for generations. We went with a mule called Josepepitta. Very old the mule was with ribs like a bird cage, clattering with tins and pans for sifting and storing the gold which didn't exist. My father let me go with Drager because he was his best friend, his only friend. Besides, he thought it would do me good ... my father. He thought it would ...' For the first time Manello faltered. Softly he finished: 'He thought it would make me into a man.' When the girl didn't say anything and the long silence was filled only by the car noise and the rising wind, Manello regained his composure and went on.

'I don't know why I tell you this. We went into the hills. For three days we walked and climbed in the heat and dust. We found nothing, of course, there was nothing to find. As we prepared camp Drager's friend, the man whose name I forget, reached under a ball of scrub to find firewood and was bitten by a snake. I didn't see the snake, nor did Drager or his friend. It vanished among the little rocks and bushes. But this man, this friend of the crazy Drager, lay on the ground holding his left arm and screaming and twitching. His body became taut like a bow string and then would have spasms of movement as though some invisible finger played him. Drager took a knife. He poured a little paraffin into one of the tins and set it alight. Then he passed the knife blade through the flames. He said to me: 'Hold him, boy . . . hold him good.' I took the man by the shoulders and pressed him to the ground. Drager ripped away his sleeve. He drew the knife across the man's vein, where it bulged like a bloated leech in the crook of his elbow. He drew it quickly and the man's blood dribbled out. Drager put his lips to the wound and sucked out the blood. We sat there for about ten minutes. I held the man's shoulders and Drager squatted sucking and spitting until the blood had caked in his dirty beard and the man was dead. We buried him there and left a cross made from a broken spade handle. Then we came back home.'

'Why have you told me this? Why did you bring me here?'

'Here we are.' Manello spun the wheel and the headlights drifted in a circle. Suddenly, where desert and scrub had been there was a house. One storey with dirty white walls patched by rusted iron sheets like dried scabs. Some tumble-down out-buildings formed a right angle with the house. That was all. Around was the desert and the sand blew up to the walls like sea spray dashing a rock, wearing it with sure patience into the sea.

'What is this place?'

Manello said simply: 'It is my father's house.'

It was quite dark now and they could see the feeble trickle of oil light dribbling between the broken shutter slats. The sound of their car and its lights drawn across the house front, had roused the old man. He came to the door and opened it cautiously. He had an oil lamp in one hand, a shot gun in the other.

'Who is it?' His voice was cracked and querulous, but the girl knew that it must once have been strong and vibrant. Manello switched off the engine.

'It is Manello, your son Manello.'

The old man came out towards the car. When he killed the engine, Manello had cut the main beams, now as the old man approached he switched them back on, blinding the weak eyes.

'Let me see you, Father,' Manello called. 'It's a long time. Let me take a good look at you.'

The cold white light was merciless. Before it the old man seemed like some specimen on a dissecting board. He had covered his eyes with one hand, laying down the lantern but keeping tight hold of the gun. He half bent forward and his tattered, unbuttoned shirt showed thin ribs and grey flesh folding down from his hairless paps.

'You are still a fine strong man,' Manello called.

'I can't see you. Those lights are too bright. Come into the house, Manello.'

'Why are you armed, Father? What does a strong man like you fear in the desert night?'

'I thought you might be young hooligans. They sometimes come here. They come in trucks, army trucks they have bought. They do damage here ... look at those windows which they broke.'

'Can you not catch them, Father? Catch them and beat them for their crimes?'

Manello was standing on the car seat, leaning forward across the top of the windscreen.

'Please,' said the girl softly, 'can we not go into the house?'

'Who's that with you?' The old man came forward, moving into the darkness around the car.

'It is my wife, Father. That is why I came here, to introduce you to my wife.'

They went into the house with Manello carrying the cases.

'You are very lovely,' the old man said and he reached out to touch her arm. 'It is many, many years since this house saw such beauty.'

Manello dumped the cases on the stone floor and dust and sand flew.

'If I had known you were coming,' the old man said uncomfortably. 'If Manello had told me you were coming here.'

'We are staying in the city,' the girl said. 'When Manello said we would go away for the night he did not say we should stay here.'

'My home is very poor now. It is unworthy of you.'

'Does old age always bring such humility?' Manello demanded. 'If so there is a lot to commend it.'

There was a silence, then Manello said: 'We are on our honeymoon. We are staying in the city because the picture I am directing is filming locations near here.'

'It makes me very proud to know how you have succeeded.' The old man took the girl by the hand and drew her towards the centre of the room. 'Manello was always a bright boy. Headstrong, a little too soft for this life, but always clever. I knew that he would get on in the world.'

'What the hell happened to the lights?' Manello demanded. He moved the light switch angrily.

'There is a fault in the geuerator. It has been like that for weeks, Manello. I am too weak in the legs to climb the tower and fix it. The wind turns the sails but no power comes. Perhaps you would fix it for me now. It is bad being without light. This oil makes the place smell.'

'Perhaps I will fix it,' Manello smiled quietly. 'Perhaps now I am not afraid to climb the tower, eh, Father?'

The old man made an awkward gesture with his hands and turned away. He said: 'You must be tired and hot after the drive. Manello, take your wife to the main bedroom. I have little food here but I will make you a meal such as I can.'

Manello took up an oil lamp and handed it to the girl. He lifted the cases and they went through an arched doorway. Halfway down the passage a door stood ajar and the girl looked in.

This room was at the back of the house. The roof had fallen in and one wall crumbled to dust. Sand had swept in and covered the floor. Alone, abandoned in the room beneath the stark, broken beams, was a rocking horse. The girl went forward with her lantern and turned the yellow light over the toy. It's colours had been burnt out by the sun, but here and there in the carved, curled mane and in each staring, detailed eyeball a scrap of paint remained. She pushed the horse and it rocked slowly with clouds of dust pouring from its flanks.

'It is so big,' the girl said in wonder.

'My mother brought it with her from the city. It had been hers since she was a child.'

She stooped, suddenly seeing the strange bonds which

circled each of the horse's legs. 'Why ropes here?' she asked. 'Who would tie up a rocking horse?'

'Come on,' Manello said roughly. 'There isn't time to stand here.'

They went to their rooms and the girl unpacked a case. Manello found a jug of dirt-filmed water under the wooden wash stand. He tipped it into the basin. 'You go first.'

The girl pulled off her clothes quickly and stooped over the basin. Manello watched the curve of her firm thighs. When she straightened and turned, the lamp cast a soft shadow in the deep cleft of her uptilted breasts.

'When did your father come out here?' The girl sat on the bottom of the great iron-framed bed and dried herself.

'My grandfather settled here with some friends and his family. He had a large family. My father was one of eight boys.' Manello pulled off his shirt and unbuckled his belt. 'They built this farmhouse and other houses. It was a prosperous community.' Manello dropped his trousers and stepped out of them, aware of the girl's eyes on his body. 'But the young men grew tired of the quietness. They drifted off. The war came and some were killed. My father went to the city and married my mother. Then the depression came and he couldn't find work any more so he came back here.'

'He had many children?'

'Only me. I was a great disappointment to him. My mother died bringing me into this godforsaken world so I was a killer as well as a failure.' There was no bitterness in his voice. He finished washing and came back to the bed.

'Why did you bring me here?' she asked. Then after a moment: 'Was it because of last night?'

Manello turned his head away. She reached out and stroked his shoulder, letting her hand smoothe down the fair hair which curled on the nape of his neck.

'Are you ashamed? There's no cause for shame, Manello.' She turned his face towards hers, tracing the shape of his lips with her fingers. She tried to draw him closer, but he resisted. 'There is no cause for shame,' she repeated gently. 'You are my husband.'

'In name . . . in law . . . My father is right — I am a half man.'

'That is not true,' she drew him down beside her, rubbing her body against his.

'Please,' Manello said softly. 'Not yet . . .'

They returned to the living room to find that the old man had set the table and heated some thick vegetable soup. Manello was sullen and silent, the girl, as though to make up for it, chattered loudly. She complimented the old man on the pretty china.

'It was my wife's. She brought it with her from the city. Her family was wealthy. It was a good catch for me to marry a woman so beautiful and rich. All my friends said what a good catch I had made. But her family lost everything during the thirties.'

'That rocking horse was hers? I saw it when we went to our room.'

'It was a lovely thing. Hand carved you know, hand painted in bright colours. She had it especially sent from the city. It must have cost a fortune to send it all the way out here. But she had money . . . her family was rich.' He sucked greedily at the soup and the greasy liquid dribbled down his chin and neck. 'When I can afford the paint I shall re-decorate it as it was.'

'That would be nice,' the girl said.

'It's all I have to remind me of her. She was very lovely.'

'It's a pity you didn't have a little girl to . . .' the words, the bright unthinking flow of words halted in confusion. Timidly she finished . . . 'to play with it.'

'Oh, but I used to play on it,' Manello said suddenly. 'My father invented a very special game for little boys to play on the rocking horse. Do you remember, Father?'

'It was a long time ago. I forget things.' The old man's voice was peevish.

'Surely not so long? Ten years since we last played together with the rocking horse, Father?'

'I tell you I don't remember. Is that why you came here – to fight with me?'

'Fight with you? Your half-man son. A strong man like you and a half man.'

'What is it?' the girl asked urgently. She looked from one to the other.

'My father made that rocking horse into a whipping post,' Manello said. 'That is why there are ropes on the feet. To bind my wrists and ankles when he beat me, and he beat me many times, my father.'

'It was for your own good ... you were soft, stupid as a boy. Weak things do not survive in this world. Nature kills the weak.'

'But you weren't allowed to kill me, were you, Father?'

'I loved you.' The old man looked appealingly at the girl. 'You understand that. I only did it because I loved him.'

'And Margarette. Was that for love too?'

'She was a tramp. No good for you.'

'When I was seventeen I had a girl called Margarette.' Manello was speaking directly to the girl, ignoring the old man. He spoke slowly and carefully like a witness making a deposition before an attorney. He weighed each word as though it might later be held against him. 'My father and I were building the tower for the electricity generator. It is a very tall tower to catch the faintest gasp of air. I have an allergy that makes me go in mortal terror of heights. Not then, but now with my greater knowledge, I understand that this fear is real and not weakness. But then I thought it was only because I was a coward, a half man as my father constantly told me.

'That day, we had to fix the generator on to its platform high on the tower. My father had done the high work while I sawed the timber and pulled it up to him. He promised that he would secure the generator. But Margarette came to see us work and he decided I must be taught a lesson. Before my girl, he ordered me to climb the tower and work on the platform. I tried. I climbed a little way, a few yards and then the terror overcame me and I could go neither up nor back. He stood there cursing me, shouting that I was a coward, threatening that unless I did as he ordered he would beat me.

'I could not go up, you understand, no threat or promise on this earth could have made me. Somehow I struggled back to the ground. My fear was so great that I could not move. I was trembling and covered in sweat, my legs numb and useless.

'He grasped me by one arm and shouting and jeering pulled me to the house. He called for Margarette to follow, to see my disgrace. When we were all in the room where that horse stood, he locked the door. Then before my girl he stripped me naked and bound me to the legs and beat me until in fear and pain and disgrace my bladder opened and I fouled myself before them. That is what he did to me.'

Manello pushed his chair away from the table. The old man's gun lay on the sideboard. He picked it up and swung the barrels towards his father.

'Get up,' he ordered. The old man clung to the table edge.

'Manello, it was for love.'

'Get to your feet.'

'Will you kill your own father?'

Manello didn't bother to reply. To the girl he said: 'Take the lantern and go to the room with the rocking horse.'

Manello pushed the gun against the old man's cheek. Trembling, his father rose and followed the girl.

The rocking horse stood cold white under the risen moon. It might have been carved of ivory or bone. It might have lain, fish-pecked beneath the sea for a millennium, so pure and clean the timber seemed. Their feet stirred the fine sand and it seeped into Manello's shoes.

'Remove your clothes.'

The old man looked at his son and at the girl. He started to cry, the sobs sounding dry in his husk of throat.

'Hurry.'

Hands trembling, he unbuttoned his shirt and pulled it off. His skin had lost its deep tan and grown grey and loose like an ill-fitting shroud.

'It was for love,' he insisted through his tears. But he let his baggy trousers fall and exposed his flabby thighs and wrinkled, hairless body. The girl turned her head away.

'Lie over the horse,' Manello commanded. The old man obeyed painfully and the horse creaked in protest against his weight. Manello stooped quickly and bound the wrists and ankles. The rope was almost rotted but the old man made no move to struggle, and the binding was no more than a gesture.

The old man's legs and arms were spindles, his backbone jutted through the painfully thin flesh like a partly submerged reef.

How in ten years? Manello wondered. He had been so powerful, so muscled. Or was it just that a boy's fear had put pounds on to the frame and created a strength which never in reality existed. But the old man probably had been strong. Ten years alone, without hope, in the silence of the desert would drain a man of everything . . . even of a desire to live. Perhaps especially of the desire to live. Was that the real punishment? The long, hot silence among the decay of a lifetime's work. Without even a dog for company. But the old man couldn't stand dogs and had drowned the only stray Manello ever brought home. If any came begging for food he'd shoot at them, and now none came.

'You should have kept a dog,' Manello said suddenly. 'It would have kept off the roughs . . . it would have been something that mourned your passing.'

'Will you kill him?' The girl demanded.

'If I do, then he killed himself.' Manello stroked the cold steel of the gun along the old man's naked body. 'Everything I am he made.' He looked hard at the girl. 'Everything that I am not as well.'

He raised the gun to his shoulder and his finger went across the triggers. For a moment the blunt, round mouths caressed his father's chest and groin.

'Goodbye, old man,' he said. He fired and the explosion was like some massive orgasm. The sound rocked to and fro between the decayed walls and set the horse in gentle motion. On the far wall, two black smears stained the white baked mud where the pellets had landed.

The old man sobbed, his body swaying with the movement of the horse, the stench of his spilled fear filling the cool night.

Manello and the girl didn't bother about their belongings. They left the cases and clothes to the old man. They went out to the car and drove back to the city.

TERROR OF TWO HUNDRED BELOW

By William Sinclair

AN ICY HAND gripped Linda Reynolds' heart when the dark figure of a man stepped out from the side street into her path.

Although she tried to sidestep him, she waited with terror-stricken anticipation for his vice-like grip to clamp on to her arm. Instead, he mumbled an apology, as she brushed past, and ambled down the street without a backward glance. The scream, which had risen to her throat, subsided in a sob of fear when she realized that she was still free, but her knees felt rubbery, as she trotted on through the dimly lit streets.

It was a deserted neighbourhood of gaunt warehouses and high tenement buildings and the wet, black pavements reflected the sickly gleam of the infrequently spaced street lights. Few people passed this way at this time of the night and tonight, the rain seemed to have kept even these indoors.

Linda's breath came in rasping gulps now and her body, under the long raincoat, was bathed in a sweat of panic and cruel exertion. She knew she must stop soon or her legs would collapse beneath her and yet the imagined sound of pursuit drove her on beyond any normal limits of endurance.

Then she saw the lone figure ahead. He was walking away from her, his head bent against the wind and rain, intent, no doubt, on reaching a blazing fire and a warm bed. Her flagging limbs closed the gap between them, but when she was no more than twenty yards behind, he turned sharply into one of the tenement openings.

She staggered in after him, her footsteps echoing noisily round the narrow stone walls. The close was lit by a solitary, stuttering gas light, but it was sufficient to reveal the look of surprise on his face as he whirled to see who was behind him.

'Please help me,' she sobbed. 'They mustn't catch me.'

She almost collapsed in his arms and then drew back, with her head bowed, gasping for breath.

'Whatever's the matter?' he asked in a low voice. For all his surprise, he still remembered that two families lived on every floor and loud voices at midnight would penetrate to each and every one of them.

'They mustn't catch me, please don't let them,' she pleaded again.

'Now, steady on. No one's going to catch you.' He put a comforting arm round her. 'Come on up to my flat and have a drink. Then I'll see that you get home safely.'

She went unprotestingly, comforted slightly by his calm assurance.

He lived on the third floor and a welcoming fire lit the room with dancing shadows even before he switched on the light.

'Let me take your coat, and come and sit by the fire while I get you a drink,' he invited, noting that she was extremely pretty with long blonde hair and a slim, shapely figure.

'I have whisky or would you prefer a hot drink?'

'I wouldn't mind a cup of coffee if it's not too much trouble,' she said gratefully.

'No trouble at all. Now you sit there and warm yourself while I make it.'

He disappeared into the kitchenette to reappear after a few minutes with two mugs.

'My name is Paul Rogers, what's yours?' he asked chattily, handing her one of the mugs.

'Linda Reynolds,' she replied, feeling some of the fear and tension of the past few hours lift, as she looked up at his rugged, smiling face.

'Well, supposing you tell me what got you into such a state? Then we'll see what we can do about it.'

Linda wrapped both her hands round the mug and sipped silently for several moments. Paul sat across from her and the only sound in the room came from the hearth, where the coal crumbled gently into ashes.

When she spoke at last, her voice had an almost eager ring as if she longed to tell someone of her experiences. The high pitched note of hysteria had gone and she spoke calmly.

'It all began about a year ago. I don't know if you have ever heard of Professor Gordon Maxwell, but he was a brilliant man and I was fortunate enough to be one of a small research team which he formed. There were four of us in the team, the names of the other two being John Byrne and Martin Saunders, and the project we became totally dedicated to was basic enough. We were looking for a cure for the common cold. Science has been looking for a prevention and cure for many years without success, but we made a radical breakthrough, which as far as we knew, put us ahead of anything so far achieved in this field. In fact we thought we were very near to producing a vaccine which would give a person complete immunity from colds for up to five years.

'Unfortunately, like most research projects, ours was always hampered by inadequate funds. The nearer we got to success, the more serious the financial situation became and then something came up which we hoped might solve all our worries.

'I'm sure you've heard of Sir Arthur Wayne. He is a very rich man and a very generous one, and all his life he has donated large sum of money to charity. He is a great showman as well and you can imagine our hopes when it was announced, in a blaze of publicity, that Sir Arthur had decided to donate half a million pounds to the research project which, at that time, was thought to be the most worthwhile in terms of benefiting mankind. Any person or team engaged in medical research was eligible to enter for the award and the winner was to be chosen by a Board of experts who would study the merits of each project and the progress so far achieved.

'We felt that our cause was as worthy as anybody's and so, with nothing to lose, we entered. Professor Maxwell made sure that our application was well presented and in due course, to our surprise and delight, we were adjudged the winners.

'All the other competitors were very magnanimous, when our victory was announced, with the exception of one. This was a man called Jason Sloane, who in fact came second in the Board's assessment of the various projects. Little was known of his work until he put it before Sir Arthur's adjudicating Board. It was concerned apparently with the suspension of life by freezing and he claimed to have had considerable success. Anyway, when the Board came to the final stages of making their decision, it was strongly rumoured that he was the favourite to win the award.

'The announcement of our success was made at a reception at Sir Arthur's home. In his speech, the Chairman of the Board praised all the projects which had come before them, giving special mention to Sloane's. He explained that he and his colleagues felt that our work was of more immediate benefit to mankind and that had been the deciding factor. They believed that current problems should be tackled before schemes which appeared to have more long-term implications. The reason for announcing a second and third at all was in case the winners, for some unforeseen reason, were unable to proceed with their work. In such an eventuality, the award would be passed on to the next in line.

'We were naturally cock-a-hoop, but I remember feeling an inexplicable uneasiness when Jason Sloane came over to our group afterwards. Professor Maxwell commiserated with him for coming second, but Sloane refused to shake hands. He just looked slowly at the four of us with those cold fish-like eyes of his and I remember his words very clearly.

' "The Board made a bad mistake in passing over my work. Fortunately it is not an irrevocable one." '

'Then he turned on his heel and walked away.

' "He's a damned bad loser," John Byrne remarked in the awkward silence that followed, but Professor Maxwell was his usual diplomatic self.

' "Forget it," he advised. "He's disappointed, that's all. It's only natural when he got so near to winning. We would have been the same if we had come second, but we might not have shown it in the same way."

'In the weeks that followed we didn't have time to think about Jason Sloane or anyone else for that matter. We were all far too busy revising our schedules, deciding what new equipment we needed and generally pushing ahead with Project A.W. as we renamed it after its new benefactor. Although money was going to be much more plentiful from now on, Professor Maxwell was determined that not a penny should be wasted or misappropriated.

'The grant had an important personal influence on my life as well. John Byrne and I had been engaged for some time, but we had postponed our wedding since the future of the project looked so uncertain. Now the team were welded even closer together and, since the project's future seemed to be assured, we fixed a date for the wedding.

'Everything seemed to be perfect and then it happened, just a month to the day after the Wayne Award had been made to us. It was discovered that some specialized equipment could only be obtained from a German firm in Hamburg, so Professor Maxwell decided to charter a special place and take the team over to examine it and, if suitable, bring it back with them.

' "There's no need for you to come, Linda," he told me. "I'm sure you've plenty to do with your wedding only a fortnight away. If you'd just grade that latest batch of cultures, you can have the rest of the time off while we're away."

'I made some remark about the men not wanting to be hindered by female company in a city like Hamburg and warned them to ensure that John behaved himself. Although I would miss him, of course, I was glad enough to have some spare time before the wedding and I didn't really mind being left behind. I saw them off at Luton Airport in the early evening and motored back to my parents' home in Buckinghamshire, where we were going to be married. John had promised to phone me when they arrived, but I waited in vain. In the end I went to bed feeling annoyed and thinking he had either not bothered or had forgotten.

'My mother woke me with the news next morning. Normally I'm pretty dozy when I wake up, but the look on her face and the note in her voice had me wide awake, even before I understood what she was saying. It was almost as if I had been expecting something.

' "It's just been reported on the news that a light plane went missing over the North Sea last night," she said. "I don't want to alarm you unnecessarily, dear, but it seems almost certain that it's John's."

'When we checked with the authorities, my mother's fears were confirmed. The last routine exchanges with the aircraft had been made as they crossed the English coast and after that, nothing. An intensive air-sea search failed to find any sign of the plane or its occupants, until about three days later when they were about to give up. Then an aircraft spotted some wreckage, which was picked up and confirmed to be part of the missing aeroplane. Subsequent tests showed that an explosion had taken place in the air. There was still no sign of the passengers, however, and in fact none ever was found.

'I was absolutely shattered. In a flash, my future husband, two of my best friends, and a job to which I had been completely dedicated since I left college, had been snatched away from me for ever. Perhaps, worst of all, was the lingering doubt about what had really happened to the aircraft and those in it. More than one newspaper suggested how strange it was that no trace of any of the passengers had been found and so I suppose it left me with the forlorn hope that perhaps they weren't dead after all.

'The uncertainty persisted even as I slowly picked up the pieces of my life. It took a long time, but you can't live in the past forever and I gradually came to terms with myself. The problem of finding another job, however, was unbelievably difficult. I could have taken plenty of routine research posts, but after the sense of excitement and achievement which Professor Maxwell had engendered in all of us on Project A.W., I just couldn't face any of them.

'My parents were very good and said I could stay with them for as long as I liked. Dad has a small market garden, and I helped him with that to try and repay my board, but it was all very temporary and unsatisfactory. Anyway, this lasted for about six months when I received another big surprise.

'I was picking apples in the orchard when my mother called out to say that a gentleman wished to see me. Imagine my surprise when I got to the house and saw Jason Sloane waiting for me. I was so taken aback that I just took his hand when he offered it.

' "I expect you're surprised to see me, Miss Reynolds," he smiled. He actually looked pleased to see me.

' "I must confess I am," I replied.

' "As I'm sure you will remember, the last time we met was at Sir Arthur Wayne's home."

' "I remember." My memory of his behaviour on that occasion probably made me sound rather hostile, because he added hastily. "I see you do and I blush with shame every time I think about it. My conduct was quite inexcusable and I can only offer my profound apologies. All I can say is that my disappointment at not winning the Wayne Award got the better of me and I have regretted it ever since."

'He really looked sorry and I found myself wondering if we had misjudged him.

' "We all do things we regret afterwards," I conceded.

' "But unfortunately I will never be able to make my apologies to Professor Maxwell and his associates. That was a most tragic accident."

' "Yes it was," I said sharply.

' "I'm sure you don't wish to be reminded of it, as I believe you also suffered a great personal loss, but I am bound to say how deeply shocked I was when I read about it. Professor Maxwell was a brilliant man and, of course, although I badly needed the Wayne donation for my own work, that was the last way I wanted to win it."

' "I'm sure you are putting the money to good use, Doctor Sloane," I said politely.

' "I think I am," he nodded. "But perhaps you would like to decide that for yourself."

' "What do you mean by that?" I asked.

' "Simply that I would like you to come and work with me."

' "But . . ."

' "Before you say anything, let me explain," he interrupted.

' "I have wanted to ask you ever since the accident. Unfortunately, I have only just succeeded in tracing you. At

Professor Maxwell's laboratories they could only tell me the address of your flat. No one seemed to know of your parents' home, nor had any idea where you might be. Consequently, it's taken me all this time to track you down. Now that I have, let me say that I feel that if you were to work with me, it would be a tribute to Professor Maxwell in a way. It won't be his project, it's true, but part of his team would live on, working in another field of research which I think will greatly benefit mankind in the future, just as his would have done."

'He paused for a moment and then admitted. "Besides, I need a good assistant."

' "But you don't know anything about me," I protested. "I might not meet your requirements."

' "I knew Professor Maxwell," he insisted. "He wouldn't have had anyone in his team who wasn't first class. No, I've no fear on that score, so what do you say?"

'I hesitated.

' "I understand you haven't followed up your vocation since . . ." he prompted.

' "No, I haven't." I admitted.

' "Which is surely a great waste of your training and experience," he urged.

'He was a persuasive talker all right, but I still couldn't make up my mind. I wasn't even sure if I approved of the work he was engaged in, but it was difficult to counter his final argument.

' "Look," he said at last. "Don't make your mind up now, but come and see my work for yourself. I'll show you round my laboratory and then you can decide if you would like to work with me."

'Sloane had argued reasonably and indeed had shown considerable charm. Yet something at the back of my mind bothered me. Anyway, after some further persuasion I agreed to visit his laboratory, without any obligation, and he took his leave.

'Two days later I caught an early evening train into London and the night sleeper to Glasgow. Sloane met me personally at Queen Street, but then to my surprise drove northwards out of the city. When I asked him where we were going, he told me that his laboratory was up in the hills. He explained that when he had set up his headquarters originally, lack of money had been a major problem and in deciding upon a less central position, he had been able to spend more on equipment and less on ground, bricks, and mortar. Having known similar financial difficulties under Professor Maxwell, I could sympathize with his point of view.

'Glasgow was soon left behind and so too was the sullen drizzle which had persisted since I got off the train. Soon we were twisting through the foothills of Dunbartonshire and then Argyll, and the sun peered spasmodically at us through banks of dark clouds. The volume of traffic gradually fell to a trickle, but nearly two hours had elapsed before we finally turned off a narrow B road on to an even narrower track, which was deeply rutted and bordered by stone dykes. A jolting mile farther on, we rounded a hill and before us lay a thickly wooded valley. I thought I saw the square grey chimneys of our destination, as we got nearer, but apart from a thin trickle of smoke, which curled aimlessly above the trees, there was no sign of life. Even the birds seemed unnaturally quiet.

'Jason Sloane may have been principally concerned with saving money in choosing this place for his work, but he had also found perfect isolation.

'As we approached the house through the trees, I had my first good view of it, a grey, forbidding edifice of tall square chimneys, stone block walls and tiny windows. From the outside, it projected as much warmth as a medieval castle and it had the welcoming aspect of a Victorian prison.

' "It's an old hunting lodge," Sloane explained as we drew up at the massive front door.

' "Not exactly what I'd call cosy," I suggested.

' "Don't be put off by the exterior," he advised. "It's really quite comfortable inside."

'His assurances were hardly borne out by the great vaulted hall, which echoed to our footsteps, nor by the lounge, a large room of solid oak furniture, blackened beams, and faded paintings. The huge fire that blazed cheerfully in the open hearth, however, did help to push back the cold clammy air which seemed to cloak the house. I tried to imagine the same room a generation earlier, echoing to the noise and laughter of a hunting party back from a day in the hills. It wasn't easy.

'Sloane poured me a sherry and himself a whisky, and we drank and talked in front of the fire.

'"I was very fortunate to find this place," he explained cheerfully. "It belonged to a Mr Everett Lauder, who owned a distillery in Glasgow. In the twenties and thirties he used to entertain his friends to hunting and fishing weekends and many famous people have warmed their behinds in front of this very fire. Unfortunately, the war put an end to all that. The army took it over as a commando training headquarters, the country around here being ideal, of course, for endurance and initiative training and that kind of thing. By the time the war ended, Lauder had sold out his business and gone abroad, so this place stood empty for years before the Youth Hostels Association took it over. That didn't last long though. Apparently it was too out of the way, and so when I got to know of it, it was pretty run down and I bought it for a song."

'He offered me another drink and though I declined, he poured himself one before continuing.

'"The house is really too big for my needs, although besides myself, there are a couple of servants, who live in and do the cooking and cleaning. I also have two assistants, but they have only limited experience and I have to personally supervise all the scientific side of the work we do. Of course, with the extra money now available, I hope to be able to attract other scientists of the calibre I really need and then we will move ahead very much faster."

'At that moment, a big, bearded man in a white coat burst into the room. He stopped in his tracks when he saw me, but only for a moment.

'"Doctor Sloane," he said in a deep, breathless voice. "Would you come quickly please, we're having trouble with one of the patients. She's not responding."

'A flicker of annoyance and concern crossed Sloane's face, but it disappeared almost as quickly.

' "Very well, Branston, I'll be along in a moment," he replied.

'As Branston withdrew, Sloane turned to me.

' "I must ask you to excuse me for a little while, Miss Reynolds. As you heard, an emergency seems to have arisen and I am needed downstairs. You may like to use one of the visitors' bedrooms to freshen up, so I'll get the housekeeper to show you the way. Please make yourself at home and I will rejoin you presently. Then after lunch I'll show you round."

'In response to his call, an elderly woman in a sombre black dress led me upstairs and along a corridor to a bedroom at the far end. I tried to make conversation, but she was quite un-communicative and blunted all my questions with non-committal grunts.

'The bedroom was at the rear of the house and the view from the high, leaded windows took in rough pastureland, which rose gently to craggy hills that seemed to surround the house on all sides.

'I had already made up my mind, whatever Sloane showed me. I couldn't possibly live and work in such complete isolation, however beautiful and peaceful the surrounding countryside was. The loneliness would give me too much time to think and the plane crash was still too close in time for that to be healthy. I realized at that moment that I was still a long way from getting over John's death, if indeed I ever would. And so I decided I would thank Sloane at the first opportunity for his kindness, catch the night sleeper back to London and that would be the end of it.

'Lunch was an uncomfortable affair in spite of the excellence of the meal itself. At the table, besides Sloane, were his two assistants, Branston, whom I had already seen briefly, and Davies, a younger man with a thin face and close-set eyes. I wasn't particularly drawn to either of them and the way they kept stealing glances at me, when they thought I wasn't look-ing, made me glad when the coffee arrived. Sloane made some pretence at keeping the conversation going, but his mind was clearly pre-occupied. If this was an average lunch, then the decision I had already made, to decline Sloane's invitation, was fully reinforced.

' "And now Miss Reynolds, let us get down to business. If you'll follow me, I'll show you round."

'He led the way across the hall to a small door set back in a dark alcove. Opening this, we descended a well-lit stairway.

'It was like stepping into another world. The walls were plastered and painted and the very effective air conditioning made a welcome contrast to the damp, cold atmosphere of the house above. We passed through another door at the foot of the stairs and along a narrow passage. Then another door, and I found myself in a large, well-equipped laboratory.

' "This is no doubt a familiar sight to you," Sloane remarked. "Another feature of this place, which made it fit my requirements so well, was the tremendous amount of room beneath the Lodge itself. I'm not sure what all this space was used for, originally, but I imagine part of it was a wine cellar. It was also probably used for storing fuel and for skinning and hanging the deer which were shot by the hunting parties. Anyway, I've been very glad of it although, as you can probably imagine, it cost a great deal to convert into acceptable working premises. Latterly, the Wayne money has been most useful and in fact the air conditioning has only recently been installed. Before that, we had to rely upon rather more primitive and less effective oil heaters. We also have our own electric generating plant now, which is an absolute necessity when you live this far out. Also, with our type of work, we couldn't possibly risk the chance of a power failure at any time."

'I wandered round the laboratory, casting a professional eye over the apparatus. Some of it was familiar to me, but the purpose of most of it was completely foreign.

' "Before we go any farther, let me explain my work in a little more detail," said Sloane at last. " Basically, there are three categories of people with whom I am working. The first are those who, according to all present medical knowledge, are dead. At the point of death, their physical deterioration is arrested and they are placed in, for want of a better layman's expression, cold storage. There, I'm afraid, my contribution ends. The theory is that as long as their body tissue is perfectly preserved, if in the future a cure can be found for the disease which killed them, it should be possible to bring them back to life again. There is a society in the States, which has been working along similar lines, but as far as I know I am well ahead of anything they have achieved so far.

' "My early efforts were unsuccessful and when the bodies were examined, some time after they had been processed and stored away, we found that decomposition of some of the organs had set in. In the past few years, however, I think I have found how to stop the normal decay of a dead human body and I hope in the very near future to find out if the second part of the theory has any hope of success.

' "You see, one of my clients died five years ago of a bad heart. As you know, heart transplant operations, which were then unknown, are now an almost everyday occurrence and so I hope that it will be possible to carry one out on him. I need hardly say what a medical triumph it would be if we were to succeed, but first I need a suitable donor and then a surgeon with the necessary skill to do the actual transplant."

'As he described his work, Sloane had a far-away look in his eyes. Although he was talking to me, I felt that he also wanted to hear his own theories and hopes expounded to himself. His complete dedication was unquestionable, but it seemed to have an almost fanatical and unnatural quality.

' "What about the second category?" I asked, intrigued in spite of my uneasiness.

' "The second type are those people who are dying of some fatal illness, but are not yet dead. The same principle applies, but naturally the chances of success with these are very much higher. The emergency this morning concerned one such case. A young girl, who was dying, was recently brought here, but unfortunately we were unable to start the freezing process in time and she died just before lunch. We will, of course, still freeze her, but her chances in the future have obviously deteriorated."

'I had heard enough. If there had been any doubt about my

staying on to work with Jason Sloane, what I knew now would have finally decided me. Whatever the merits, or otherwise, of what he was trying to achieve, it was far too macabre for me.

' "Look, Doctor Sloane," I said. "I think it is only fair to tell you that I have made up my mind about your invitation to work here. I'm grateful that you have gone to all this trouble, but I just don't think I could fit in. Therefore, so as not to waste any more of your time, perhaps you could arrange for someone to take me back to Glasgow and I'll catch the night sleeper."

'Sloane did not reply for a moment, but when he did, there was an edge to his voice that hadn't been there before. For some reason it made me shiver.

' "That is a pity, Miss Reynolds, a great pity," he said at last. "However, now that you are here, you must let me show you the third category of patients which I mentioned."

' "I really don't think there is any point . . ." I began.

' "But I insist," he interrupted, with a strange smile. "I'm sure you will find that what I have to show you next is of particular interest. Now, if you will please come this way."

'We passed through a door at the far end of the laboratory into a cold gloomy passage. It was as if we had moved upstairs again. A single pale orange glow revealed a series of small doors on either side of the passage.

' "Behind these doors lie my patients," Sloane explained. "Half of them are already dead, the others were dying before they came here, but now that process has been arrested. All of them, however, have been treated and then permanently cocooned in a temperature of —200 degrees Centigrade. Various attachments to their bodies enable us to record any changes that might occur and a running case history is kept on each."

'This was the nearest I had ever been to a mortuary and I could sense the atmosphere of death which hung about me like a heavy shroud. I was now very nervous and yet at the same time fascinated.

' "How long have they been in there?" I asked, trembling slightly.

' "The earliest patient died about ten years ago," Sloane replied. "Of those not actually dead, the earliest client is coming up for five years."

'By now we had reached a door at the far end of the passage. Sloane opened it to reveal another flight of steps leading down still farther.

' "Unfortunately," he continued as we negotiated these in the same sickly light, "we have been running short of accommodation for patients during the last year or two and it became necessary to open up this lower chamber."

'We reached the bottom and Sloane touched a switch which improved the lighting, although it was still far from brilliant. I saw that we were in a long, narrow, vault-like room with a roof which curved down into the walls and was so low that we could hardly stand upright.

'A bank of dials and switches took up most of one end, but it was the long wall opposite that drew all my attention. Several deep square cavities had been dug out of the solid rock. Fresh brickwork suggested that three of these had already been closed in again, but the others stood empty. In front of the end one stood what looked like a large metal canister. It was about seven feet long and cylindrically shaped with a diameter of three to four feet. It was obviously destined to go into the hole which gaped open behind it. The canister was divided along it's entire length and it looked as if the top could be separated from the bottom, like an elongated Easter egg.

'I realized that Sloane was watching me closely as I looked around. All the friendliness had gone from his face when at last I turned to him again. His smile was cold and mocking and made me shiver even more than the cold damp air around us.

' "To use your own phrase, Miss Reynolds, not exactly what you'd call cosy. But let me explain."

He tapped the metal canister.

' "In here and in three similar metal containers, bricked in behind the wall there, lie people who are neither dead nor dying."

' "I don't understand," I said.

' "I mean that when they were placed in there, they were all in perfect health."

' "But what for?" I asked in bewilderment. "How is this supposed to benefit them?"

' "It wasn't meant to benefit them, although it might ultimately. My intention, though, was to benefit mankind as a whole."

' "You mean they volunteered for such an experiment?" I asked incredulously.

' "Not exactly." Sloane's smile was positively evil. "In fact their incarceration had to be enforced, but what does that matter when science stands to gain so much?"

' "You mean that men were put away in those things against their will?" My voice rose in indignation. "That's the most inhuman thing I've ever heard."

' "Before you go any farther, there is something else I want to show you," Sloane interrupted. "Come over here."

'As I moved nearer, he raised the top half of the canister clear of the base to which it was hinged. All I saw at first was a mist of frozen vapour rising into the relatively warmer atmosphere of the chamber. Then as the vapour thinned, I saw the body of a man lying in the capsule. He was completely naked and his flesh looked so unnaturally white and firmly angular that he might have been carved from a block of marble. He lay as still as death and as my eyes travelled up the length of him from his feet, I felt my senses reeling when at last I gazed unbelievingly at his head. Although it had been completely shaved of hair and his eyes were closed in a face that looked to be moulded in death, I had seen that face too many times to mistake its owner.

' "John" was all I could gasp, before the shock of seeing the fiancé I thought to be dead became too much for me and I fainted.

'I was probably only unconscious for a few moments. At least when I came round, nothing had changed. We were still in that dreadful lower chamber and that metal tomb still stood open with my poor John's frozen body lying in it.

'Sloane helped me to my feet, but as I remembered where I was, I pulled away from him.

' "What have you done to him, you fiend?" I shouted, though still feeling shaky. "And how did he get here in the first place?"

' "One question at a time," said Sloane, looking quite unperturbed by my outburst. "He and his two friends and, of course, the pilot of their aircraft, are all here and that is all you need to know at present. The others are in similar containers behind those bricked up portions of the wall and your fiancé is about to be sealed up in the same way. I kept him out till last as I thought you might like to see him once more."

'He raised his hand when he saw I was about to interrupt.

' "Let me finish, if you want an explanation."

'I stifled my protest and listened in an agony of horror and bewilderment.

' "The work, on which I had made so much progress, was at a standstill because I had run out of money and then, when it looked as if it might be saved, you people snatched away my last chance. When your Professor Maxwell won the Wayne Award with his project, I was lost.

' "Then I thought, why should I not share in your good fortune? Half a million pounds is a lot of money and more than enough to keep both our projects going. So I had the plane hi-jacked and brought here. Then I put my proposition to the Professor, but unfortunately he would not cooperate and so I had no alternative but to make the three of them disappear for good. I would then gain control of all the money by default.

' "The question of what to do with them presented something of a problem. Although I was desperate, I am a scientist and murdering them was out of the question. Then I had my brainwave. For a long time I had thought how desirable it would be to apply my technique to perfectly healthy human beings instead of dead or dying ones. I wanted fit young people to store away indefinitely in the same way as my less fortunate clients to see if their natural ageing process could be completely arrested. Don't you see? In a hundred or two hundred years' time your fiancé will be resurrected and, physically, he won't have changed from the day you last saw him."

' "You're mad," I exclaimed, unable to contain myself any longer.

'Sloane merely shrugged.

' "Maybe. We all have our idiosyncracies and how does one differentiate between madness and sanity? At best it is a very narrow dividing line. All I know is that the fulfilment of a lifetime's work lies around us." He waved his arms. "The possibilities for mankind are so enormous as to be beyond his wildest dreams, so what are three lives and half a million pounds in that context?"

' "Why you . . ." I began, but Sloane stopped me again.

' "Careful what you say now," he admonished. "Or you may shock your fiancé. He is bound to be listening."

' "What?" His words stopped me in my tracks. I wasn't sure if he was making a cruel joke, but he looked quite serious.

' "That's right, although he is frozen solid and all the blood has been drained from his body, his brain is still functioning normally and he can hear everything we are saying. In fact that is one of the problems I have so far failed to solve. Although the body can be immobilized and all its functions completely halted, I have been unable to de-activate the brain and some of the senses. For example, the subject can still hear and smell and feel certain sensations.

' "Once the brain stops functioning for any length of time, it is very difficult to revive it again and so the patient's ultimate recovery becomes less probable. That is why I have less confidence over the long term success of my category one patients, compared with those not yet dead. On the other hand, for those who live in a deep freeze, time must weigh very heavily, with their brains conscious year after year inside a body that is to all intents and purposes dead."

'The implications of his words were almost too ghastly to contemplate.

' "You can't be serious," I gasped.

' "But I am and I can assure you that he has heard every word since we came down here."

' "You won't get away with this." I found myself screaming at him now with a mixture of fear and anger. "When I tell the authorities, you'll end up in a mental institute for the rest of your life."

' "You disappoint me, Miss Reynolds," he said, shaking his head solemnly. "Knowing what you do now, you surely don't think that you will be allowed to leave here?"

'The implied threat stopped me short. I suppose my mind had been first of all too confused and latterly too horrified over the monstrous nature of Sloane's work to even consider that my own personal safety might also be in jeopardy. Sloane appeared to read my thoughts.

' "Yes, I have very definite plans for you," he affirmed. "When I asked you to come here, I really did want you to help me with my work, but now I realize that it was a foolish hope. Of course you need never have known who were in these capsules, but when you declined my offer, I decided I was going to use you in another way. It also gives me the opportunity to punish your fiancé a little more.

' "I believe he loves you, and knowing that you are now going to join him in his cold vigil may make him regret even more the unpleasant things he said to me when he was brought here. Do you know, he tried to get away and smashed some valuable apparatus before we could restrain him?" Sloane's eyes blazed angrily. It was the first time I had seen him in a temper since that day at the Wayne house. "The fool could have delayed my work for years and it was what finally made me decide to use him and his friends as guinea-pigs."

'He calmed down a little before he continued, but the way he looked at me now was almost inhuman.

' "And now you are here, my dear, I will be able to complete this series of experiments. You will shortly join your three friends, but first of all you will be made pregnant. Then we will also discover if a pregnancy can be arrested for an indefinite number of years and then continued when you are released."

'He looked down at John.

' "Do you hear that, Mr Byrne?" he shouted. "I'm sure, as

a scientist, you will approve of my thoroughness and attention to detail. Shortly, you will be sealed away for a lifetime, or perhaps even longer, but at least you can be comforted in the knowledge that your expectant fiancée will be lying only a few feet away from you."

' "You really are mad," I gasped. "And I'm getting out of here."

'I turned towards the stairs intent only on fleeing from this dreadful chamber, which a twisted mind had turned into a place far more fearful than any tomb. To my surprise, Sloane made no attempt to stop me, and then I realized why. Standing silently at the foot of the stairs were his two assistants.

' "Branston," Sloane instructed. "Take Miss Reynolds up to her room and see that she cannot leave. Help him, Davies. Afterwards, I will need you both down here again to help me close up the capsule and put it away."

'I struggled and screamed as I was hauled up the stairs and along the dimly lit passage, but it was to no avail. I was taken back into the laboratory and through another door, which I hadn't noticed previously, to a room near the foot of the stairs. The room contained only a bed and the solid door was slammed shut when I had been pushed inside. I heard the lock click and the footsteps receding, as the two men returned to help their unbalanced master in his devilish work.

'For the next few weeks I lived in a perpetual nightmare of humiliation, terror, and uncertainty. Apart from being taken to Sloane's laboratory for various physical tests and examinations, I was confined all the time in that one room. My meals were served regularly by one of the three men and, although I hated and feared them for what they had already done and still proposed to do to me, I was gradually able to piece together how John, Martin, and Professor Maxwell came to be there.

'It was really very simple, as Sloane explained to me one day when he was in one of his expansive moods. Branston, who was a trained pilot, waylaid the original pilot, tied him up and hid him in the back of the plane. Having taken over the aircraft, he set course for Germany, but changed course and headed for Scotland after crossing the coast. Since they flew above cloud most of the way and it was dark anyway, the passengers had no suspicion of foul play until the plane actually landed at an old airfield near the lodge. The first inkling they had that anything was wrong, was when they were met by Sloane and Davies. At gunpoint, they were brought to the lodge, where Sloane made his proposition to them. The rest I already knew, except how the pieces of the plane came to be found in the North Sea. Sloane was equally communicative on this point.

'Fearing that the complete disappearance of the aircraft and its occupants might be too indicative of foul play, and that any subsequent search might unearth the truth, Sloane had had the aircraft blown up on the ground. Parts of the wreckage were then flown back over the original route and dropped into the sea to be found in the search. Any investigation farther afield was thus averted, in spite of the half-voiced suspicions in the press over the complete disappearance of pilot and passengers.

'Although I discovered how it had been brought about, it did nothing to alleviate my position or frame of mind. My three friends were now far worse off than if they had been killed outright, and soon I would join them.

'The worst part of my captivity, however, were the other visits of Branston and Davies, sometimes together and sometimes with Sloane in attendance as well. On these occasions, the two men forced me to have sexual relations with them, and although they took obvious pleasure in this, they were also acting under Sloane's instructions with a very definite end in view.

'I think they also administered a fertility drug to me in the meantime. Anyway, after two months or so I became pregnant and, of course, Sloane soon found out as well. Such a discovery is a big emotional experience for any woman, but in my case, it was no cause for happiness. Instead, I knew that very soon now, like John, I would be lying in a tomb of ice, neither dead nor yet alive, with my baby frozen inside me.

'My terrible predicament almost drove me crazy at times and thoughts of suicide were never far away. Only the forlorn hope that I might somehow be saved, kept me sane. I thought how my mother and father must be frantic with worry about me, but although they would inform the police, when I didn't return, I held out little hope from that quarter. Sloane was bound to have covered his tracks far too well. I discovered that he had a laboratory in Glasgow and he only had to say that he had shown me around there and then seen me on to the train for London.

'Finally, I knew the day was approaching. No one said anything, but from the activity, the tests, and the way they all looked at me, I knew instinctively that my time was running out.

'I could often hear snatches of conversation, as Sloane and his men passed my door, and this evening I learnt that Branston and Davies were going into Glasgow to the other laboratory, to pick up some additional apparatus and drugs. It strengthened my belief that they had decided the time had come to put me away.

'All the time I had been a prisoner, my one overriding thought was how to escape. No clear-cut opportunity ever presented itself, however, so now I decided that I must try out the one idea that had occurred to me during the long weeks of my captivity. The success of it depended on two pieces of wood, which I had seen lying in the laboratory and had managed to smuggle back to my room. One was only about a cubic inch in size, the other was flat and about three inches square. Both were probably off-cuts of the wood used in the recent modernization, which Sloane had commissioned, and since I had got them back to my room I had worked furiously on them, paring down the small cube and honing the square piece until it was wedge shaped. My only tools were the floor and wall, which I used as though they were sandpaper.

'In the early evening, Branston came to take me to the laboratory for more tests.

' "Come with me," he instructed from the doorway and, without waiting, walked ahead of me.

'The door was secured by a yale lock with the keyhole on the outside. Inside, however, the usual opening mechanism was missing. As I left the room, I slipped the small block of wood in the hole, into which the lock normally springs when the door is drawn shut. I breathed a sigh of relief that Branston didn't look round and that the wooden block, though fitting flush, was still tight enough not to fall out. It was the first piece of luck I'd had in a very long time and it was certainly overdue.

'Sloane only kept me for a few minutes and when he had finished he said to Branston.

' "Right, I'll prepare the list and tell Davies to get the car out of the garage. Take her back and then be on your way. As it is, it'll be after midnight by the time you return."

'Sloane left the laboratory without as much as another glance at me and Branston stood and watched me put on my cardigan before escorting me back to my room.

'When I was inside, he pulled the door shut behind me and in the split second before he leant on it to ensure that the yale had caught, I thrust the wedge into the crack near the lock and pushed with all my weight. It held against his push and I heard his footsteps moving away up the stairs.

'With my heart thumping I pulled out the wedge and fearfully tried the door, hoping that the small block of wood had kept it from locking. I sobbed with relief when the door opened. It had worked! I stepped out into the passage, picked out the piece of wood, and drew the door shut behind me. Then I moved softly up the stairs and peered out of the door at the top, into the dimly lit hall. The air was as cold and clammy as I remembered it when I first arrived at the house. It seemed so long ago.

'At that moment I heard a car pull up at the front door and footsteps coming up the steps. I ducked back out of sight as Davies entered the house and strode across the hall towards a door at the far side.

'It was now or never. I crept through the hall but paused at the door when I heard the rain falling outside. A raincoat was hanging just inside the door and on an impulse I grabbed it, drew it on, and slipped out. Looking frantically around, I realized it would be madness to run off into the night in this remote part of the country. I had no idea how far the nearest house was and I would be lost in five minutes. On top of that, they might have dogs which could track me down before I reached safety. I decided that I must ride my luck to the full, so I ran down the steps, hauled open the boot of the car and climbed in, pulling it shut behind me.

'A few minutes later I heard voices coming from the house and then approaching the car. If they opened the boot, for any reason, I was lost, and I held my breath as one of the men walked round behind the car. I was sure he must hear the pounding of my heart as he passed within inches, but he kept going and climbed in and slammed the door. The engine started and I wept with relief as I felt us pulling away from that hellish place.

'I was bitterly cold and terribly uncomfortable in the boot, but I didn't mind. I knew that with every minute, I was being taken nearer to civilization and safety. I thought how angry and frustrated Sloane would be when he brought me my supper to find me gone. I wondered if he would suspect that I had stolen a ride in the car, but in any case he had no way of contacting Branston and Davies to find out, at least not until they reached the laboratory.

'The thought made me tingle with renewed fear. Of course he could phone the laboratory in Glasgow constantly and when they eventually answered, they would be told and would doubtless race back to the lodge. This meant that I had to get out of the car as soon as it stopped.

'After what seemed an eternity, I guessed that we must be approaching the city from the increasing sound of passing cars. It being late in the evening and wet, though, there was relatively little traffic about to hold up our progress and so our first real stop was at our destination. I heard Branston get out of the car.

' "You go on up and I'll back in off the road," Davies called out to him.

'I was in a panic as I knew Branston might be made aware of my disappearance as soon as he entered the building. The car reversed, painfully slowly it seemed, the engine stopped and Davies got out. I waited ten seconds and then heaved open the boot, leapt out and ran for my life. I thought I heard shouts behind me, but I didn't even dare to glance back. All the time I looked for someone to help me, but there was no one about until I saw you.'

The fire had burnt low as Linda completed her incredible story. All through, Paul had listened silently, without comment, but as she finished, he saw that the fear and agitation had returned. The recent memory of her ordeal and the nerve-racking escape had caught up with her again.

He placed a calming hand on her shoulder and took the empty mug from her.

'Take it easy,' he said gently. 'You're quite safe now.'

'But they might have seen me come in here and be waiting for me,' she cried.

'I don't think so. Anyway, we won't take any chances. I'll telephone for the police and get them to come and pick you up, all right?'

'Oh, yes please,' she said gratefully.

He rose to put on his coat.

'Where are you going?' she asked.

'To telephone. The nearest box is down the road, but it won't take me five minutes.'

'You aren't going to leave me are you?' she gasped.

'I'll have to, unless you want to come with me.'

'Oh, no, I couldn't go out into those streets again,' she protested.

'That's what I thought,' he agreed. 'But you'll be perfectly all right here. Lock the door when I've gone and I won't be long.'

He smiled, but failed to banish the look of fear that was engraved on her lovely face.

'Please be quick,' she pleaded.

'I will,' he assured her. 'And don't let anyone in till I get back.'

She waited alone with bated breath. Every sound made her heart leap fearfully and when the knock came on the door at last, she jumped nervously.

'Who is it?' she whispered.

'Paul,' said the muffled voice and, with a grateful sob, she drew back the bolt and opened the door.

The relief on her face faded when she saw the two men standing there. One of them was big and bearded, the other was younger with a thin face and close-set eyes. Linda knew that her freedom was at an end and in that split second all her hopes crumbled in overwhelming despair. Fate had been playing a cruel cat and mouse game with her all along. It had never intended that she should escape. She had no fight left and Branston's warning was totally unnecessary.

'If you make a sound, I'll be forced to hit you,' he said.

'Doctor Sloane is very worried and angry,' Davies admonished her, as though she were a naughty child.

'How did you know his name?' was all she could think to say.

'It was on the nameplate on the door,' Davies explained simply.

'Come on,' said Branston, taking her arm.

In dazed resignation she walked out of the cosy warmth of the flat, leaving the door ajar. The two men closed in on either side of her and they descended the echoing stairway to the waiting car below.

When Paul returned to his flat a few minutes later to find Linda gone, he did not know what to think. Neither was his uncertainty in any way dispelled by the two policemen who eventually arrived in a squad car.

'Sounds a pretty far-fetched tale if you ask me,' commented one of them, when Paul had finished his story, repeating in as much detail as he could remember, what Linda had told him.

'I'm not so sure,' he said doubtfully. 'She was absolutely terrified of something, I'm certain of that.'

'Well, there doesn't appear to be anything else we can do here tonight,' said the other policeman, finally closing his notebook. 'Of course, you will let us know if she returns, won't you, sir?'

'Surely there are several facts which you can check out,' insisted Paul.

'We'll make our report, sir,' the first policeman assured him. 'And you can be sure that everything will be checked out that can be. Now we'll bid you goodnight.'

Paul wandered thoughtfully round the living room when they had gone. Her story had certainly seemed far fetched, but somehow in his heart he knew that Linda Reynolds was in very great danger. Furthermore, there was nothing he could do about it.

Paul Rogers was right.

In the laboratory beneath the old hunting lodge, Doctor Sloane's experiments in suspended animation had reached a grim personal finale for Linda Reynolds.

As if in a hypnotic trance, she walked out of the room from which she had escaped, only a few hours before, with such high hopes. Branston's light grip on her arm guided her into the laboratory, where Sloane and Davies waited.

'You have put us to a lot of trouble,' Sloane intoned, as though repeating a centuries-old incantation. 'It means that I will now have to take extra precautions in case the authorities ask awkward questions, although it will make no difference to you.'

Linda showed no sign that she had even heard him. Her face was calm, all emotion and fear having drained away. She was now far beyond tears and terror, and hope.

When Sloane nodded, his assistants made the preliminary preparations. Although the low temperatures were expected to take care of any bacteria, every precaution had to be taken before the final processing.

She neither hindered nor helped them while they stripped her of all her clothes. Her beautiful long hair was cropped as close as possible before her scalp was shaved to the bone, and then her entire body, too, was carefully and meticulously shaved of all its hair. She was bathed and placed in a steam container until her pores had surrendered every molecule of dirt. Jets of hot air were then directed over her to dry her skin.

Sloane watched his assistants in silence until at last he was satisfied and the girl lay naked on a cold sterilized table. Her eyes met his in a blank stare as he stood over her, a hypodermic poised in his hand.

'The time has come,' he announced solemnly. 'Apart from a slight prick from this needle, you will feel no pain. After that, you will see nothing more, although a little later you will hear us storing you away. Then I'm afraid it will be an eternal silence.'

She gazed unseeingly at the ceiling above her as he plunged the needle into her arm.

They worked quickly and expertly on her body during the next few hours. Finally, when all the blood had been drained from her and been replaced by a glyco-saline solution, which would not expand in the extreme cold and rupture her organs, she was placed in a bright green metal canister. Wires were attached to her body to be connected up with the instruments in the lower chamber, to which they carried her in her scientifically prepared coffin. Sloane adjusted some switches and the temperature in the canister started to fall rapidly.

'Close it,' he said at last and the lid was lowered and sealed. The canister was manhandled into the opening in the wall, which had been prepared for it, and the two assistants quickly completed the entombment by bricking in the entrance.

Sloane took a last look at their handiwork and, as he turned towards the stairs, murmured to himself. 'You will hate me now, my dear, but in a hundred years you might think differently.'

THE CURE

By Dorothy K. Haynes

THE WOMEN came early, calling and crowding at the door. 'Are you ready, Missis? We thought we'd go with you for the company, like. Just one or two of us . . .'

'You might want some help with the boy.'

She had not bargained for that. All night she had lain awake and worried, and now she had made up her mind. She would do as the neighbours said; but if David was to go, he must go with her alone, so that he could change his mind and run back if he wanted to. After all, he might be twelve years old, but he was little more than a baby.

She told them, but they would not listen. 'You're too soft with him, Mrs Weir. I wouldn't put up with his capers.'

'It's time he started acting like a man. With his father gone, you could do with a man in the house.'

Her lips were white, but she kept her temper, seeing their food on the table, and so many other things, the very coat the boy was wearing. 'I told you I'd bring him. You can come if you want to; but I'll need time. It's not a thing you can do in a minute.'

They withdrew, not very willingly, and she stood crumpling her apron, looking down at her son. The clock whirred, but did not strike, and the lid of the kettle lifted on a slow puff of steam. 'Come on, David,' she said, trying to force a sprightliness into her voice. 'Wash your face, now. I've warmed the water for you.'

The boy did not answer. He hardly ever answered, and sometimes she wondered if he heard properly. Unless, of course, it was too much bother to him to speak. Everything was a bother to him nowadays.

'Do you hear me, son? You can't go up dirty.'

The child began to blubber, his face turned to the fire. 'I don't want to go,' he mumbled. 'I don't *want* to!'

A finger tapped at the window and a face peered through the pane, and suddenly, her anger at the neighbours was transferred to her son, so that, for the moment, the fear of failure was less than the fear of his being a coward. She went over to the fire and shook the snivelling boy by the shoulder. 'Get up now, David. Wash your face and get outside. Do you think your father made this fuss when *he* went?'

It was cruel, but the snivelling stopped. Wiping his eyes, David got up and laved his eyes at the basin. His legs trembled, thin as sticks, but he said nothing as his mother brushed the hair out of his eyes and straightened his clothes. 'Now,' she said. 'It's for your own good, son. Don't look, don't think. Just walk straight on, and keep your eyes shut at the end . . .'

Holding his hand, her own hand trembling, she led him outside, and his weak eyes screwed against the sun. The clouds were incredibly white, puffed up and sailing, the trees and grass too green to be true. He had not been out for so long . . . the brightness puckered her own forehead, so that she looked at the ground; and then she forced herself to face the neighbours.

They stared at her, impatient, their faces half hidden in their great hoods, and she could see that they were itching to get away up the hill. She did not want to see them gabbing and whispering in front of her. Her lips quivering, she held her son's hand tighter, and went to the head of the procession.

They went slowly, because the road was bad, full of spring puddles and ruts and potholes. There were great splashes of dung where cattle had passed, and all the gutters were swimming. The houses leaned over the street, one side in sun, the other in shadow, and everywhere windows opened, and heads poked out to ask questions. 'Davie Weir,' the women who were following told them. 'Going to be *touched*. Him whose father was hanged,' and the word was passed back, eagerly, impatiently, to the old folk by the fire. 'Dick Weir's wife. Taking her son to the gallows. Up to the *gallows*!'

'Oh!' They had heard of it, this dreadful thing, the old

superstition that the touch of a hanged corpse could heal, but few of them had seen it carried out. There weren't so many hangings nowadays. There had been no excitement in the town since Dick Weir had been hoisted a month ago, and there were some people who said that the law had been too hard on him. Weir had always been a sober, steady man, but his son was a weakling, never without coughs or fevers or aches in his bones, and the only way for a poor man to get medicine and dainties was by stealing.

Well, now that he was dead, it looked as if he might be more use to the boy than when he was alive. It was worth going to find out. The weavers came from their narrow houses, fluff in their hair, their looms silent. The baker left his shop, and a smell of new bread came with him, warm and delicious. He stuck his floury hands in his apron and ambled after the crowd, and the blacksmith left his forge to the apprentice and the horses stamping and jingling in the gloom. 'Going to be *touched*,' they mouthed, and nodded to each other. 'Dick Weir's son,' and they shook their heads with the pity of it; but there was a brightness and stir about the morning, just as there had been a month ago, and more of the people followed on, Old Andra, the bellringer, the two idiots who were propped all day against the church railings, and a squatter of children whose mothers were glad to be rid of them for a while.

The woman walked on, leading her son, seeing and acknowledging no one. She had not been out since the hanging, and it was like the first walk after illness, light-headed and unreal. She could not fix her mind on what would happen at the top of the hill; and maybe Dick had been the same. It should have been a comfort to her; but surely he must have realized, as the chains were put on him, and he faced away over the wide view . . . He had always been an outdoor man. He must have screamed and fought, if he were human. She herself, sitting with the boy, had stuffed her hands into her mouth till she choked. Outside, the noise had increased, and then quietened again, except for one awful sound, like a groan or a sigh, that she heard, and yet did not hear; then the people had come back to the streets again, in twos and threes, but they did not tell her what it had been like. 'He carried himself well,' was all they said.

They had been more than good to her. She had looked for work, cleaning or washing at the big houses, but nobody would employ a woman whose husband had been hanged. It was the neighbours who kept her going with small gifts, oil for the lamp, loaves and logs, and their company in case she felt lonely.

Sometimes she almost longed for loneliness. They were kind, but they never left her, talking, talking from dawn till dark. They sat about the kitchen, loth to forget about the hanging and let the excitement die. She did not want to speak about her husband. What she wanted was quite to remember him – or to forget. They asked about David, and tried to rally him, and laugh him out of his turns, and she could not explain that David did not like to be teased. Everything was out of order. There was spilt milk on the table, and the fire smouldered bitterly; but without the neighbours there would have been no milk and no fire.

And then, out of kindness, they made their suggestion, a word, a nudge, a hint behind the hands.

'They say it's a great cure, Missis. Rachael, the orphan, they took her . . .'

'You owe it to your son, Missis. What's a wee unpleasantness? He's not too far gone . . .'

'No!' she screamed at them. 'I couldn't! It's not right . . .'

'It's his own father,' they argued. 'If you thought anything of the boy . . .'

She was angry at that, but they kept their patience, talk, talk, talk, till at last, out of weariness and dutiful gratitude, she gave in.

Up past the school, where the houses began to thin out, the path mounted the hill. Lambs leaped, wobbly-legged, and the turf smelled sweet. They climbed like pilgrims, stopping sometimes because the boy was tired, and soon the ones behind began to press forward to see what was happening. They looked ahead, pointing to the top of the hill, but Mrs Weir and her son never looked up. She kept her head down, and led the boy by the arm, like a blind man.

The ground was levelling now, and a wind blew against their faces. The woman felt rather than saw what was about her; behind, the babble of voices, and in front, nothing but a faint swish, like cloth rubbing on wood, and a sickly smell . . .

The boy looked sideways at her, for guidance. His face was sick, green-looking, but she could not help him. She could not lift her hands to cover her eyes, although what was above seemed to be drawing her. She stood there, as if in prayer, and there was nothing she could do. Nothing.

Suddenly, one of the women pushed forward, grabbed the boy by the waist, and half lifted him. 'Go on, son. Up. Let him touch you . . .'

Something creaked, and chains clinked a little. Other hands lifted him up from behind, thrusting roughly, hurting him. 'That's it. His hand . . .'

He was light in their arms, for all his struggles. His eyes were tight shut, but his fists threshed pettishly, landing weak blows on arms and faces. Higher they pushed him, and there was something on his shoulder, cold, listless, something that slid off again uncaringly. The boy began to scream, shrilly, thinly, and at the sound his mother looked up, in spite of herself.

She made no sound, but her breath gagged back in her mouth, and her face was grey. This limp thing, bumping about like a sack, this was not her husband. If it had been recognizable, it would have broken her heart. Now, she felt only fear of it, the thin hair fluttering, the faint whiff of decay as it swung. Even the clamorous women were retreating, their handkerchiefs spread to their faces. The body turned again, grinning and suddenly she felt herself swinging with it, round and round and down in a cold dampness and roaring . . .

And then, her son was beside her, no longer screaming. His thin arms circled her, his slight body leaned in to support her. There were tears on his cheeks, and his mouth puckered childishly with crying, but there was the first hint of maturity in his face. 'Get away!' he shouted to the crowds pressing in to stare at him. 'Get away from her. Can't you leave us alone?'

'Davie!' His mother shivered, and pulled at his sleeve to

quieten him. 'Mind yourself now, Davie. They wanted to help—'

'Look at them,' he said.

Her hands at her mouth, her mouth nibbling, she looked, and the hooded women stared back at her, callous, curious, licking their lips over the drama. For a moment, it seemed to her that the judge and the hangman were innocent, and that these were the real people who had strung her husband on the gibbet.

But now it no longer mattered. She stood in a daze, her hands still at her mouth, and her son seemed to tower above her, older, wiser, with infinite power to protect. As he pushed forward, they fell away on each side of him, the weavers, the blacksmith, and the mob who had followed for the fun of it. He passed through them without a glance. They stood for all the things he had learned and spurned at the foot of the gallows – the poverty that forced a man to steal, the cruelty of those who hanged him; and the ignorance of those who, even now, were rejoicing that the touch of a hanged corpse could really heal.

THE IMAGE OF THE DAMNED

By Alex Hamilton

I SERVED MY apprenticeship with heads which impatient hands tore from mine, in order to set them on pikes. It could be said, therefore, that almost from the start the efforts of my fingers were succeeded by frantic applause from the gallery. I cannot forget how they cheered – the executioners for hurrying, myself for taking my time. These frantic, clambering wretches who thronged to see the guillotine fall, who fought, literally, for better vantage points on roof gutters and tradesmen's ladders, gave their workaday, sporting plaudits to the executioners who loomed over the scaffold, and their respectful souls to me, who worked in wax in its shadow. But it was chance that it happened that way; I would not have chosen to begin with the dead, but I was young and opportunist and I seized my chance. An artist looks for power only to use it – power, at the moment that my fingers first felt their dexterity, chanced to be in the hands of cut-throats. It gave a direction to my life, but the sequel was my own doing.

In the later days of my fame my waxes have been applauded by soft and delicate palms. I have bowed, and been sleek and grateful (for there is power and patronage in white, feminine palms) but their acknowledgement of my skill, like the sound of velvet waterfalls in the halls of the great, has never ceased to evoke for me that first stupendous, crashing enthusiasm of the mob, at a time when a white uncalloused hand was an offending hand. Spontaneous applause, unfaked and unreflective, is the one influence, among so many, that we who worked in wax share with artists in every medium. Once in my life I had a tribute to my work which went beyond the praise of any palms, be they white as bridal sheets, be they red as scaffold steps.

Who knows what strange superstition in the revolutionaries compelled these beasts, who wanted to obliterate a world, to perpetuate the image of their dead in wax? Was it first as a joke that they caused poor Marie Grosholtz (whom you may know as Mme Tussaud), that sweet Royalist lady, to cast the death masks of so many of her friends? Was it as a rider to this bitter jest that they brought me from the slaughterhouse, who had never used better material for his little statues than the tallow melted down from ox-tripes, to help her? They thought my aplomb was due to the oceans of blood I had seen flow in the abattoir, but they were wrong. I learnt it from Marie who saw, not a herd going to its death, but every time a separate, special way of meeting death which is not to be found in ox and sheep and swine. Look at her waxes – she was an artist.

And we had our revenges. In time we collected the executioners themselves. The terrorist Robespierre sneezed into the basket and we blew his nose for him. Charlotte Corday dealt with Marat in his bath, and we were tempted to agree with her that he died not as a man but as a beast – only the scruples of our art overcame this human weakness. And then came the great day when the public accuser himself, Fouquier-Tinville, whispered 'I am not well – I see the shadows of the dead following me.' It was indeed a mortal sickness – how dark with shadows must the basket have looked to Fouquier-Tinville, when he in his turn waited those seconds before the knife fell.

Of course Marie herself worked on in this shambles with the knowledge that the joke might cease to be amusing – at which point she would no doubt be invited to take a ride in a tumbril. Only once did she ever reveal this thought to me, when she remarked quietly, one day when more heads had been severed than we had wax for, that she 'hoped when you are required by the new despots to make the image of Marie Grosholtz, you will remember the mind that animated her, not merely the sin that killed her. In her case at least, you have had the opportunity of study.'

Naturally I answered that I did not believe it could ever come to that, and I thank the fates that it never did. 'Shame,' they used to say to us, 'lies not in the scaffold but in the crime,' but had she died there, I could not have endured to work on without her. Yet that exchange between us itself deepened my understanding of her, and the attention she gave to her – because of her I can say *our* – art. She taught me not merely the secret process of mixing chalk and clay and paint, and the potency of wax, but the deeper, more secret routes into the psyche of our subjects. She taught me to understand the skeleton as the natural man, and to study whether the flesh had been its friend or its enemy. From these beginnings I came to perceive how many men and women conceal themselves from themselves. And I perceived the beginning of knowledge in myself when one night, during that time of carnage, I picked up with a plump young trollop in a tavern, and did her will, to drive the reeking daylight scenes from my brain, only to see behind the fat thighs and globular breasts of a carefree voluptuary, the suffering femur and close little ribs of a seamstress. But I fancy that another man would never have seen any deeper than her dimples. All the same we made love? Of course. I'm not daft. And I'm not wax – yet.

We knew the prison officers, Marie and I. She made it plain that was important. I thought at first that she insisted on this for the sake of our own survival, but as the business got into my blood and the joke turned to earnest, I realized again that all this great little lady's reasons derived from the love of her art. I was to get to know the workings of the prisons, the tricks and the triumphs of the men who administered them, their dust and their damps, their corridors and cells, their tortures and their pleasures-on-the-side, their very architecture and where the light might fall on a murderer's pallet – for a great scheme of hers which I was to bring to fruition. We would travel the world together with waxen figures – hers would be the gallery of the famous, while my lot, my province, my novelty, would be the infamous. 'You shall see,' she said, 'how grand you will become with your chamber of horrors.'

I need not tell you how true a prophet she was. I am bold enough in my turn to prophecy that our collection will last until the sun comes close enough to melt not only our waxes but the flesh of the men who guard it. I owe it all to Marie, but she would not say I have not repaid the debt. She lent me a talent and, as the parable recommends, I have returned it ten-fold. This, I avow, at some cost to the shape of my own flesh, which has compromised with my virtuous skeleton. For in the dreams which shrouded my working studies I have lifted the knives of murderers, yes and scissors and hatchets too, to drive them into quivering, startled flesh. I have brooded over poisons in hidden cabinets, and uttered hypocritical kindnesses at the bedside of stricken victims. I have laid my sights along the massed barrels of a regicide's infernal machine, and watched the random blast extinguishing the lives of blameless spec-tators. I have waited down alleys with the stink of cabbage and fish-heads carried in the fog about me, with a hook in my hand and walnut juice darkening my skin, to sweep the pedestrian with a few shillings into oblivion. I have torn the clothing from women foolish enough to cross the heath while the moon was a baby, and like a baby swaddled – in clouds. And I've begged them, exhorted them, prayed to them, not to struggle while I doused the ungovernable brand at my crotch; and then cursed them for obliging me to quench their spark of life.

All these and a thousand other mazes I wandered, in search of the quality of the Minotaur, talking in condemned cells to men and women who in the main had not known the maze lay beyond the picturesque kissing-gate where they entered. And I must not forget that there were among these creatures of strange experiences a certain few whose flesh was at one with their unnatural skeletons. I waxed them accordingly, while they looked on with a smile and usually, before I had done, they were offering me their clothes, to perfect the job! Well, of course I accepted graciously, and forbore telling them that was the arrangement I had with the executioners anyway, that for a consideration they should rescue the clothes from the line. These were the criminals whose appetite was whetted by my activities, who made a hearty meal of their last dinner on pig and plum sauce, and smacked their lips at the idea of im-mortality in my chamber.

For the great majority, however, the moment when their cell door was unlocked for me, and my pots and my colours, was a dreadful moment. It was the instant of doom itself. For I liked time in which to work, and to get time I had to make my decision long before the jury came to theirs. In prison every man's action has its special meaning, every gesture and expression carries its prediction of hope or despair, and when we had removed to England and my career was set on a regular, official footing, my purpose was clear enough to the inmates. Once it was known that I had a 'nose' for a conviction, even the Governor understood that the scaffold carpenters could be called upon to look out their equipment. I did not discourage the spread of my reputation as a shrewd tradesman – in England particularly it is the quality above all others which bears with it the idea of discretion of word and action. I came and went from my appointed rendezvous without interference. As my little gallery grew I was proud to play host, in my turn, to all the elements of the law. There were the men who had apprehended the miscreants, the turnkeys who had helped me, the prison officers who preened themselves before the evidence of their usefulness to society, the Members of Parliament who went from my presence with a renewed assurance that the country was in need of more stringent measures to make war on the underworld. Lastly – I at least could pick them out from our visitors – we welcomed the underworld itself, awed at my skill and fearful of being the object of my special study.

All these, and the thousands who came in off the streets to stare, to remember, and to fall silent if the idea crossed their minds that these deadly figures were not unlike those living beings among whom they were then jostling, gave me praise for the verisimilitude of my craftsmanship, and I never wearied of it. But an artist is never content – he is always hoping for an event which will be a proof of his mastery, beyond all critical expression that his fellows can utter. Of all the tributes which were given me, none pleased me more than the astonished children who shrank into the skirts of their mothers at sight of my waxen rogues – but even this fell somewhat short of unqualified proof of success. You may have seen me, passing through your town on tour with our collection, and you may have heard me speak, gracefully acknowledging the world's enthusiasm. But you have never before heard from me of the event which gave me proof positive. Until now the secret has been kept as faithfully as we have guarded the knowledge of how we make up our wax. I tell it now because my fingers are stiffening and the wax will no longer mould as my still-eager mind would have it – I shall never again lift the knocker at Newgate.

Very often patrons of our show inquire why we do not include the Hon James Berrisford among our exhibits. To which I am wont to reply that an untimely aggravation of the chronic gout, which had first afflicted me in the days when I stood ankle deep in the slaughterhouse bloodbath, crippled me and kept me in my bed during the time that that remarkable rake awaited sentence and the carrying out of that same. But the truth is elsewhere. The truth is that I was never so well in my life, that I spent many hours until the very eve of the execution date with the Hon James and that the wax that I made of him, with his generous help and well-informed comment, was among the very best of my creations, fit to stand in the front rank before royalty itself. But neither the curious eye of royalty, nor the speculative eye of the paying customer, ever looked into the defiant blue of the eyes I set into my study of the Hon James.

He had been a great gambler, of a kind that Crockford's, in these weak days when women have more bottom than the men, never sees. He would gamble thousands on a race between two unknown beggars, on the breed of the next dog to come round the corner, on the depth of a newly-discovered cave, on the leader in next day's *Times*, on the colour of a beauty's under-pinnings. It was while resolving a bet of this last kind that he gambled on the absence of the lady's husband and, while he won the first part of the bet, he lost the second. The cuckold died there that night, and he was brought to justice.

He made a brave figure in the dock, being tall and well-built, while I flatter myself that among observers I was one of the very few who could read the story of his dissipations in his countenance. So at the outset he was not without his sympathizers among the fair who flocked into the well of the court. Had these ladies troubled to ask my advice they would have stayed away – a court is a kennel for the hounds of fate: once in it there is no reputation, however gay, which can long sustain itself without being torn to splinters of greed and the bleeding tissue of lust. Shall I ever forget the shock on the faces of his admirers when it became plain that the greatest erotic capacity that the Hon James could muster was a direct consequence of his laying a wager? Then only could he guarantee his ante. As this whisper spread I could see, looking about me, that they would not forgive him for that. It was, as I say, a whisper that put the news about – which I believe m'Lud was never conscious of, for had he been so, he would most certainly have cleared the court in a trice and conducted the remainder in camera. Nevertheless there was enough said in question and answer, appearing in the records, to prove the Hon James Berrisford thought and felt very differently from the ways natural to flesh and blood (and not forgetting, bone). Those who wish to look up the records may do so – I will only here recall the amazing defence of the Hon James that he had sat down to cards with the lady's husband, while she looked on from the great four-poster, and played for it and all it contained. Her evidence corroborated this, but took the story farther perhaps than he had bargained. For she averred that when her husband lost (and thereupon put a pistol ball through his right eye), she turned away from her lover in horror, and now for the first time, in all the long parade of his gallantry, was he able and determined to possess her in good earnest. The Hon James Berrisford was sentenced to wear the devil's hempen collar, not for murder, but for rape.

Myself, already interested in the Hon James as a potential subject, had no need wait on this conclusion before preparing my wax. The facts which led me to appear in his cell while there were yet five-and-thirty witnesses to be called, were plain to me in the list of women tabled for a hearing by the prosecution. They were four, much above average in their looks, with money enough to show these to advantage – and all of them recent widows. It was as obvious as their heaving bosoms that they lined up as the Hon James's winning streak, which now at last was ended. As I sat in my regular seat at the Bailey (which the ushers are now kind enough to reserve for me on those days when I am detained by urgent business when the court first sits), you can suppose that I figured myself a pretty tableau for our show, with pink and blue lights playing on handsome shoulders. The public for wax loves a story revealing passion in the quality. I am not insensible to it myself – more especially when I have been the architect of its presentation, and am able to gloss it with anecdotes learnt from the mouths of the principals.

Once having determined (or let vaulting ambition determine) the intention of a tableau, it behoved me to work with some expedition. My days I spent in making sketches of the prosecution's armoury of ladies, to play them into an extra dimension at my leisure. Otherwhiles I was engaged chiefly with the accused man himself and . . . But I am resolved to hide nothing, since milady did not. She was gracious and complaisant enough to allow me the great bed itself, at cost. And previous to its removal from her boudoir she attired herself in the same shift she wore on the fatal night. Thus deliciously disposed, she assumed the posture of anxious vigilance she had taken while those two gambling men laid the burden of decision on a pack of cards. She was pleased as I worked to inquire if my mind dwelt always on the 'straight line to posterity'. And in the same spirit I answered that I was able to find as much joy in the contemplation of the perfect curve of a posterior. The practice of my art necessitates on occasion some indulgence in sentiment.

No concessions of any kind were required in furtherance of work on the centrepiece of my grand design, whose impact on an admiring world would be doubled if I could exhibit it for the first time on the very morning our egregious gambler finally turned in his chips. From the moment that I entered his cell to make his acquaintance, and he appreciated that the playing-out of his hand was henceforth a mere formality, I had not the least trouble in securing his interest and support. In his solicitous care to ensure that I was master of every detail of mind and body, so that the facsimile might be perfect, his conduct was exemplary. Once he knew from me that he must hang, he showed the breeding of an earlier age, before the Jacobin virus infected the common mind everywhere with envy and hatred, and destroyed the belief of the aristocracy in their own blood. It is my opinion that nature intended the Hon James to be a first-born son, for he was far worthier of the title than his elder brother. Once I expressed this view to him, and he replied that eldest sons were the real prisoners today – of tradesmen and their columns of figures. He said it very well, considering that at the moment of the remark he was surrounded by walls thirty inches thick, and a ring of destruction even more impenetrable was closing on him.

An account of the whole life of the Hon James is not to my purpose here, though he supplied it all when he understood my concern to be clear how flesh and skeleton might have combined or fought in his case. He told me all, and a tenth of it might have been enough to bring his trial to a summary conclusion, had I wished to retail it to the authorities. But of course his great quality as a gambler was the instinctive perception of every hand played, and he saw that I was among those who play for keeps. In my turn I spoke with great frankness and he paid me the compliment of being a most attentive listener. He was most admiring of my diligence in researching the byways of the penal system, and heartily entertained by my account of the intimate relationship I had undergone to secure a true wax of his paramour. 'More truth perhaps, my dear fellow,' he inquired at the end, 'than you could expect wax to convey?' Which suggestion I was confident enough to deny. This assurance seemed to intensify the enthusiasm of his interest in the wax of himself, if that were possible.

Such was our mutual encouragement and my absorption in my task, which I had begun to hope might evolve a masterpiece, that the court proceedings dwindled into the background, as a shallow mockery of reality. The concluding speeches, the verdict and the sentence came and went as almost imperceptible scratches in the armour of our concentration. (Though I was obliged for periods to break off, to secure waxes of the other ladies who must take a place in my tableau, they were cooked, one might say, as vegetable adjuncts in a heat controlled to perfect the roast. I owe the phrase to the ever-active brain of the Hon James.)

It was a scene which must have affected even the turnkeys, had their fancy ever been capable of soaring free of those dreary catacombs, when two nights before the dawn appointed for his execution, I at last stood back from the wax, and he wrung my hand and declared that it only wanted breath to be himself. From the look in his eye, he added, he was sure the thing was pining for a gamble. In the fullness of my heart I swore that if it were a gamble he wanted, as his last pleasure on earth, I would endeavour to provide him with one.

He seemed struck with the idea, and paced about the cell several turns before speaking again. Then he came forward and put out both arms, said gravely 'I am in your power!' and dropped them again. He stood motionless, his attitude a replica of the posture I had given his copy. It was, naturally, an attitude very characteristic of him. But whether the urgency of completing my task had led me to overtire myself, or the burden of the impending break between us had suddenly become too heavy, I cannot say, but seeing the two of them, identical, resplendent with action, my head seemed to swim for a minute, and I was unable to distinguish which was the Hon James, and which the copy. I said nothing for a time – had I spoken I might have imitated those credulous visitors to our show who address the dummies in the apparent hope of communication with them.

Then, after an unconscionable pause, he moved again and I felt the warm blood of his hand on mine. 'You are a great artist, my dear fellow,' he said, 'for you've put into the wax even those elements which you have never yourself experienced. That wax speaks the excitement of the gambler about to make a great *coup*!' I looked at the wax, and thought it a fair judgement. I shook my head. 'The credit,' I responded, 'belongs equally to you. You have entered voluntarily into the make-up of the wax itself.'

'What a lark,' he remarked, his lips smiling, but his eyes glittering with a quality deeper than laughter, 'if they should hang the wax and the original go free!' I heard the words, but they merely echoed the message I had already read in his eyes. I said softly, speaking willy-nilly, out of habit, as a partner: 'Then my tableau would be missing its central figure.' He laughed outright, triumphantly: 'I will stand in its place.' He stood back and observed me, and whispered 'My dear fellow, I do believe you are beginning actually to experience the excitement of a gamble. Is there anything in this world to beat it?' I must confess there is not – but it was his next argument which really persuaded me to throw in my hand with his: 'You have told me that it is Mr Marwood's pride that between his entry into the condemned cell and the movement of his hand on the lever to let the trapdoor fall, a mere eleven seconds elapses. He is an old friend of yours – I make no doubt that a wax of Mr Marwood travels in your show. If he were persuaded to join in – and I can muster a jolly sum to help him make up his mind – the thing might be done. And then, my dear old miracle-worker, what a tribute to your art might be included in your epitaph!' Of all my subjects, the Hon James Berrisford was the only one to have seen past the contours of my flesh, to the skeleton in me which lived before, and lives after. I shook his hand in silence and the deal was made. Then we put our heads together for the details.

The following night, in the early hours which should have preceded the execution, my perfect work of art was laid under a blanket in the condemned cell, and I bore out on my shoulder the nearly naked, living body of the Hon James Berrisford, with his face and hands and feet lightly waxed over, and the rest of him wrapped in a canvas. He maintained rigidity of pose with the concentration of a gymnast, and before we made our exit his muscles must have ached even more than mine. But for the rest, it was easier than you might have expected. For

neither the silent prisoners we passed in their cells, nor the
turnkeys padding down the corridors, were willing to gaze on
even the wax of a man who must quit this life in a few hours.
Indeed I was already used to this reaction, for to them no
doubt, as I went out with my trophies, I must have
seemed like the shadow of death some hours in advance of its
time.

At the gate of the prison waited the conveyance which I had
arranged, to remove us to the secrecy of the exhibition. This
secrecy would be brilliantly cast aside under the eyes of the
thousands we expected to visit us, a short hour after the news
of execution was posted on the prison gates. The interval
passed more slowly for us than it does for any condemned man,
albeit we were busy enough – for not merely had the Hon
James to be clothed in the articles the wax would have worn,
but it was necessary he should stand on his pedestal and there
be waxed over, early enough for the patina to be dry before the
crowds should come to cast their rapt scrutiny upon him. I had
little mental energy to spare for jokes, but the Hon James kept
up a running fire of pleasantries, even when the wax allowed
only his lips to move. I remember especially that as he mounted
his stand he appreciatively surveyed the tableau and con-
gratulated me on the circles of ladies. 'The fear that confronts
me now,' he said, 'is that this excitement will have its wonted
effect, and I shall give everything away by enfolding one of
these beautiful creatures in my passionate embrace!' The
witticism was plausible enough to make me tremble, and I
begged him to face away from them if that were the case. He
reassured me, saying that he was too old a gambler not to be
able to distinguish between the game and the spoils; nevertheless it was some time before I could steady my hand sufficiently
to proceed with my work.

It was always chilly in that subterranean chamber, for we
never allowed the heat of summer to mar the tone of our
waxes. But for all that, a further sudden fall in the temperature
seemed to invade the precincts as the first notes of Newgate's
great bell, tolling for a departed villain, assaulted our ears.
Briefly a faint ironic smile touched the Hon James's lips, as the

sonorous echoes swirled about us. His gaze settled on the ormolu clock which had once been on the mantelpiece of Marie Antoinette, whose severed head Marie had cast, and had passed into the possession of her executioner and from him into my hands, when I took the impression of *his* severed head. The clock now showed a few beats before eight, and with every throb of its movement the golden spot of satisfaction glistened more brightly in the eye of the Hon James.

But I could not smile, nor could my own dilated pupil have evinced other than the blackest and deepest horror. For in that chamber the sounds of the street are never heard, much less the booming of Newgate's bell, which was a good cab journey distant from us. The awful clanging came from within. Without moving I could detect its source. Some years earlier we had cast a copy of the Newgate bell, to accompany a tableau illustrating the dreadful end of a lad of fifteen, who had butchered a youthful companion in larceny in a jealous fit over the division of their gains. The clapper of this property, which had never moved before, now wildly swung heralding the death of a capital offender. But to judge from the ecstatic brilliance of his eyes, the Hon James had no suspicion that he was hearing not the dreaded reality, but a grimmer, weirder proxy. Then abruptly, as I thought the breath I held must burst my body, the tolling ceased. It was immediately succeeded by the bright, tinkling chimes of Marie Antoinette's clock, announcing eight. I stood a few paces from the Hon James, as rigid as the waxes.

A strange alteration spread across the face of the man, as if the wax unreasonably were softening. A mysterious grey pallor came and went, as if the shadow of a pufflet of cloud had chased across it. The sequel was a swift infusion of scarlet, as when one of my apprentices miscalculates the strength of his dye. Perhaps I make an unreliable witness, for my amazement and horror were extreme, but it seemed to me now that no trace of his former gloating anticipation remained on the Hon James's features, but had indeed been parcelled out among his motionless retinue of paramours.

Then the eighth note sounded. His head jerked upwards and

his face was convulsed. Fissures appeared everywhere in the wax coating of his cheeks and forehead, and a hideous blasphemy exploded from his lips. It echoed in the stone recesses of our underground chamber, to linger afterwards in my brain like the startled cry of a man who falls among thieves where he had expected a friendly welcome. Then, as I stood, no more able to move than any of my creations, his body stretched and arched spasmodically, one leg rose till his knee almost pressed his stomach and gradually subsided again. His tongue protruded from his lips, and in place of the stars in his eyes I looked into the stygian vortex of death. Waxen flakes scattered about the floor at my feet, as the centrepiece of my tableau crashed down from its podium, and sprawled before me in unfeigned stillness.

I had rather less than an hour in which to set matters to rights before the customers would pour in. I cannot say how many of those valuable minutes I spent still standing, aghast at what had befallen. I owe it to my experience in the early years of carnage and terror that I achieved enough to pass muster, and not one pair of eyes, among the many discerning commentators who visited us that day, ever guessed at the dreadful drama which had been enacted just prior to their arrival.

But it was all singularly disappointing. The work of weeks had to stand by its journeyman effects. There was no life in the centrepiece – several critics in their notices of the show next day drew my attention, and that of their readers, to this irrefutable truth, while the man from *The Times*, commenting sympathetically on the devotion of my scholarly attention to detail, nevertheless opined in conclusion: 'In the last analysis, perspiration is after all no substitute for inspiration.' It gave me my excuse for withdrawing the tableau from public exhibition, but it was obvious that I should have featured my wax, and not the original. A gambler's whim had tricked me into losing a masterpiece. The proof of this claim is that in the prison that morning, nothing untoward was noticed. Mr Marwood the hangman later reported to me that he had very speedily dealt with the 'corpse', beyond chance of discovery. Of course I showed Mr Marwood, by raising a flagstone, the real results of his handiwork.

I had thought Mr Marwood to be made of sterner stuff. The sight must have addled his wits, for he never officiated with the rope again. But he was no great loss to any of us: what I think of the flesh and skeleton of Mr Marwood may be seen by any man or woman who cares to visit our collection.

A SHARP LOSS OF WEIGHT

By Norman P. Kaufman

THEY GAVE ME twenty years, so I behaved myself, did only thirteen. ONLY thirteen! Come to sunny Wormwood Scrubs, bridge the gap between innocent teens and soured, embittered early thirties! Excuse the twisted attempt at humour: the Scrubs is hardly the ideal spot for developing one's talent for light banter.

I was known as the model prisoner during my stay. If ever I'd felt like laughing at anything during those long and sickening years, then this at least was worth a chuckle. Model indeed! Oh, yes, I was quiet enough: no sit-down strikes, no swearing, no riots, no nothing, that was me. Maybe I'd thought of livening things up a little, right at the beginning. But the Scrubs can gouge the fibre from the proudest of backbones.

And there was something else on my mind that may have added to my apparent air of couldn't-care-less – something apart from the company of thieves, rapists, murderers, and the like; or the nerve-stretching clang of the cell doors at nine each night; or the pervading, all-enveloping, putrid stench of unwashed bodies, the stink of the whole rotten place that eats its way into the skin, so that the reek of it is with you for evermore . . .

But yes, there were other things on my mind: like what I would do when I got out, and where I would go, and whom I would see. Especially Morrie. The idea of one day meeting up again with Morrie occupied a very special niche in my waking dreams. I could recall his great bloated drink-raddled face easily enough, and the convex mound of flesh that strained at his waistband, and the snorting breath that wheezed wetly from those sausage lips of his. But I had never seen the engrained sneer on his pockmarked features turn into a grimace of sheer unsullied fright; I had never been privileged to witness runnels of sweat coursing down his cheeks, as he begged me not to shoot . . .

For that was my avowed intention: that was the notion I clung to throughout the endless years, the ambition that helped me retain the remnants of my sanity. Very likely they would put me back in again if I were caught; but then it would be for a crime I actually HAD committed, and not one for which Morrie had set me up. 'Extenuating circumstances,' the learned judge had told me. 'You are so young,' he had continued, 'or I might well have had you detained for the rest of your natural life . . .' That pompous old fool, what could he know? Doubtless his youth had been spent in some other environment than the dungeons of Wormwood Scrubs. But now . . . now I was out: and the first, last, and only thing that mattered was to arrange for the extermination of a certain Morrie.

So, thirteen years to the day since I had stepped across its grim threshold, the Scrubs spewed me out on to the pavement. It didn't occur to me that I was free at last, that I was still young, that the sun was shining. For cold single-mindedness, there was no one to touch me that morning. I had two pounds in my pocket, and thirty shillings of that went on a second-hand Luger. Pay your money and no questions asked, was the shop-owner's attitude – and I was thankful for it. The remaining cash bought me a double helping of ham and chips, and a trip across town to where Morrie had lived, and would, if all went well, shortly die.

I stepped off the bus, aware that my mouth was dry, my heart beating a little faster. It was not unlike the feeling I had experienced eighteen years before, when I had met my very first date. I swallowed a smile at the incongruity of the comparison: the joys of youth, the vengeance of a two-time loser.

The house was still there, just as I remembered it, as beautiful as Morrie had never been. I stared at the long, winding drive, the acacia trees that lined it, the mansion-like spread of the building ahead of me. That a man should sink so low and yet have possessions such as these . . .! My grip tightened on the Luger, shoving it deeper into my coat pocket.

The woman who answered the bell was quite unlike anyone I had ever seen in Morrie's company. For one thing, she was short and dumpy. Wisps of grey stood out from her colourless hair, done up as it was in a nondescript bun. She was well past fifty, and made no attempt to conceal the fact. 'Is Morrie available?' I inquired, and tried a smile on her; but either she was too old for my charm to work on her, or maybe I wasn't as handsome as I liked to believe. Perhaps the Scrubs had had something to do with that.

'Won't you come in?' she said in a voice that plainly said: I don't care whether you come in or not. But in I went: I had no reason to be proud any more – and getting into the house as easily as this was the best thing I could have hoped for.

This oh-so-plain-little-woman led me down the gloomiest hallway in the world, and stopped at a door at the far end. Whether or not she was intended to knock, I didn't know, but without so much as a by-your-leave she twisted the handle and flounced in, letting me stand behind her like a humble school-boy. If this were part of Morrie's softening-up process, then things had certainly changed since the old days. Or could it be that he had actually had an attack of respectability? Whatever the case, the answer would be something Morrie himself could understand, if not appreciate: I would shoot his face off.

She stood just inside the room, which itself was lighted by about a dozen candles that stood along the skirting board to the left-hand wall. Just for a second, I hesitated: there was something odd about this set-up. But ... I hadn't waited all this time just to back out now. And all I could lose was my life. With a kind of mental shrug, I followed her into the room.

Morrie was there. And I was right, things certainly had changed. Like some gross fly caught in a mechanized web, he hung suspended from great steel chains that were stapled to the ceiling and wall. His clothes hung in shreds from his now emaciated body; the greasy black hair was now white, what was left of it; his limbs were shrivelled, fleshless. Only the muted glint in his shadowy eyes showed that he lived.

The woman met my gaze of instinctive horror with a calm that itself held a terrible fascination of its own. If she were aware of my slackly open mouth, my dilated eyes, my shallow breathing, she gave no sign. 'Shirley was my daughter,' she said. Her voice was as empty as her face: I turned away from those sad eyes. 'She was seventeen when Morrie – took her away. And you – you must be the boy who got the blame.' I forced myself to meet her stare. 'My daughter was violated and strangled,' the woman went on. 'But Morrie lived.' She paused. 'And to me, mister, that seemed unfair. Very very unfair.'

She moved towards what was left of Fat Morrie. 'So ... I got a job here as housekeeper. At first he wasn't keen on someone of my age and looks, but I managed to persuade him that good cooking and cleaning is a great substitute for the giggling young things he ... kept here.' She waved a work-coarsened hand towards her victim. 'Naturally, he didn't know who I was – until one morning I knocked him over the head, trussed him up until I could get the proper equipment—' She gestured at the chains with a certain pride, as if she were a child with a new toy. 'He's been like this for close on thirteen years, mister. I feed him now and again, just to keep the spark of life going. No one comes here – I get my own provisions, there was plenty of money in the house for the rest of my – our – lives.' For the first time, there was a sheen of tears in her washed-out blue eyes.

'I came here to kill him.' Somehow, my voice sounded like that of a stranger.

'No ... please don't do that.' The woman's tone was tense, urgent. She knuckled the tears away savagely. 'You lost all those years of your life – I know that. But I lost my daughter.' She turned to stare at what had once been Morrie. 'Don't you understand, mister? He's no more fit to die than he is to live.'

We stood looking at each other for a moment or two, the dowdy little woman and the ex-convict. Then, without another word I turned and made my way out of that darkened, dreadful little room, along the corridor, out into the eye-aching sunlight.

The rest is history: ditching the Luger in the nearest waste bin, walking to the nearest Employment Exchange, and eventually getting fixed up with a fair job.

But I still think back to that house, to Morrie and what might have been. And in my heart I'm satisfied that for Fat Morrie at least, death would be infinitely more preferable than life.

AN EXPERIMENT IN CHOICE

Desmond Stewart

As THE young man crossed the square he was not sure that he was followed; he was certainly not worried. In this city it was always likely that one was being investigated; the people who worked for the police had to put in reports; otherwise they might be dismissed, or investigated themselves. You did not notice spies more than you noticed beggars.

He passed the statues without returning their blank stares, and was lost in the crowd buying tickets at the various windows. Three trains were waiting at different bays. There was comfort in crowds, an anonymity that came as a relief, like a cigarette.

As he lit up, he was aware – it was the last thing he was aware of – that the cigarette had fallen to the ground; then darkness, without pain.

He awoke under the sun, his eyes staring at a sky innocently blue; no smell of industry trailed the cloud that moved from right to left. His body was agreeably warm.

But he could not move. His naked legs and arms were clamped in iron grips. The grips were not painful; they simply kept him where he was, spreadeagled on his back. A bird scooped near him, a small bird, carried on the breeze. He sensed that it was early.

Time passed, and his first strugglings against the iron bonds eased. The drug they had given him perhaps made him languid, and as he gazed at the sky he remembered days from his childhood, long ago, and fishing in small ponds. The clouds had been diaphanous then, sailing through noons that lasted, it seemed, for ever.

Suddenly the ponds were gone. Noiselessly, smoothly, they

had retracted. He sat up. Then trembled. For as he realized where he was, a vertiginous nausea banished the idyllic fantasies which had kept him quiet.

He wanted to scream; but he was so high above the world that to scream seemed pointless. And on so narrow a wall. It seemed a wall. He was lying naked on a flat ledge with a narrow slot down its centre. It was not a ledge. It was a catwalk, and not straight. It was circular. And he was high above the world, hundreds of feet above a green and blue morning world, with trees like bushes, they were so far below, and no sign of factories, except where in the distance a grey haze was moored to chimneys.

He was lying on the lips of one such chimney and he was alone. The polished surface on which he lay was empty, except that a few feet behind his head was a plastic flask and a plate, with bread. Outside – he recoiled as he looked – outside was a drop of hundreds of feet, a drop only inches from his left arm and leg.

He lay back, his breath panting, looking at the sky, which now seemed ironical and cruel. Winged creatures had vanished. He half sat up again, terrified that vertigo might send him crashing to his death.

He looked to the right, a few inches from his scrabbling hand. There it was dark, the inner darkness of a funnel, a cold abyss. There were no fires, there was no soot, only darkness, a receding inner darkness going down and down.

A helicopter must have brought him here. He imagined it hovering, and figures in helmets gingerly stepping, acrobats, with heads for heights, on to this curving wall, and strapping him here.

He looked where the bonds had been: sockets in the surface. Controlled manacles could come up and could retreat. He moved his limbs so that they were invulnerable to any counter-attack from this silent machinery.

And he noticed idly that the curving platform on which he lay had, down its centre, a long dark slit. He wondered what it was for.

His heartbeats grew more normal and, still gingerly, he sat

up. He needed the flask, he wanted to drink. Very slowly he pulled himself back and round towards the flask and the bread.

In truth, the ledge was not dangerous, if he kept his head; the chimney was sufficiently large for the curve to be gradual. If he had been a steeplejack, he could have stood up and walked, even run, round the circle. He shuddered, knowing how bad he was at heights. Under the flask lay a sheet of typed paper. He pulled it free and found a message, or rather, a set of instructions.

'Drink the water, eat the bread: they are sufficient for your needs.'

He sipped the water. Its presence could only mean that he would soon be rescued. Even so he should eke it out, and there were only two small loaves.

He continued reading.

'You are the subject of an experiment; you have had 147 predecessors. You are situated on the summit of a steel-topped chimney. Here there is no deception: all is as you see it, a dark interior, an exterior whitewashed wall. You were laid here shortly before dawn. You can leave by jumping outwards, or inwards. But you will decide before noon.'

This was ridiculous. He had been brought by helicopter, he could be rescued by helicopter. Why should he be so insane as to jump either way? He read on.

'You will be perusing this at about 8 AM. You will eat your breakfast at 8.10. Soon you will observe a change in your environment. You have already remarked a narrow aperture in the platform on which you are lying. At 9 AM, a steel blade, knife-sharp, in the form of a cylinder, will emerge from its slot and begin to rise. By noon it will have reached a height of seven feet.

'Why did we select YOU?'

He put the paper down and felt cautiously inside the slot. There was barely room for his small finger. There was nothing to feel; the walls were polished.

'We wished to add a quota of intellectuals to our selectees for this test. We inform you, for your interest, that 93 of the previous subjects of this experiment chose to jump inwards;

but of those only nine could be classed as educated, and not one was above the average in intellect.

'Finally, may we thank you for your cooperation?'

It was nightmare, but under a fine sky, in a pastoral landscape.

This tower: what lay at the bottom? Inside, all was dark. Those who jumped inwards could never have known what they jumped towards. Outwards . . . He peered prudently over the edge, then withdrew from the frightening perspective.

He drank more water and chewed a loaf. He would simply wait. His adrenalin had pumped alarm to his veins. Now he was calm again. They had put him here; they could rescue him. The experiment was on his nerves. He would have liked to smoke, but there were no cigarettes and no matches.

Then suddenly his senses came alert.

There was, not a sound, but a movement, below him, in the slot. He could see nothing, but he sensed motion and then he knew what it was: the slot was empty no longer, it was filled as with ink; what filled it was blue-black and flush with the ledge. Flush only for a moment. A ridge of oiled steel began to rise in slow and inexorable silence. His narrow space was now bisected. He could lie down no longer. He felt the edge, now a thumb height above the surface: sharp as a Japanese sword of execution. He crouched, his legs each side of the silent cylinder.

Wildly, he looked over the side. Perhaps somewhere there were steps, a steeplejack's ladder?

He crawled round the chimney: this was it, a test of nerve, to lower himself over, to cling like a fly and descend the four hundred feet of gently curving wall. He crawled the agonizing circuit back to the plastic flask.

There were no steps.

Inside then? Perhaps just lower than the darkness was a ladder to safety.

But who could know? Who could see?

He wondered what impelled those who had jumped before.

Crouching there beneath the sun, in a tortured dialogue he rehearsed reasons.

Inwards, back to the womb, in to darkness. That was the impulse. The hope, below reason, that as they fell it would be to some warm, enfolding cushion.

And outwards? He calculated: only fifty-three had jumped outwards. They were the vigorous ones, the hopeful? And yet hopeless. At least in darkness there were hopes. Outwards . . .

He peered, but from this height the scrubby, uneven ground was indecipherable. There was a tattooing of small black points on the earth. Were they stones or bushes? There must be some hope in this situation. Perhaps the dark points were the meshes of a net. But as he squinted again, he doubted. More likely they were spikes. And at this thought his body began to tremble as with a fever.

By now, the slow sliding steel was fast approaching his groin so he half stood, and lightly laid his hand for support against the side of the rising cylinder. He wondered about the men before him. The paper spoke of them as not above average intellect. He thought of sewage-workers or taxi-drivers and the shadow of a smile passed over his lips.

He wanted a drink. It was with difficulty that he turned and stooped, avoiding the steel, and drank what was left of the water.

He found that he could stand straight, with the rising wall between his legs, up to his knees, only its knife-edge dangerous. He threw the flask to his right, down towards the earth and lost sight of it. He kicked the plate into the chimney, and listened, but heard nothing.

He looked up. The sky was ironic and remote, as indifferent to him as to a chimpanzee shot among the stars. He could not believe that the universe concerned itself with the morality of man. Which side should he stand? Bifurcated on the summit of this alien tower, he asked the idle question. The sky did not care, and neither did the earth. Only somewhere a cold human intelligence, if human it was, recorded his decision, for reasons of its own.

But suddenly he recognized: it was too late to make a decision – the steel had come too high, he could not lift his leg over without falling, and still the steel rose, smooth and silent.

At this moment, careless whether the sky heard or not, he began to scream.

It was afternoon. The colour and most of the people had fled from the square. A statue cast a narrow shade in which fruit stalls sheltered.

A man dressed as a vendor, hardly bothering to play the part, scrutinized the few travellers crossing the white space towards the station.

The apparent vendor was alert. A young man was approaching with an old copy of *The New Yorker* under his arm.

'Guard my stall.' He threw a coin to a nearby beggar. 'I'll be back.'

Preparing his needle, he followed his next victim into the station where, by the ticket-window few people, but enough, formed an anonymous throng.

THE EVIL ONE

By Robert Duncan

WHEN THE last tickling trickle of sweat, with its small addition to ecstasy, had rolled down their sides, together they lay still, neck to neck, leg to leg, arms about one another. Evie sighed, reflecting on how this had come about. It seemed strange to her that she had just made love with someone she had not known six hours previously. Yet it seemed perfectly natural as well.

In the same way it had seemed natural when Jane said 'I don't remember inviting that chap over there,' for her to reply 'Oh, it's all right. He came with me,' and move away towards the stranger before Jane could ask any questions. It was not true. She had come alone, for Alan was in London to be interviewed for a job. She did not know what had prompted her to lie, but it gave her an opportunity to approach the strange, uninvited guest. She had noticed him earlier, standing slightly apart from those nearest to him, not talking to anyone, seeming just to be watching and listening. From then on, she had paid little attention to anyone else in the room. Once or twice the dark young man had looked straight at her, held her eyes for a moment, then dropped or averted his.

Now she went straight over to him and said 'Hello.'

'Hello' – a quiet return, not questioning, as one might have expected.

'Our hostess just said to me she didn't remember inviting you. I told her you came with me. I hope you don't mind.'

'No. Thank you.' – still quiet and, she sensed, friendly. He went on: 'Anyway, I feel as if I did come to see you.'

The only thing that seemed odd to her was that it did not seem odd that he should say such a thing, but indeed very

right and natural. She herself had not intended to come to
the party at first, with Alan being away, but then something
made her change her mind, and now she too felt as if she had
come just to meet this stranger. She found herself saying 'I
know what you mean.'

Her going towards him had not started any general trend.
Now, instead of his standing alone, watching and listening,
there were two of them, talking apart from anyone else. No
one else approached. Even people she was acquainted with
did not come near, appearing to divine that their conversation
was special and private, not to be interrupted. It started slowly,
but not awkwardly, and continued so. It was not that they
had difficulty finding things to say, but the conversation was
economical and the pauses were as much part of it as the
words, the communion remaining unbroken.

He told her his name was Luke. It reminded her of cowboys
in the Wild West, and of the writer of the third Gospel, the
beloved physician, a historian and an artist. The latter seemed
more apt. Not a common name in Glasgow in an age that
was not strongly religious. But it seemed to fit him, and
anyway he did not sound as if he had lived in Glasgow all
his life. His surname lent support to this – Morningstar, not
a Scots name. But beautiful. Luke Morningstar. Yes, there
was something of the West in the whole name, but not the
Wild and Woolly. Rather the romantic Old West. But also
Luke, travelling with Paul in the Mediterranean. And the
morning star, Venus in the East, at dawn. Her own was a bit
plainer, and more Scots – Evie Adams – but it sounded nice,
she thought, and she probably had Celtic blood in her somewhere, so she wasn't all that plain either. Not that her looks
were – chestnut-coloured hair, blue eyes, healthy skin, and a
firm figure. She was not bad herself.

It was difficult to say about Luke. He had dark hair, dark
eyes, and a skin that had seen the sun, from what she could
make out under the dimmed party lights. He was fairly tall,
and well-made. Older than her twenty-one years, but how
old it was hard to say. He had the appearance of a man in his
late twenties, but something in his eyes and voice suggested

greater experience than that. They both seemed deep with experience, although his voice was not physically deep. But Evie did not ask his age, nor he hers. It did not seem very important. A superficiality, like so many other things they felt no need to mention. He did not mention his parents, whether they were alive or dead. She did not mention hers, or Alan. He talked more about places he had been, what he had seen and done, how he always felt he was looking for something, an experience, or a person, that would bring about something of the nature of a revelation in his life, give it the direction he felt he needed. She knew what he meant, she agreed with him.

He played about with their initials, L.M. and E.A. They could be rearranged to form M-A-L-E, or A-L-M-E, Latin vocative case of *almus*, meaning nourishing or kindly.

'ALME MALE – O, kindly male,' he intoned. She laughed. 'M-E-A-L.'

She suggested 'L-A-M-E' and they both laughed.

It would have made no sense to anyone else, but it was part of the communion, their initials joining in symbolic combinations, sometimes straight, sometimes ironic. She was not tipsy, and Luke was obviously sober. So it was not wine that had caused the heady feeling she was experiencing. It was just the effect they had on each other, for she knew Luke was feeling it too. Their talk seemed ethereal.

When more than a third of the guests had already dispersed, they decided to leave, so as not to become conspicuous among the dwindling numbers. No one paid very much attention to them, so Evie did not bother to say any formal goodbyes.

Her landlady was rather strict, which meant they headed for Luke's place, where no one would mind. There was no question of their going their separate ways.

He had a room in a flat in a street unfamiliar to her, off Great Western Road. They arrived there just before two o'clock. Luke switched on a table lamp and they made coffee in the kitchen and brought it through. They sat drinking it, speaking when words came, happy not to when none did.

Again she felt overwhelmingly how much the silence was

part of the conversation. They felt impulses from each other that transcended the field of vocal communication. The periods of stillness were like music, conveying meanings without the explicitness of words, but at a deeper, more fully understood level. If she had had to sum up what he told her, she would have said he made paradoxes clear to her, and she thought this was because he was himself paradox. What had before appeared strange and anomalous to her was now resolved, and seemed quite natural.

At length the words died out, and they sat silent for a long time, sometimes not even having to look at each other. They rose and went and washed-up the cups in the kitchen. Then came back through to Luke's room. He kissed her and switched off the light. They began to undress in the darkness, not hastily but eagerly. They could hear the brush of clothes and the sound of each other's breathing. Then they went to bed.

It was only a continuation of the intercourse that had begun before a word was spoken between them. As their bodies came together, the paradox she had sensed in him became tangible. She held him, and it seemed that his flesh was young but his bones were old. Older than time. And his spirit was older than his bones by as much as they were older than his flesh. Boy-man and man-god in one. His love was what she had hoped Alan's would be, but at heart had known it would not. Her hymen was ruptured in pain and joy, and the imagery was of the curtain of the inner sanctuary of the temple rent in two, and the rocks split and the graves opened, and a darkness before her eyes, as of the sun in eclipse. She cried out. The pain was splitting her, but she held on in her joy, and the climax when it came to her arched body was the fulfilment of the communion, the satisfaction of her hunger, what she had been looking for.

Now they lay still. Luke was sleeping beside her. She felt at peace, but thirsty. It had been hot. She would go and get a drink of water in the kitchen. Easing herself out of bed so as not to disturb him, she padded through to the kitchen and poured herself a glass of water. Drinking it in the quiet of half past four, she let her eyes run idly over the various utensils scattered about. She finished it and returned softly.

Luke's rhythmic breathing told her he was still asleep. She felt an urge to look at him, and switched on the table lamp. His hair was tousled down over his forehead. He frowned slightly in his sleep, and his lips pouted moistly. The blankets were pulled out at his side of the bed. Evie bent down to tuck them in. One of his knees was bent upward. It would be funny to tickle his feet and see him toss. Grinning to herself, she lifted the bedclothes and slid her hand under. She felt for his foot. Then a galvanic chill plated her skin as her fingers met something hard and cold.

The lamina held her motionless for some seconds. She did not know exactly what it was she had felt, or why it gave her a shock, but the fear was very real. Slowly she withdrew her hand, took the blankets and began to fold them back. Her body palpitated with sickness and horror. She felt it in her head and her legs, her throat and her abdomen, her breasts and her stomach, as she uncovered, not a human foot, but a perfectly formed animal hoof. Awed, she could not help putting out her hand again and touching it, letting her palm rest for a minute on the evil, horny thing. She was just struggling to take it all in. Satan incarnate had made love to her.

It was grotesque. She pulled her hand away and shook her head. Oh, the grotesque! Was this her consummation, the end of her hunger, the resolution of paradox? Only bizarre. When she had thought some kind of truth was in her grasp, it was only another unholy version of the old absurdity. 'ALME MALE – O, kindly male.' Yes, M-A-L-E, Latin vocative, O Evil One. He had been aware of this, it was deliberate. She had appreciated and laughed at certain ironies, but he had others, concealed, that were not funny. And his name! – Luke Morningstar. The Old West, the Gospel writer, the beloved physician? No, only a ludicrous abbreviation of Lucifer, Son of the Morning, the Fallen. Now, in the second half of the twentieth century, who would have believed it? Was there to be nothing in her life but this ridiculous, unresolved grotesquerie, this chaos?

What was she to do? Just dress and leave as quickly as she could, afraid and ashamed? How could she? What was the meaning of shame in a situation like this, how could she have protected herself against him? Wake him and challenge him? What good would that do? He would laugh at her. She was powerless before him, and he could tie knots in her in an argument.

It struck her like ice on her back that he might not be sleeping at all. She looked at his face, half buried in the pillow. Maybe he was lying there enjoying himself wondering how she would react. He looked as if he were asleep, but how could you be sure with him? He could deceive anybody. She thought of Alan. What was she going to say to him? Would one of those who had been at the party tell him what she had been doing? Oh, she was so confused. Even if she tried to leave, there was no guarantee that that thing in the bed would let her. And could she just go away like that and think of him laughing at her? She did have her pride. How she hated that creature now who had been so fond to her just recently. If only she could avenge herself on him. How she hated him.

She did not know how long she sat there thinking of what he had done to her and hating him. But all at once an idea came to her. Among the utensils in the kitchen she had seen a sharp carving knife. If he really was asleep, that might rid the world of this devil for ever. He had been human enough for copulation, there was no reason why he shouldn't be human enough in that shape to be killed as well. And the chances were he was human enough in his present guise to have to sleep.

Once she had resolved on it, she did not waste any time. She went through to the kitchen and found the knife. Of course there was still a chance he was just waiting for her to make a move like this, but even if he discovered her, things could not be much worse than they were.

Back in his room, she approached the bed softly. He had not moved. She bent down and gently pulled back the bed-clothes to his waist. Over his heart there was the symbol of an inverted cross. No wonder he had switched off the light to undress, with that and the hooves. Modesty, hah! She placed the point of the knife over the junction of the arms of the cross. He did not stir. With a downward thrust she sent the blade between his ribs and through his heart. Blood spouted up and gushed over her hands and arms. She leaned on the knife momentarily, feeling sick, and then pushed herself away. He was dead, but his eyes and mouth had opened.

She stood with her eyes closed and her head back, her bloody arms held out from her sides, sucking in the hot air through her mouth till she recovered her self-control. Then she looked towards the bed and shuddered. A crimson flow from his heart reddened the sheets, and he still stared upward open-mouthed. She went to the kitchen to wash her hands of his blood.

It occurred to her to wonder whether anyone else lived in this flat. Probably not. In fact it was quite possible that he had set up the flat solely for this occasion. Once she left it, it would probably disappear, and never be discovered. So no one would find out what she had done. It was a pity in a way, but at least she would have the satisfaction of knowing herself. She would have liked some recognition, but no one would believe her story without proof, not even Alan. Not that she could tell Alan, of course. She was actually beginning to look forward to seeing him again now. He did lack something, it was true, but she felt that she had after all gained something from the night's experience which would enable her to come to terms with him. Her spirits were rising rapidly. This might in fact have been what she was looking for all the time, and in order to gain great strength it might have been necessary first to come through a great trauma.

By the time she left the kitchen she was feeling quite cheerful. She felt no trepidation walking back to the bedroom. She could have laughed that she could actually have felt something akin to guilt at first after killing him. By no stretch of the imagination could it be classified as murder, and it was silly to think of it as such. She could not have murdered anyone. It was different, a necessary evil. Not even evil. He was evil.

She opened the door and stepped into the room. The floors did not seem so noiseless after his death. She could hear her footsteps quite clearly now. She would dress and leave, and if the body was discovered no one was likely to call it murder. But it was more probable that it would never be heard of. Without compunction she looked at the corpse. It lay unmoved, with the blankets turned down and the same large bloodstain over the torso and sheet. Unmoved. But something was different.

It took her several seconds to realize what had changed. The foot protruding from under the blankets where she had lifted them. It was a foot, a human foot.

She could not have been mistaken. There had been a hoof before, and now there was a foot. There was no question of that. But what explanation could there be? Had being killed, pouring out the evil blood, in his veins from time immemorial, somehow purified him? Had she somehow released his spirit to return to its pristine state? But if so, what about the body she was left with? If anybody saw it now, they would most definitely think she had committed murder. How was she supposed to explain that away? She hated him even more than when he had been the devil. He had done that to her, and now he was saved. And if the body were found, she would be the one who would have to explain. How?

She sat down in a chair and lowered her eyes from that blasted corpse, and she saw the answer to her question. With terror and a growing feeling of pleasure she sat for a long time contemplating her newly acquired set of perfectly formed hooves. Then she rose and set about arranging things.

MARMALADE WINE

By Joan Aiken

'PARADISE,' Blacker said to himself, moving forward into the wood. 'Paradise. Fairyland.'

He was a man given to exaggeration; poetic licence he called it, and his friends called it 'Blacker's little flights of fancy,' or something less polite, but on this occasion he spoke nothing but the truth. The wood stood silent about him, tall, golden, with afternoon sunlight slanting through the half-unfurled leaves of early summer. Underfoot, anemones palely carpeted the ground. A cuckoo called.

'Paradise,' Blacker repeated, closed the gate behind him, and strode down the overgrown path, looking for a spot in which to eat his ham sandwich. Hazel bushes thickened at either side until the circular blue eye of the gateway by which he had come in dwindled to a pinpoint and vanished. The taller trees over-topping the hazels were not yet in full leaf and gave little cover; it was very hot in the wood and very still.

Suddenly Blacker stopped short with an exclamation of surprise and regret: lying among the dog's-mercury by the path was the body of a cock-pheasant in the full splendour of its spring plumage. Blacker turned the bird over with the townsman's pity and curiosity at such evidence of nature's unkindness; the feathers, purple-bronze, green, and gold, were smooth under his hand as a girl's hair.

'Poor thing,' he said aloud, 'what can have happened to it?'

He walked on, wondering if he could turn the incident to account. 'Threnody for a Pheasant in May.' Too precious? Too sentimental? Perhaps a weekly would take it. He began choosing rhymes, staring at his feet as he walked, abandoning his conscious rapture at the beauty around him.

> *Stricken to death . . . and something . . . leafy ride,*
> *Before his . . . something . . . fully flaunt his pride.*

Or would a shorter line be better, something utterly simple and heartfelt, limpid tears of grief like spring rain dripping off the petals of a flower?

It was odd, Blacker thought, increasing his pace, how difficult he found writing nature poetry; nature was beautiful, maybe, but it was not stimulating. And it was nature poetry that *Field and Garden* wanted. Still, that pheasant ought to be worth five guineas. *Tread lightly past, Where he lies still, And something last . . .*

Damn! In his absorption he had nearly trodden on *another* pheasant. What was happening to the birds? Blacker, who objected to occurrences with no visible explanation, walked on frowning. The path bore downhill to the right, and leaving the hazel coppice, crossed a tiny valley. Below him Blacker was surprised to see a small, secretive flint cottage, surrounded on three sides by trees. In front of it was a patch of turf. A deck-chair stood there, and a man was peacefully stretched out in it, enjoying the afternoon sun.

Blacker's first impulse was to turn back; he felt as if he had walked into somebody's garden, and was filled with mild irritation at the unexpectedness of the encounter; there ought to have been some warning signs, dash it all. The wood had seemed as deserted as Eden itself. But his turning round would have an appearance of guilt and furtiveness; on second thoughts he decided to go boldly past the cottage. After all there was no fence, and the path was not marked private in any way; he had a perfect right to be there.

'Good afternoon,' said the man pleasantly as Blacker approached. 'Remarkably fine weather, is it not?'

'I do hope I'm not trespassing.'

Studying the man, Blacker revised his first guess. This was no gamekeeper; there was distinction in every line of the thin, sculptured face. What most attracted Blacker's attention were the hands, holding a small gilt coffee-cup; they were as white, frail, and attenuated as the pale roots of water-plants.

'Not at all,' the man said cordially. 'In fact you arrive at a most opportune moment; you are very welcome. I was just wishing for a little company. Delightful as I find this sylvan retreat, it becomes, all of a sudden, a little *dull*, a little *banal*. I do trust that you have time to sit down and share my after-lunch coffee and liqueur.'

As he spoke he reached behind him and brought out a second deck-chair from the cottage porch.

'Why, thank you; I should be delighted,' said Blacker, wondering if he had the strength of character to take out the ham sandwich and eat it in front of this patrician hermit.

Before he made up his mind the man had gone into the house and returned with another gilt cup full of black, fragrant coffee, hot as Tartarus, which he handed to Blacker. He carried also a tiny glass, and into this, from a blackcurrant-cordial bottle, he carefully poured a clear, colourless liquor. Blacker sniffed his glassful with caution, mistrusting the bottle and its evidence of home brewing, but the scent, aromatic and powerful, was similar to that of curaçao, and the liquid moved in its glass with an oily smoothness. It certainly was not cowslip wine.

'Well,' said his host, re-seating himself and gesturing slightly with his glass, 'how do you do?' He sipped delicately.

'Cheers,' said Blacker, and added, 'My name's Roger Blacker.' It sounded a little lame. The liqueur was not curaçao, but akin to it, and quite remarkable potent; Blacker, who was very hungry, felt the fumes rise up inside his head as if an orange tree had taken root there and was putting out leaves and golden glowing fruit.

'Sir Francis Deeking,' the other man said, and then Blacker understood why his hands had seemed so spectacular, so portentously out of the common.

'The surgeon? But surely you don't live down here?'

Deeking waved a hand deprecatingly. 'A weekend retreat.

A hermitage, to which I can retire from the strain of my calling.'

'It certainly is very remote,' Blacker remarked. 'It must be five miles from the nearest road.'

'Six. And you, my dear Mr Blacker, what is your profession?'

'Oh, a writer,' said Blacker modestly. The drink was having its usual effect on him; he managed to convey not that he was a journalist on a twopenny daily with literary yearnings, but that he was a philosopher and essayist of rare quality, a sort of second Bacon. All the time he spoke, while drawn out most flatteringly by the questions of Sir Francis, he was recalling journalistic scraps of information about his host: the operation on the Indian Prince; the Cabinet Minister's appendix; the amputation performed on that unfortunate ballerina who had both feet crushed in a railway accident; the major operation which proved so miraculously successful on the American heiress.

'You must feel like a god,' he said suddenly, noticing with surprise that his glass was empty. Sir Francis waved the remark aside.

'We all have our godlike attributes,' he said, leaning forward. 'Now you, Mr Blacker, a writer, a creative artist – do you not know a power akin to godhead when you transfer your thought to paper?'

'Well, not exactly then,' said Blacker, feeling the liqueur moving inside his head in golden and russet-coloured clouds. 'Not *so* much then, but I do have one unusual power, a power not shared by many people, of foretelling the future. For instance, as I was coming through the wood, I *knew* this house would be here. I knew I should find you sitting in front of it. I can look at the list of runners in a race, and the name of the winner fairly leaps out at me from the page, as if it was printed in golden ink. Forthcoming events – air disasters, train crashes – I always sense in advance. I begin to have a terrible feeling of impending doom, as if my brain was a volcano just on the point of eruption.'

What was that other item of news about Sir Francis Deeking, he wondered, a recent report, a tiny paragraph that had caught his eye in *The Times*? He could not recall it.

'*Really?*' Sir Francis was looking at him with the keenest interest; his eyes, hooded and fanatical under their heavy lids, held brilliant points of light. 'I have always longed to know somebody with such a power. It must be a terrifying responsibility.'

'Oh, it is,' Blacker said. He contrived to look bowed under the weight of supernatural cares; noticed that his glass was full again, and drained it. 'Of course I don't use the faculty for my own ends; something fundamental in me rises up to prevent that. It's as basic, you know, as the instinct forbidding cannibalism or incest—'

'Quite, quite,' Sir Francis agreed. 'But for another person you would be able to give warnings, advise profitable courses of action—? My dear fellow, your glass is empty. Allow me.'

'This is marvellous stuff,' Blacker said hazily. 'It's like a wreath of orange blossom.' He gestured with his finger.

'I distil it myself; from marmalade. But do go on with what you were saying. Could you, for instance, tell me the winner of this afternoon's Manchester Plate?'

'Bow Bells,' Blacker said unhesitatingly. It was the only name he could remember.

'You interest me enormously. And the result of today's Aldwych by-election? Do you know that?'

'Unwin, the Liberal, will get in by a majority of two hundred and eighty-two. He won't take his seat, though. He'll be killed at seven this evening in a lift accident at his hotel.' Blacker was well away by now.

'Will he, indeed?' Sir Francis appeared delighted. 'A pestilent fellow. I have sat on several boards with him. Do continue.'

Blacker required little encouragement. He told the story of the financier whom he had warned in time of the oil company crash; the dream about the famous violinist which had resulted in the man's cancelling his passage on the ill-fated *Orion*; and the tragic tale of the bullfighter who had ignored his warning.

'But I'm talking too much about myself,' he said at length, partly because he noticed an ominous clogging of his tongue, a refusal of his thoughts to marshal themselves. He cast about for an impersonal topic, something simple.

'The pheasants,' he said. 'What's happened to the pheasants? Cut down in their prime. It – it's terrible. I found four in the wood up there, four or five.'

'Really?' Sir Francis seemed callously uninterested in the fate of the pheasants. 'It's the chemical sprays they use on the crops, I understand. Bound to upset the ecology; they never work out the probable results beforehand. Now if *you* were in charge, my dear Mr Blacker – but forgive me, it is a hot afternoon and you must be tired and footsore if you have walked from Witherstow this morning – let me suggest that you have a short sleep . . .'

His voice seemed to come from farther and farther away; a network of sun-coloured leaves laced themselves in front of Blacker's eyes. Gratefully he leaned back and stretched out his aching feet.

Some time after this Blacker roused a little – or was it only a dream? – to see Sir Francis standing by him, rubbing his hands, with a face of jubilation.

'My dear fellow, my dear Mr Blacker, what a *lusus naturae* you are. I can never be sufficiently grateful that you came my way. Bow Bells walked home – positively *ambled*. I have been listening to the commentary. What a misfortune that I had no time to place money on the horse – but never mind, never mind, that can be remedied another time.

'It is unkind of me to disturb your well-earned rest, though; drink this last thimblefull and finish your nap while the sun is on the wood.'

As Blacker's head sank back against the deck-chair again, Sir Francis leaned forward and gently took the glass from his hand.

Sweet river of dreams, thought Blacker, fancy the horse actually winning. I wish I'd had a fiver on it myself; I could do with a new pair of shoes. I should have undone these before I dozed off, they're too tight or something. I must wake up soon, ought to be on my way in half an hour or so . . .

When Blacker finally woke he found that he was lying on a narrow bed, indoors, covered with a couple of blankets. His head ached and throbbed with a shattering intensity, and it took a few minutes for his vision to clear; then he saw that he was in a small white cell-like room which contained nothing but the bed he was on and a chair. It was very nearly dark.

He tried to struggle up but a strange numbness and heaviness had invaded the lower part of his body, and after hoisting himself on to his elbow he felt so sick that he abandoned the effort and lay down again.

That stuff must have the effect of a knockout drop, he thought ruefully; what a fool I was to drink it. I'll have to apologize to Sir Francis. What time can it be?

Brisk light footsteps approached the door and Sir Francis came in. He was carrying a portable radio which he placed on the window sill.

'Ah, my dear Blacker, I see you have come round. Allow me to offer you a drink.'

He raised Blacker skilfully, and gave him a drink of water from a cup with a rim and a spout.

'Now let me settle you down again. Excellent. We shall soon have you – well, not on your feet, but sitting up and taking nourishment.' He laughed a little. 'You can have some beef tea presently.'

'I am so sorry,' Blacker said. 'I really need not trespass on your hospitality any longer. I shall be quite all right in a minute.'

'No trespass, my dear friend. You are not at all in the way. I hope that you will be here for a long and pleasant stay. These surroundings, so restful, so conducive to a writer's inspiration – what could be more suitable for you? You need not think that I shall disturb you. I am in London all week, but shall keep you company at weekends – pray, pray don't think that you will be nuisance or *de trop*. On the contrary, I am hoping that you can do me the kindness of giving me the Stock Exchange prices in advance, which will amply compensate for any small trouble I have taken. No, no, you must feel quite at home – please consider, indeed, that this *is* your home.'

Stock Exchange prices? It took Blacker a moment to remember, then he thought, Oh Lord, my tongue has played me false as usual. He tried to recall what stupidities he had been guilty of. 'Those stories,' he said lamely, 'they were all a bit exaggerated, you know. About my foretelling the future. I can't really. That horse's winning was a pure coincidence, I'm afraid.'

'Modesty, modesty.' Sir Francis was smiling, but he had gone rather pale, and Blacker noticed a beading of sweat along his cheekbones. 'I am sure you will be invaluable. Since my retirement I find it absolutely necessary to augment my income by judicious investment.'

All of a sudden Blacker remembered the gist of that small paragraph in *The Times*. Nervous breakdown. Complete rest. Retirement.

'I – really must go now,' he said uneasily, trying to push himself upright. 'I meant to be back in town by seven.'

'Oh, but Mr Blacker, that is quite out of the question. Indeed, so as to preclude any such action, I have amputated your feet. But you need not worry; I know you will be very happy here. And I feel certain that you are wrong to doubt your own powers. Let us listen to the nine o'clock news in order to be quite satisfied that the detestable Unwin did fall down the hotel lift shaft.'

He walked over to the portable radio and switched it on.

MONKEY BUSINESS

By John Arthur

RICHARD CLARKE left his air-conditioned bungalow and stepped straight out into the clammy, oppressive grip of the tropical morning. Before he had walked a hundred yards his thin cotton shirt was clinging to his back in large, damp patches. Beads of perspiration trickled from his forehead and into his eyes. He blinked rapidly and flicked the salty droplets from his eyebrows with a time-worn movement of his right hand. He looked out from his elevated vantage point at Pasir Panjang, across the water to where dozens of sea-going freighters sat moored in Singapore harbour, waiting patiently for their cargoes of copra and rubber to be loaded before proceeding on their lazy way around the world.

The weather never varied. It was January now but it could just as well have been June or September. Month to month, day in and day out, the temperature remained at a steady ninety degrees fahrenheit, extremely high humidity adding to the discomfort. Even the heavy, steaming rain of the monsoon season failed to break the inexorable grip of the equatorial greenhouse heat.

Clarke was used to it and the climate no longer bothered him. During the last six years he had learned to accept the ways of both the island and its inhabitants. He had reached the stage where he felt that he belonged there as he did nowhere else in the world. He had many friends among both the caucasian and the oriental populations and managed to enjoy a social life which many considered to have died with the end of colonialism. He mixed freely with the natives. The withered, opium-smoking Chinese laundryman, the ebony Indian money-changer, the gold-toothed satay man – they all knew and respected him. He, in turn, acknowledged their beliefs, respected their customs, and was accepted as a friend. Many of his European friends had even said that they suspected that he was beginning to think like an oriental himself, but he knew, only too well that he still had much to learn. In fact it was his desire to learn and to understand that stopped him ever thinking of England and home.

A yellow-topped Mercedes taxi roared past him. He waved to the driver and the taxi, braking dangerously hard, skidded to a halt in a cloud of red dust some fifty yards farther on down the road. A head popped out of the nearside window and a grinning yellow face called back to him.

'Taxi, John?'

Clarke walked up, climbed into the rear seat and was thrown violently backwards as the driver put his foot down and they shot off down the road. Clarke smiled to himself. After all, he was used to it.

'Where to, John?' the driver asked. To him, everybody was John.

'Paya Lebar Airport.'

'Five dollars – OK?' He looked at Clarke and smiled widely as he asked the question. Clarke laughed.

'You cheeky sod! What do you think I am, a bloody tourist? Three dollars, and that's all you'll get!'

'OK, John – Three dollars fifty cents.'

'Three dollars only.'

'OK, John – three dollars.' The driver was still smiling and they were friends already.

They drove past Collier Quay, up through the city and bustling Chinatown, out to the far side of the island. When they reached the airport Clarke gave the driver three dollars plus an extra fifty cents. The young Chinese waved and drove off grinning even more enormously than before. Clarke went to the bar and bought himself a long brandy-sour which he took up to the observation balcony to await the arrival of his client.

Within thirty minutes, all being well, Wayne Harrison would arrive and Clarke would be there to meet him. They would shake hands, exchange meaningless greetings, and for the next three days it would be Clarke's duty to escort the American on a lightning tour of Singapore at the end of which time he would receive the generous sum of three hundred dollars – American, of course – for services rendered. It was not very demanding work but it paid well, and that suited Clarke admirably. He never experienced difficulty in obtaining clients as most of the tourists, and especially the Americans, seemed to prefer being shown around by someone who spoke the same language – albeit with a slightly different accent. The only distasteful thing about the work, as far as Clarke was concerned, was the people he had to deal with. He saw them as a crowd of pasty-faced, money-spending, camera-clicking, empty-headed idiots who gawked and gasped at anything and everything they saw. Some of them showed disgust at the squalor and filth they found in certain run-down corners of the city, taking it for granted that the sanitary granite and marble civilization of their home towns was a world-wide heritage. They didn't for one moment attempt to sympathize with the poor or, in any way, to bridge the vast gulf between East and West. They simply stood apart in splendid isolation, clicking their cameras and remaining totally uninvolved. Clarke found himself gripping the balcony rail tightly as he thought about it. Perhaps he was, after all, beginning to think like an oriental. He looked beyond the airfield and saw the giant silver airliner whispering in above the unstirring palm trees.

Clarke stood outside the Arrival Lounge and watched through the plate-glass window as the motley band of passengers battled their way through customs and immigration. They came in all shapes and sizes, but it wasn't difficult to pick out Harrison. He stood slightly apart from the rest of the passport-waving crowd, a look of childish expectancy on his flabby white face, already pointing and clicking his camera at anything that took his fancy. Within the space of a minute he 'bagged' three customs officials, a 'Welcome to Singapore' sign, written in four languages, and several of his fellow passengers. He was a tall man, vastly overweight, with thinning grey hair cropped close to his head. He was wearing a poorly tailored, but undoubtedly expensive, dark blue suit, the baggy trousers of which flapped above a highly polished pair of brown brogue shoes. His crisp white shirt was choked with a bright yellow tie. Clarke estimated that he must have been in his early fifties. Obviously over-fed, probably over-paid, and well on his way to a coronary thrombosis.

Clarke waited patiently until Harrison had completed the formalities of arrival and had assembled his luggage before walking over and introducing himself. He tried to appear genial.

'Mr Harrison? – I'm Richard Clarke. Hope you had a pleasant trip.' The American's face split into an over-friendly smile and he extended a podgy, but well manicured, hand.

'Well, hello there! Glad you made it on time. Never met a Limey yet who wasn't punctual. Fine! Fine!' The American's voice, like everything else about him, was too loud.

Clarke shook the proffered hand but Harrison withdrew it quickly and raised his camera just in time to snap an attractive young Malay girl, dressed in a sarong-kebaya, before she disappeared round a corner of the building. He turned to face Clarke once more and gave him a stupid look which seemed to indicate how pleased he was with his sharp-shooting. He spoke hurriedly.

'Well now, let's get started. Only three days here, then I'm off up to Hong Kong on business. Must be plenty to see and tell the folks back home about!'

They took a taxi back towards the city. Throughout the journey Harrison used his camera to immortalize anything which was new or strange to him. He captured the noisy, explosive colour of a Chinese funeral procession, the mysterious majesty of a Buddhist temple, the weary face of a trishaw driver and countless other things besides. The clicking didn't stop until they reached the Goodwood Hotel. The taxi-driver winked at Clarke as Harrison paid him off in American dollars. Clarke winked back and said nothing. After all, he and the driver were in the same business.

Clarke had expected Harrison to spend the rest of the day settling in at the hotel. Harrison, however, had other ideas.

Within three hours of his arrival they were fishing from a sampan off Blakang Mati Island. The big American was in his element, despite the fact that all he caught was an assortment of venomous sea snakes. Twice during the afternoon Clarke, and the wildly jabbering boatman, had to cut the American's fishing line to prevent him dragging the deadly reptiles into the boat. Harrison's misplaced enthusiasm made him impervious both to their warnings and to the immediate danger. He spent most of the time, however, flat out in the bottom of the boat with a large straw hat over his face, singing 'Home on the Range' while the sun beat mercilessly down upon his rainbow-coloured shirt and his knee-length Bermuda shorts.

That same evening they dined sumptuously at the Troika restaurant and then returned to the Goodwood for a quiet drink and to plan their activities for the coming day.

'Tomorrow' said Clarke, running his index finger lightly round the lip of his brandy glass, 'is Thaipusam.'

'Tie Poo what?' exclaimed Harrison, nearly biting through his inevitable cigar.

Clarke decided to give Harrison the full treatment.

'In Singapore there are two million people, give or take a few thousand. Most of them are Chinese and can be subdivided into groups of Hokkien, Teochew, Cantonese, Hainanese, and Hakka peoples, speaking several different dialects between them. There are also large numbers of Indians, Ceylonese, and Malays.

'Thaipusam is a Hindu festival during which the Indian devotees of the faith parade through the streets doing penance. If we watch the parade tomorrow you may well be amazed, if not a little frightened, by what you see. Those doing penance have their bodies pierced with scores of sharp needles and sometimes wear sandals which are nothing less than small beds of nails. Others have their noses, tongues, cheeks, any loose skin in fact, skewered with silver arrows or fishing hooks.'

Clarke sat back in the deep leather armchair and paused to see what effect his words had on the American. It annoyed

Clarke to see that the American was showing mild interest but nothing more. He continued.

'The wearing of the kavadi is yet another form of penance. It consists of a heavy wooden framework and is edged with razor-sharp blades which rest upon the shoulders of the wearer.'

Harrison wasn't listening. He was far too preoccupied with the legs of the petite Chinese waitress whose smooth ivory thigh was showing tantalizingly through the slit in her cheongsam as she brought fresh drinks to their table. Harrison watched her walk away, then leered across the table at Clarke.

'Say, is it true what they say about the Chinese?' He laughed loudly, his fat face wobbling with each separate guffaw.

Clarke experienced what he thought was a suitable feeling of disgust and at the same time determined to make another assault on the American's credulity in order to regain his interest.

'The Chinese, whatever may have been said about them, are a very interesting race of people and their customs are the strangest of all.' Once again he sat back and waited for Harrison to take the bait. Harrison was hidden behind a thick cloud of cigar smoke, but he waved it aside impatiently as his curiosity got the better of him.

'For instance?' The fish had bitten. Clarke was ready to elaborate.

'Some sections of the Chinese community consider the head of the Songfish to be a great delicacy. They eat every part of it, except for the bone of course. Strange by Western standards, don't you think?'

Harrison raised one eyebrow and twisted his slack mouth into a wry smile, but said nothing. Clarke warmed to his subject.

'There is still an isolated group of old-world Chinese here in Singapore who indulge in a ritual which even I refused to believe existed until I actually saw it take place.'

Harrison was sitting on the edge of his seat, a look of intense interest on his face. Clarke was pleased that he had managed to shake Harrison out of his state of apathy. He continued once more.

'These people believe that the brain of a monkey, if eaten, will increase one's mental capacity, restore virility, and also guarantee long life. However, these qualities are lost unless the brain is removed from the animal while it is still alive and eaten immediately. The unfortunate creature is tightly bound, the top of its skull is removed and the brain is torn from the cranial cavity to be eaten, if possible, before the furry corpse has stopped twitching. I can assure you that to watch it happen is quite an unnerving experience. Believe me, nothing screams as loudly or as horribly as a petrified monkey.'

Harrison's expression reflected sheer disbelief.

'I guess that's one tall story that you guys throw in for the tourists! Hell, I won't believe that until I see it. It's inhuman!'

Clarke smiled. 'It justs depends on your upbringing. After all, we don't all share a common sense of values. The few people who indulge in this sort of thing find it perfectly natural I assure you.'

They sat in silence for several minutes. Harrison was still sceptical with regard to what Clarke had told him and he sat deep in thought. When he started to speak he had changed the subject.

'I think we agreed on three hundred dollars.' He reached into his hip pocket and produced a bulging wallet from which he took more than the required sum. He leaned forward and handed the money across the table to Clarke.

'I like to settle money matters well in advance. It makes for good service. Besides, if I throw in another fifty maybe you can arrange something special.'

Clarke got the point and, as he took the money, decided that he definitely could arrange something. Harrison seemed to deserve it.

Clarke hired a car and early the following morning drove back up to the Goodwood. He gathered from what Harrison told him that, after he had left the hotel the night before, the big American had taken a taxi into the city and had found himself a woman. In this way he had managed to discover that what they said about the Chinese was not true at all, and what pleased him most of all was that it had only cost him twenty dollars to put his mind at rest. Clarke smiled dutifully when he heard the story, but his thoughts were elsewhere.

They spent most of the morning watching the Thaipusam procession, during which time Harrison's perennial camera was constantly on the move, busy taking photographs to astound 'the folks back home'. Harrison seemed to enjoy the spectacle, but it was obvious that he wasn't intrigued, as Clarke always was, by the strength of the devotees' faith, which enabled them to withstand terrible pain and to escape permanent injury.

Later in the day they surveyed the island from the top of Mount Faber, studied minutely the macabre statuettes in the Tiger Balm Gardens, and inspected the dazzling green world of The House of Jade. All the while Clarke supplied Harrison with the relevant details.

Night found them sitting on a wooden bench outside a bar in Bugis Street, surrounded by the dregs of humanity. The street was full of pimps, prostitutes, drunks, beggars, pedlars, and pickpockets. Here you were supposed to be able to satisfy any lust, practise any vice, buy anything or anybody. Clarke had never had any reason to believe that you couldn't do just that. The place and the people were unique, save for those that had just come to watch. Harrison was greatly amused by the antics of a pair of queers who were trying to solicit the attention of a group of British sailors. It had taken Clarke a full twenty minutes to convince him that they were, in fact, male and not female. Harrison hadn't taken his eyes off them since.

'I can guarantee' Clarke had said, between sips of a long, cool, lager beer, 'that the most attractive woman in this street at present is a man.' Harrison had laughed loudly, too loudly in fact. He wasn't used to a great deal of drink and it was going to his head. A short while later he lost five dollars trying to beat a young Malay boy at noughts and crosses. His heavy loss was partly due to the drink, but mainly due to the fact that the boy was a professional and he was not.

Clarke sat back and savoured the warm, spicy aroma of the
night air. The distinctive smell of fresh Durians, displayed
on a nearby fruit stall, mingled with the faint odour of beer
and the wafting clouds of cooking smoke issuing from countless
kitchens. It was the smell of humanity and Clarke loved it.

Several drinks later Clarke reintroduced their old topic of
conversation.

'How would you like to see something a little extreme?'
he asked.

'Whadya mean?' slurred Harrison, his mouth flapping
loosely, at the same time slopping a great deal of his beer
across the bare wooden table, 'a blue movie or somethin'?'

'No,' replied Clarke.

Harrison opened his eyes wide and managed a beery smile.

'Aw, you mean that damned monkey business!'

'Yes, if you still want to see it.' Clarke waited, with bated
breath, for the reply.

'Fine! When?' Harrison was hooked.

'As soon as you're ready to leave.'

Within ten minutes they were driving away from the lights
and the sounds of the city.

The car bumped along a rough dirt track that led off the
main road and down into a black wilderness of rubber and
palm trees. The dripping green vegetation and an occasional
scuttling rat were all that could be seen within the arc of the
headlights. They moved slowly and somewhere close at hand
Clarke could hear a colony of bullfrogs booming out their
mournful song. Harrison had collapsed in the rear seat. He
was snoring loudly and remained undisturbed by the buffeting
he was receiving from the rough passage of the vehicle. Clarke
caught a glimpse of a rapidly fluttering bat, momentarily
caught in the headlights. A short while later an emerald-green
snake fled across their path in a lightning whiplash zigzag.

After they had travelled a mile or more through the blackness they came upon a small kampong consisting of several
atap huts grouped closely together in a small clearing. Clarke
climbed out of the car as an old Chinese, bent double with

age, hobbled towards him carrying an oil lamp. He held the lamp high so that he could see Clarke's face more clearly. As soon as he recognized him he gave a crooked smile of welcome. The flickering lamp cast long shadows and gave the old man's face a satanic appearance. His smiling mouth was a black cave, guarded by a solitary gold tooth and several decaying stumps. Long black hairs drooped down from a large wart on his chin. His heavily lined face took on the appearance of a ploughed field and his eye sockets looked black and empty. He leaned forward into the light and his eyes sparkled and came alive when he saw Harrison slumped in the back of the car.

'Good, Mr Clarke. You bring us a visitor!'

Harrison stirred, sat up, shook his head and, with great effort, swung his legs out of the car, and pulled himself to his feet. He hung on to the open door to steady himself.

'Are we there?' he asked in a daze, staring curiously about him with half-closed eyes.

'Yes' replied Clarke. 'Old Lim Chong will take you inside. I'll wait for you here. I've seen it all before.'

Harrison murmured his assent and the old Chinese led him towards the nearest hut. He had barely stepped inside before he collapsed on the floor in a senseless heap.

The first thing Harrison thought when he regained consciousness was how badly he had underestimated the potency of the local beer. He tried to raise a hand to his throbbing head but found that he was unable to do so. He almost panicked but managed to fight back his fear and tried his best to assess the situation. His brain was still befuddled and he couldn't see very well. He was sitting in almost pitch darkness and he couldn't move his arms or legs. He could see an oil lamp hanging in the doorway, but it was burning so weakly that it shed hardly any light at all. His heart jumped violently when the lamp started to move towards him. He heard a shuffling and the light became brighter. He was considerably relieved when he saw that it was carried by the old man. Lim Chong turned up the wick of the lamp with a horny hand and the bare hut was filled with a light that hurt Harrison's eyes.

'What's going on?' Harrison shouted. 'Where's Clarke?'

Lim hung the lamp from a wooden beam, then thrust his wizened face close to that of the American.

'Mr Clarke not very far away,' he breathed softly.

Harrison tried to turn his face away from the foul stench that issued from the old man's mouth. But he couldn't move his head either. In a moment of terror he realized his position. He was stoutly lashed to a heavy wooden chair and his head was clamped in some kind of wooden vice which was presumably, in turn, fastened to one of the vertical hut supports somewhere behind him. For some reason he had been rendered totally immobile. But why? All he knew was that he was scared stiff.

'What is it you want? My money? Then take it, but for God's sake get me out of this contraption!' He was screaming, but he couldn't help himself.

Lim Chong had moved behind him and the vile smell returned as the old man whispered in his ear.

'No, sir. We no want your money.'

Harrison only began to realize what it was all about when he experienced the first stinging pain as Lim Chong deftly drew a razor-edged knife across his forehead, just below the hairline. Then he knew. He struggled like a madman, but to no avail. He screamed for Clarke to help him, but when nobody came he just screamed. And screamed. And kept screaming.

The pain was almost unbearable. He could feel the hair and the flesh being ripped and stripped away from his skull and he could feel the warm, sticky blood seeping down his neck and running down his face, blurring his vision so that he saw everything through a red mist. His screams increased in both volume and intensity and his heart pounded in his chest like a sledge-hammer. His fear became so total that it began to paralyse him. He could find no strength to continue his useless struggle and he was finding it hard to breathe. His screams were reduced to babbling pleas for mercy and finally broke off into hoarse, choking sobs. He began to cry like a child, the salt tears mingling with the blood in his mouth.

There was a quick rasping sound and sensation that reached down to every one of his nerve ends as Lim Chong started to saw away the obstructive bone. He shivered with horror and stared with disbelief as the brittle white fragments began to litter the floor around him.

Harrison moaned and cast his eyes upwards. He saw several wickedly smiling faces before him, all ghastly yellow in the light of the lamp. The terrible thing was that Clarke's face was among them. He saw each one of them eagerly raise a claw-like hand towards his head. Their hands remained out of his vision for a few seconds, but he managed to glimpse two of them ravenously stuffing some of the bloody grey spongy matter into their mouths before everything finally went black.

Clarke drove slowly back to Pasir Panjang. He knew now that he would never return to England. Business was good and the mysteries of the Orient fascinated him.

David Morrell
The Totem £1.25

The young hitch-hiker appeared to be the victim of a hit-and-run driver – except for the unexplained claw marks. The coroner died suddenly of a heart attack before he could conduct the autopsy, and more sinister still, the cadaver disappeared from the mortuary slab. High in the night sky a full moon shines over Wyoming.

'A knockout . . . even better than *First Blood*'
STEPHEN KING

Jay Anson
The Amityville Horror £1.50

On 18 December 1975, George and Kathy Lutz, with their three children, moved into their new home at 112 Ocean Avenue, Amityville. Twenty-eight days later they fled from the house in terror . . .

'One of the most terrifying cases ever of haunting and possession by demons . . . heart stopping . . . chilling'
SUNDAY EXPRESS

Ira Levin
Rosemary's Baby £1.75

'At last I have got my wish. I am ridden by a book that plagues my mind and continues to squeeze my heart with fingers of bone. I swear that *Rosemary's Baby* is the most unnerving story I've read' KENNETH ALLSOP, EVENING NEWS

'A darkly brilliant tale of modern devilry that, like James's *Turn of the Screw*, induces the reader to believe the unbelievable. I believed it and was altogether enthralled' TRUMAN CAPOTE

A Kiss Before Dying £1.75

'A remarkably constructed story, depicting an inconceivably vicious character in episodes of chilling horror'
CHICAGO SUNDAY TRIBUNE

'An all-time suspense classic and award-winning novel that brings you an evening of incomparable excitement' NEW YORK TIMES

The Stepford Wives £1.75

Irrational changes of personality occur almost overnight among wives soon after they move to the suburbs of Stepford. What is the unspeakable menace that overshadows this strange community? Why does the secretive Men's Association meet every night in the old house with the shuttered windows?

'Taut, rapid, frightening, quite ferociously readable'
THE TIMES LITERARY SUPPLEMENT

Fiction

☐ **Options**	Freda Bright	£1.50p
☐ **The Thirty-nine Steps**	John Buchan	£1.50p
☐ **Secret of Blackoaks**	Ashley Carter	£1.50p
☐ **Hercule Poirot's Christmas**	Agatha Christie	£1.25p
☐ **Dupe**	Liza Cody	£1.25p
☐ **Lovers and Gamblers**	Jackie Collins	£2.50p
☐ **Sphinx**	Robin Cook	£1.25p
☐ **Ragtime**	E. L. Doctorow	£1.50p
☐ **My Cousin Rachel**	Daphne du Maurier	£1.95p
☐ **Mr American**	George Macdonald Fraser	£2.25p
☐ **The Moneychangers**	Arthur Hailey	£2.25p
☐ **Secrets**	Unity Hall	£1.75p
☐ **Black Sheep**	Georgette Heyer	£1.75p
☐ **The Eagle Has Landed**	Jack Higgins	£1.95p
☐ **Sins of the Fathers**	Susan Howatch	£2.95p
☐ **The Master Sniper**	Stephen Hunter	£1.50p
☐ **Smiley's People**	John le Carré	£1.95p
☐ **To Kill a Mockingbird**	Harper Lee	£1.95p
☐ **Ghosts**	Ed McBain	£1.75p
☐ **Gone with the Wind**	Margaret Mitchell	£3.50p
☐ **Blood Oath**	David Morrell	£1.75p
☐ **Platinum Logic**	Tony Parsons	£1.75p
☐ **Wilt**	Tom Sharpe	£1.75p
☐ **Rage of Angels**	Sidney Sheldon	£1.95p
☐ **The Unborn**	David Shobin	£1.50p
☐ **A Town Like Alice**	Nevile Shute	£1.75p
☐ **A Falcon Flies**	Wilbur Smith	£1.95p
☐ **The Deep Well at Noon**	Jessica Stirling	£1.95p
☐ **The Ironmaster**	Jean Stubbs	£1.75p
☐ **The Music Makers**	E. V. Thompson	£1.95p

Non-fiction

☐ **Extraterrestrial Civilizations**	Isaac Asimov	£1.50p
☐ **Pregnancy**	Gordon Bourne	£2.95p
☐ **Jogging From Memory**	Rob Buckman	£1.25p
☐ **The 35mm Photographer's Handbook**	Julian Calder and John Garrett	£5.95p
☐ **Travellers' Britain**	} Arthur Eperon	£2.95p
☐ **Travellers' Italy**		£2.50p
☐ **The Complete Calorie Counter**	Eileen Fowler	75p

☐	**The Diary of Anne Frank**	Anne Frank	£1.75p
☐	**And the Walls Came Tumbling Down**	Jack Fishman	£1.95p
☐	**Linda Goodman's Sun Signs**	Linda Goodman	£2.50p
☐	**Dead Funny**	Fritz Spiegl	£1.50p
☐	**How to be a Gifted Parent**	David Lewis	£1.95p
☐	**Victoria RI**	Elizabeth Longford	£4.95p
☐	**Symptoms**	Sigmund Stephen Miller	£2.50p
☐	**Book of Worries**	Robert Morley	£1.50p
☐	**Airport International**	Brian Moynahan	£1.75p
☐	**The Alternative Holiday Catalogue**	edited by Harriet Peacock	£1.95p
☐	**The Pan Book of Card Games**	Hubert Phillips	£1.75p
☐	**Food for All the Family**	Magnus Pyke	£1.50p
☐	**Just Off for the Weekend**	John Slater	£2.50p
☐	**An Unfinished History of the World**	Hugh Thomas	£3.95p
☐	**The Baby and Child Book**	Penny and Andrew Stanway	£4.95p
☐	**The Third Wave**	Alvin Toffler	£2.75p
☐	**Pauper's Paris**	Miles Turner	£2.50p
☐	**The Flier's Handbook**		£5.95p

All these books are available at your local bookshop or newsagent, or can be ordered direct from the publisher. Indicate the number of copies required and fill in the form below

9

....

Name_____
(Block letters please)

Address_____

_____

Send to Pan Books (CS Department), Cavaye Place, London SW10 9PG
Please enclose remittance to the value of the cover price plus:
35p for the first book plus 15p per copy for each additional book ordered
to a maximum charge of £1.25 to cover postage and packing
Applicable only in the UK

While every effort is made to keep prices low, it is sometimes necessary to increase prices at short notice. Pan Books reserve the right to show on covers and charge new retail prices which may differ from those advertised in the text or elsewhere